LUCIEN JANDREAU

BY
RANDALL PROBERT

Lucien Jandreau
by Randall Probert

www.randallprobertbooks.net

email: randentr@megalink.net

Photography credits:
Cover background and Nika ~ Randall Probert
Cover photo of Lucien ~ Amy Robertson
Chapter title art and inserts of Nika ~ Randall Probert
Author's photograph ~ Patricia Gott

ISBN: 978-0-9852872-7-6

Printed in the United States of America

Published by
Randall Enterprises
P.O. Box 862
Bethel, Maine 04217

Lucien Jandreau

CHAPTER 1

1856

Lucien Jandreau, as well as the entire camp, awoke to the cookee banging a ladle against a steel pot. It was morning twilight, just before the sun breached the horizon. The air had remained hot and humid, typical for the July weather, and Lucien, like the others, awoke as sweaty as when they went to bed the night before.

Lucien's father Maurice was woods boss and he was strict about lollygagging around camp after breakfast had been eaten. He would say, "You men are here to work, not to lollygag around camp!" Maurice was tough, almost to the point of being a bully. And consequently he produced more lumber for the Eastern Lumber Company than any other of the company's crews.

Everyone hated to work in the woods in the hot humid weather and the blackflies and mosquitos and hornets. In spite of the cold weather and ice, everyone preferred to work during the winter. If they were cold Maurice would say, "Work faster and you'll warm up!" And there was the ice. If a horse slipped and fell on the ice it usually would break a leg and then would have to be put down. And on average two men a winter would slip on ice and break a leg, and/or arm. But all-in-all, everybody preferred to work in the winter.

Breakfast would consist of hot oatmeal, scrambled eggs—always scrambled, flapjacks and thick slices of bacon. This was every breakfast. And of course black coffee. Milk was a precious commodity and it was not to be used in coffee. That was Maurice's rule, not Elmo's, the cookee.

Elmo just wandered into camp one day looking for work. He was in his fifties; but he wasn't sure of his exact age. He had gotten into some trouble in Canada and left on foot. After crossing into Maine and several days later, he found the Kennebec River and followed it downstream, and just north of Skowhegan he wandered into Maurice's crew camp. No one knew Elmo's last name and Maurice paid him under the table so there would not be any trace of him. Maurice could sympathize with Elmo, because Maurice had uprooted his family and left Canada also, because of trouble.

This morning was no different than the hundreds of other mornings. Lucien sat across the table from the same face, and ate the same food, although he always ate more food than anyone else. He was always hungry. Lucien stood six foot-four. He towered above everyone else. He was twenty years old and had not filled out his frame yet. And he was stronger than four men. He had had to prove this many times.

Lucien towered over his father's five-feet-eleven, but he always cowered to Maurice's bullying ways. It was the same at home as at work. Lucien could never do anything right or please his father. No matter how hard he tried, his father would find fault with everything his son did, and he would berate him and ridicule him in front of the other men.

Lucien was just finishing his coffee when Maurice bellowed, "Breakfast is over! You eat any more and you won't work hard enough; now get out and get up into the choppings before I dock your pay!"

Everyone stood away from the table and hurriedly pulled on their coats, hats and mittens. Lucien grabbed a pancake that one of the men didn't eat. He wolfed it down so fast no one knew he had grabbed it.

They grabbed their axes and saws and started up hill to the choppings. While they were felling the first tree the third man in the crew would be harnessing the work horses. The twitch trail was so dry that dust rose with each step.

"Hey Lucien!" Maurice hollered, "a man of your size should be in the front leading the men to work!"

Lucien clinched his jaw so hard he could have bitten through nails. He never broke stride or gave any indication that he had heard his father. He ignored him. The rest of the crew were cringing also, and no one spoke.

Lucien stepped up to a beefy spruce tree and sunk his axe deep in the white wood for a notch. He swung his axes again and again working off the fury of his father. For as long as he could remember, he had had to put up with his father's contempt towards him.

Lucien was very frugal with his money. He seldom bought anything other than for work and he didn't waste his time in the bars or on the girls. He kept most of his money in a leather pouch that he kept hidden in the tool shed at home, under the anvil. The anvil alone weighed three hundred pounds and it sat on an oak block of wood that had to weigh another hundred pounds. His father could not move it and Lucien felt sure his money would be safe there. He had $400.00 hidden there and in his room at home he had another $85.00.

Lucien was so frustrated he kept chopping at the huge spruce tree until it fell. Ordinarily he and Andy would use the two-man cross-cut saw to saw through the trunk to bring it down, but this morning was different. He was feeling more anger than usual. When the tree was lying on the ground he went to work limbing it. His axe was flying back and forth so fast Andy didn't dare get near to help. He stood back and watched Lucien. He knew full well what the problem was.

Andy stood at the stump watching and said, "As big and powerful as Lucien is, it is a good thing he's good natured and not like his old man."

When Lucien had finished limbing, he turned around and saw Andy watching him and he grinned. The hostilities now gone, they worked together with the two-man cross-cut saw to buck the spruce tree into logs. They had their second tree down and limbed before Paul arrived with the team.

They worked all forenoon in the hot sun. The humidity had blown out, though. After lunch Paul and Lucien switched places and Lucien was now driving the team back-and-forth from the parbuckle yard next to the Kennebec River.

Lucien unhitched the sixteen foot saw log and using his cant-dog he rolled it over to be scaled and then he rolled it onto the sluice ramp and into the river. It usually took two men to move a sixteen foot log around, but Lucien did it alone. The pine logs were parbuckled in a pile to be driven to the saw mill later.

Maurice bad been talking with a company man most of the day. Lucien had not had to put up with his berating—that is until mid-afternoon. Lucien had just unhitched a huge spruce log when his father hollered loud enough for all to hear, "Hey, how many times do I have to tell you, Lucien, that when you come into the yard, square off with the sluice ramp to make it easier to roll the log on! Now come on boy—when are you ever going to learn!"

Everyone stopped what they were doing and all were wondering why Maurice was berating his son now. The veins and muscles in Lucien's neck, shoulders and hands were swelling as adrenaline surged through his body. He gripped his cant-dog so hard the skin on the back of his hands was beginning to crack. He had had all of his father's berating, fault-finding and ridiculing that he could stand. He threw the cant-dog back towards the parbuckled logs and said, "Shut up, old man!" He took two steps toward his father. "I have had a gut full of you and now—!"

He never got to finish that statement. When he threw his cant-dog, it hit a support pole with such force that it knocked the support pole to the ground and parbuckled logs fell and rolled to the ground, crushing Fred, the scaler.

"Damn you!" Maurice hollered. "Look what you've done now! You and that damned temper of yours."

Lucien wasn't listening. He rushed to the fallen logs and began rolling and tossing them aside. No one else dared to get near. He wasn't long clearing the logs off Fred. He was dead. His father watched as Lucien easily tossed the pine logs aside. He was now afraid of his son and what he might do. He had never seen such human strength. As had no one else.

Lucien lifted the limp body out of the fallen logs and carried it to the side of the yard and lay it down. Then he turned around and faced his father and began walking towards him. Everyone watching assumed Lucien would beat the living hell out of his father. He stopped in front of his father and said, "Damn you!" then he turned and walked off.

"Where do you think you're going Lucien?"

"I just killed a man where in the hell do you think I'm going," that's all that was said.

Two-and-a-half hours later, Lucien walked into the county sheriff's office in Skowhegan. "Well hello, Lucien. What can I do for you today?" Sheriff Ralph Collins said.

"I killed someone today, Sheriff."

"Oh come on Lucien. I don't have time for any of this nonsense. I'm late for my supper now."

"I killed the scaler, Fred Jenkins," Lucien repeated.

"You're serious, aren't you, Lucien?"

"I wish I wasn't, but yes—I'm serious."

"Great, my wife made a beef stew today and fresh biscuits. I suppose I'll have to lock you up, Lucien, while I look into this"

Lucien didn't like the sound of the steel door closing and the lock snapping into place.

"I'll have the Mrs. bring supper down to you, Lucien. We live upstairs." Sheriff Collins left and closed the door.

Mrs. Collins brought a tray down with a bowl of stew and two biscuits and a glass of water. Lucien thanked her and set the tray on the floor. He was certainly hungry, but he didn't really think he could eat anything just now. He settled for the water and drank it. Then he laid down on the bunk. His feet hung out over the bunk frame. He lay there going over and over again the day events. He always came to the same conclusion: Fred Jenkins was dead because he had lost his temper. As much as he would like to blame his father, the blame always came back to himself. And no one else.

Sheriff Collins checked in on Lucien before going upstairs to bed. "You told me exactly as it happened. Your father wasn't much help, so I talked with those who were in the yard at the time. Because you lost your temper and threw the cant-dog, a man was killed. Even though it was an accident, you will be held responsible, Lucien. So I have no choice but to hold you for court, which will be at 9 a.m. tomorrow morning."

Lucien was left alone with his thoughts about being responsible for Fred Jenkin's death. He didn't sleep at all that night. All he could do was lie on his bunk, relive the day over and over all night.

Mrs. Collins brought down breakfast the next morning. At first all Lucien wanted was coffee. "Take my advice, Lucien, force yourself to eat before we go over to see the judge."

Lucien took his advice and ate his breakfast. Afterwards Collins gave Lucien soap and water and a razor and a towel. With a full stomach and after washing he was feeling better.

At 8:30 a.m.: "Lucien, I have to put these handcuffs on. Then I'll walk with you over to the courthouse." They were early and Lucien had nothing to do but wait. Eventually Judge Ian Butler arrived and walked back to his desk.

"Well Sheriff, what have you for me this morning?" Judge Butler asked.

"A murder, Your Honor."

This interested the judge and he slid his glasses down to the end of his nose so he could look over them at Lucien and the Sheriff. "Well, you'd better explain, Sheriff."

"Your Honor, I'd like Lucien to explain. He turned himself in to me yesterday, afterwards."

"Well, son, let's hear your side of the story. But before you start let me remind you that this is a capital offense and you do not have to plead guilty now. I need to know if there is enough information to hold you over for trial. Now why don't you tell me what happened."

Lucien started to speak but Collins stopped him and said, "Stand up when you speak to the judge, Lucien."

Lucien stood and Judge Butler said, "Tall drink of water, aren't you, son."

Lucien started at the beginning and told the judge everything. "This was an accident, son, but because you lost control of your temper, you threw the cant-dog which caused the logs to topple, killing Fred Jenkins. It was an accident and that makes the offense involuntary manslaughter.

"Sheriff Collins, do you have anything to add?"

"I talked with everyone present in the yard at the time of the accident and a few of the crew and I got a clearer picture that led up to the accident."

"Go on Sheriff, you have my attention," Butler said.

"Apparently Lucien's father, Maurice, was berating him, finding fault with everything he does and ridiculing him in front of the crew, family and even people Maurice didn't know. On this particular day Lucien must have reached his breaking point, and when he lashed out at his father he caused the logs to topple, killing Mr. Jenkins."

Judge Butler sat silent for a few minutes deep in thought, then he said, "Maurice Jandreau cannot be held personally for the death of Fred Jenkins, but Sheriff Collings, before we go any farther with this case, I want to see Mr. Jandreau in this courtroom, tomorrow at 9 a.m..

"Yes, Your Honor."

"Before you leave, Sheriff, I'll issue a writ authorizing you to bring Mr. Jandreau before this court tomorrow."

Lucien sat down and waited while the judge wrote out the writ.

"The Mrs. will bring you lunch, Lucien. I have to go see your father."

"Good luck with that, Sheriff Collins."

After Sheriff Collins left, Lucien lay down on the bunk. He didn't understand why Judge Butler wanted to see his father in court. He put those worries aside and fell asleep just as Mrs. Collins opened the front door, startling Lucien.

"Maybe you'll feel more like eating something now, Lucien. Beef stew and biscuits. For supper there'll be beans and bacon and biscuits."

"Thank you, Mrs. Collins."

Lucien was hungrier than he thought and could have eaten another bowl or two. When he had finished eating there was nothing else to do but lay on the bunk again and he was soon asleep.

* * * *

Sheriff Collins hitched his team and drove up to Jandreau's crew camps near the Kennebec River in Norridgewock. It was a pleasant ride following the river. The river was full of logs heading for the saw mills. There were also a few canoes behind the booms and men fishing for brook trout.

Once at Jandreau's camp, he tied off his team and asked one of the men in the yard, "Where could I find Maurice?"

"He's in his office behind the cook camp." Collins walked over and found the door open so he walked inside.

"Hello, Mr. Jandreau."

"You back again? What do you want this time?" Maurice barked.

"Judge Butler has issued a writ to bring you before him tomorrow morning."

"What's a writ anyhow?"

"It's a written order from the judge to bring you before him, Mr. Jandreau."

"What does he want with me?"

"That's not in the writ. My orders are to bring you before him tomorrow at 9 a.m.."

"This must have to do something with Lucien. Well, I told you everything I could yesterday. I ain't going in; now get out of here!"

Sheriff Collings took two steps towards Maurice and shoved his desk to the side and grabbed Maurice by the shirt and lifted him to his feet. "You loud mouth son-of-a-bitch, you are going with me even if I have to hog-tie you and drag you out of here by your feet. Now you can either harness up your own rig so you can come back here after you see the judge or you can ride with me and walk back here tomorrow. Your choice, but you better be making it pretty soon."

"Okay, okay, I'll go peacefully and take my own rig. Do I have to stay in jail tonight or can I stay at home?"

As long as you promise to be in court before 9 a.m. you can stay at your home tonight. If you fail to come in, I'll come and get you, hog-tie you and drag you behind my rig all the way to jail where you'll spend thirty days. Do you understand me, Mr. Jandreau?"

"Yeah, yeah, I understand you all right."

Sheriff Collins was nobody to fool with.

* * * *

"What did the old man say, Sheriff?" Lucien asked.

"He agreed to come in with me. He's at his house tonight. I told him not to be late in the morning. But I think I'd better be out there at sunrise just in case."

"Why does the judge want to see my father? He didn't kill Fred. I did."

"I'm not sure, Lucien."

While they waited for Mrs. Collins to bring their supper downstairs, Collings brought out a checkerboard and opened

Lucien's cell door. He wasn't worried that Lucien might try to escape. After all, he had turned himself in right after the accident.

Checkers were a favorite passtime for both men and they both played an interesting game. Collins was only slightly better. After the third game Mrs. Collins brought down a kettle of beef stew and a loaf of new bread and a pitcher of water. She knew Lucien would probably be hungry.

Collins had two bowls of stew and told Lucien, "Eat up, Lucien. It may be a while before you get any more home cooking."

Before he was done Lucien finished off the rest of the stew and the loaf of bread. It had been a long time since he had had so much to eat.

"Sheriff, I'd like something to read. A newspaper perhaps?" Lucien asked.

"Sure thing," and he gave him his newspaper that he had read and thrown away.

He read every article on every page before it was too dark to see. Then he laid on the bunk and for the first time began to think about his future. One thing was obvious though: he would be going to prison. For how long would depend upon Judge Butler. It was after midnight before he finally went to sleep. As the clock in the church steeple rang out at midnight, he counted each bell.

He slept beyond sunrise and Collins had to wake him for breakfast. After he had eaten, he shaved and washed his face and hands and smoothed over his hair.

"It's time we went over, Lucien."

"Did the old man come in?"

"I was at his place at sunrise to make sure. He wasn't any happy to see me"

Maurice was already seated in the courtroom when Lucien walked in. He walked passed his father without any acknowledgement and sat in the front row. Sheriff Collins stood at the only exit, except through the judge's chambers.

At exactly 9 a.m. Judge Butler opened his chamber door and entered the courtroom. "All rise for the Honorable Judge Butler," Sheriff Collins said.

Lucien rose and when Maurice didn't, Collins said, "Stand up, Maurice, or the judge will find you in contempt." Begrudgingly Maurice stood. But he didn't see why he should have to.

"You may be seated, Mr. Jandreau. Lucien, you remain standing. I understand that after the accident you left the woods and turned yourself into Sheriff Collins and told him you had killed someone. Is that so, Lucien?" Judge Butler asked.

"Yes, Your Honor, it is."

"I'm going to take a judge's privilege here and ask if you plan to plead guilty today to involuntary manslaughter. A lesser charge than murder."

"Yes, Your Honor, I do. I accept full responsibility for Fred Jenkins death."

"I accept your plea, Lucien. Sheriff Collins, do you have anything to add?"

"Only that Lucien Jandreau was very honest and forthcoming immediately after the accident."

"Thank you, Sheriff. I may have a couple of questions before this is over. Mr. Maurice Jandreau, will you stand and come down in front of the bench." Maurice did as he was instructed.

Judge Butler looked sternly down at Maurice before continuing. "Sheriff Collings did a thorough investigation of this accident and after reading his report and taking everything into consideration that transpired that day, I find you equally as responsible for the death of Fred Jenkins as your son Lucien.

"I didn't get much sleep last night, Mr. Jandreau. I spent the entire night reviewing all my law books looking for a precedent case that would legally allow me to find you equally guilty for Mr. Jenkins death and send you to prison. But there just isn't a prior or precedent case that would allow me.

"It has come to my attention and Sheriff Collins' that you are a mean-spirited bully and that you have bullied your son Lucien for most of his life. It is also clear to me that actions towards your son that day precipitated the death of Fred Jenkins. It's the opinion of this court, Mr. Jandreau, that you are an abomination. That's all I have to say to you, now go sit in the back of this courtroom in the corner.

"Now, Lucien Jandreau—how old are you?"

"Twenty, Your Honor."

"For someone so young, you surely have demonstrated to this court your responsibility. I wish I could say it was an unfortunate accident and dismiss it. But someone died, Lucien, because you lost your temper. So I have no choice but to sentence you to five years in the State Prison at Thomaston. I wish I could do more for you, son.

"Sheriff Collins, when can you transport Lucien to Thomaston?"

"I know the Warden there, Lucien: Henry Farrar. You keep your nose clean and he'll do fair with you. Good luck, son," the Judge said.

As Lucien walked by his father he didn't look at him. He was free of him—not the situation that he would like, but life could only get better from here.

CHAPTER 2

It was a long, hot and dusty ride by stagecoach to Thomaston. Sheriff Collins delivered his prisoner, Lucien, to Warden Henry Farrar, and he gave Farrar a report of Lucien's case, his sentencing paper and a personal letter from Judge Butler concerning the particulars of the case.

"Thank you, Sheriff Collins."

"Good luck, Lucien," Collins said.

Lucien stood quietly before Warden Farrah as the Warden read Lucien's case report and Judge Butler's letters.

"The Judge speaks highly of you as does the Sheriff. But you have been sentenced to do five years here. You'll be kept in isolation for a week to let you adjust to prison life. Then you'll be moved to the B ward. That ward is for less violent inmates. Ward A is made up of hardcore men, murders, rapists and thugs.

"You have five years to do here; how hard or difficult that time is, is up to you. If you want to speak to me, you must ask one of the guards first. As you go along, you'll become more familiar with the prison rules. If you aren't sure of something ask one of the guards. I fill out an assessment report each month on every inmate and that report goes in your file. In case your case comes before the parole board."

There was a knock on the door and Warden Farrar was interrupted, "Come in."

"Lucien Jandreau, this is one of the guards, my second in command, Chester Adams. Chester: Lucien Jandreau, a new inmate.

"If you go with Chester he will get you your prison attire and bed makings. Any questions?"

17

"Yes sir, one."

"What is it?"

"I haven't eaten all day. Is it too late for supper?"

"The supper hour is over but if Chester was to take you to the kitchen the boys there might be able to help."

"Thank you, sir, and I won't be any trouble to you. I'm here because I belong here and I'll do my time."

Chester Adams first escorted Lucien to the kitchen, and the boys there were more than obliging to fix Lucien something to eat out of all of the leftovers. They were surprised how much he ate.

Chester next escorted Lucien to supply where he was given new prison attire. Gray shirt and pants and on the back of the shirt, sewn in with thread was Thomaston State Prison. Lucien was also given a pair of boots and bedding. Chester next escorted him down to the isolation cells. Lucien walked through the door into the cell and was surprised to see how big it was, eight feet by twelve. "You mean I get to live here all by myself, Chester, in this big room. This is better living than back home. In fact everything is better than back home."

Chester didn't reply. He just looked questioningly at Lucien. "There is no screaming or hollering allowed here. You must be quiet, Lucien. Any questions?"

"Only one. How about something to read."

"There is a small library and I'll have one of the inmates bring you something in the morning."

"Thank you, Chester."

Lucien made up his bunk and lay down. So far this prison life was better than the life he had known at home. He sat up and looked at the size of his cell. He still couldn't believe how big it was, and he had it all to himself.

Many thoughts and images were floating around in his head as he lay on his bunk. He was real sorry about the death of Fred Jenkins. Fred lived alone and never married and both parents had died and no one knew if there were any brothers and sisters or not. He saw images of him growing up at home. Once he was old enough to carry a bucket of water from the well he had chores around the house and barn. His younger brother and sister were born when he was ten and then again at twelve. So he had to shoulder a lot of responsibility watching over those two. And it was about this time when his father began finding fault with everything he did. There was no pleasing him, no matter what he did. And then the bullying began. He finished grade 9 but after that, because of his height and strength, his father made him go to work with the woods crew doing a man's job.

Lucien smiled to himself and thought, *You can bully me no more, old man. I'm free of you at last. And so far life in prison ain't that bad. I get three meals a day, clean clothes, clean bed and I don't have to sleep next to anyone. I never had any freedom living under your roof, Dad, or working for you.*

He drifted off to sleep then, thinking that this prison life was more like a vacation than what his life had been like.

 Just before the prison steam whistle blew at 6 a.m., Lucien was dreaming about a beautiful woman. He was experiencing so much love and this woman said to him, "I will always look after you." Then the whistle blew again and Lucien startled, jumped out of bed, and all the memories of this beautiful woman were fading.

Breakfast was brought to him by one of the kitchen helpers. "Any chance I could have seconds?" Lucien asked.

"You'll have to wait until everyone has eaten, then if there is anything left I'll bring you what I can."

"Thank you."

Joe, the kitchen helper, brought Lucien some more food. A half loaf of four day old bread, a bit of cheese and oatmeal without milk. "Thanks Joe." Lucien was hungry and he ate everything.

After breakfast Chester arrived. "Most everyone else is at their work station. You haven't been assigned a job yet, so

19

I'm letting you out for an hour of exercise in the yard. There will only be a few other inmates that'll be out there because of certain situations. After your isolation time is up then you'll be allowed to mingle with the other inmates. For now it is my job to keep you isolated."

"You get one shower a week on Wednesdays. Today is Wednesday, so at 11 a.m. after the exercise hour I'll take you to the showers. The inmates in the yard with you will also be taking their showers." Chester unlocked the door and escorted Lucien outside. "You're free to wander around the yard anywhere you want to go." The other inmates were already out there.

Lucien began walking around the perimeter along a well-used path. Although he was alone in a hostile place he was not sad. But then he wasn't happy to be there either. It felt good to walk and stretch his legs. He walked over to look at the quarry where there were a few men working. He was joined by three other inmates. "You must be a new inmate also," Ben said.

"Yeah, I'm Lucien." The other two were Bill and Jim, all three were new like Lucien. There were two other inmates staying by themselves.

When the hour was up they all were escorted to the showers for their weekly shower. It was a communal shower and Lucien was uneasy stripping and showering with other men. The water was cold, but refreshing. Lucien had never had a shower before. Usually all he could take was a sponge bath.

After their showers they all were escorted back to their cells. There were two books on Lucien's bunk. Lunch was brought again, "Any chance for seconds?" Lucien asked the kitchen helper.

"You have a hollow leg or something? I'll see what I can do after everyone has eaten."

"Thank you."

Lucien ate his bowl of soup and sandwich and he was still hungry.

* * * *

"Chester, how is the new prisoner Lucien handling his new surroundings?" Warden Farrar asked.

"He's acting like this is some kind of a vacation. He has not yet showed any of the usual signs of being locked up. He eats more than three men, which isn't a problem, and when he is confined to his cell he reads books. I haven't seen a new prisoner handle his new surroundings in prison as well as he is doing."

"He must have had a life at home that was more like hell. I hope he doesn't crack and go over the other way," Farrar said.

"I don't think he will, Sir," Chester added.

"What do you think about putting him in the kitchen as a helper. That way he could get all he wanted to eat," Farrar suggested.

"That might be a good idea."

* * * *

Lucien's isolation had ended and he folded up his bedding and followed Chester to his new cell on B Block. "This block is inmates with lesser crimes. A is made up with hardcore murderers, thugs, rapists and so forth. Right now you'll have a cell by yourself. This probably will change later on. For your own information, Lucien, 'cause you seem like a nice guy, there is one inmate who you will meet and he'll try to intimidate and bully you. He does this to every new prisoner. My best suggestion for you is to avoid him. He chums around with two thugs who protect him from other prisoners. They think they run the other inmates. Many times they have beaten another inmate and put him in the infirmary. So be careful, Lucien."

Chester said, "Leave your stuff here and I'll take you to the kitchen and introduce you."

Lucien put his bedding on the bunk and followed Chester to the kitchen. Everyone was watching him, making him feel uncomfortable.

"Gary, this is your new helper, Lucien Jandreau. Lucien,

21

this is Gary Hall, chief cook. He's the boss of the kitchen."

Lucien went to work first sweeping the mess hall floor. Sometimes he worked at the serving line dishing out food onto trays, sometimes he washed dishes and anything that needed doing except for cooking. And after every meal Lucien ate leftovers until he was full. This duty for him was better than Christmas morning. There were a couple of times the bully, Owen Hogg, while going through the line—he'd make a snide remark to Lucien. All Lucien could do was try to avoid him and continue serving. Hogg's two friends that were always at his side were named Larry Easle, nicknamed the 'Weasel' and the other companion was Bobbie Satchel, and his nickname was 'Suitcase'. When the weasel and the suitcase followed Hogg through the line they would stare at Lucien trying to make him feel uneasy. These two were smaller men than Hogg but they both had a reputation of being hardcore fighters.

When Lucien wasn't working and he saw Hogg and his two friends he would try to avoid them. He didn't want any trouble.

The prison had a small library and Lucien spent much of his free time there reading. Paul, the inmate in charge of the library, was an old man and Lucien treated him friendly. Paul had spent most of his life in one prison or another. And he wouldn't tell Lucien what he had done to spend so much of his life in prison. He was a used up man and certainly no threat to anyone and Lucien couldn't understand why the authorities wouldn't release him. But the truth was Paul didn't want to be released. Where would he go? His family or what was left of it, had disowned him.

Hogg and his two friends were beginning to harass and verbally harangue Lucien whenever they had a chance. When he wasn't working they would seek him out. The library was no longer a safe haven. "Sonny, the only way to stop Hogg from harassing you is to stand up to him. Show him you're not afraid of him."

"I don't want any trouble, Paul. I only want to do my time and stay out of trouble.

One day Hogg and his two buddies were waiting for Lucien when he was on his way to the kitchen.

Hogg stepped out in front of Lucien blocking his way, "You aren't very friendly, Lucien. What's the matter? You think you're better than us?"

"Look, Hogg, I just don't want any trouble."

"Well there's going to be trouble if you don't stop thinking you're better than us. People have a way of getting themselves hurt in this place. The guards aren't always watching."

Just then Chester walked around the corner, "Okay, Hogg, you and your two idiots get out of here." They walked off.

"Just remember what I said, Lucien."

"What was that all about?"

"Oh, he was just wanting to be friendly," Lucien said.

"Well maybe, but you watch yourself near him and his two cronies. There ain't nothing I or any of the guards can do unless they try something."

"I'll watch myself."

* * * *

Being able to eat leftovers working in the kitchen, Lucien had begun to put on some weight around his shoulders, arms and legs. He had settled in comfortably with his kitchen duties and prison life. Three months had passed and still Hogg and his two friends would verbally assault and taunt Lucien whenever they could.

On Wednesdays the chief cook would bake cookies and there were always a lot of leftovers and the inmates would come in after supper hour and help themselves. This particular Wednesday Lucien was cleaning the floor while the rest of the kitchen staff were still in the kitchen. Hogg and his two friends came in and there were five or six others sitting at the tables eating cookies. Weasel and Satchel, Hogg's two friends, stood by the entrance leaning back against the door jam. Lucien saw this and knew something was up. The others who knew Hogg's reputation knew what was about to happen, but they remained where they were. The kitchen help all knew what was about to happen also and they were all watching.

Lucien turned his back on purpose to Hogg and continued mopping the floor. When he was close to Hogg, Hogg stuck his foot out and tripped Lucien. Lucien fell to the floor and Hogg and his two friends roared with laughter. Lucien picked himself up and took a step closer to Hogg. Hogg wasn't expecting this. He thought Lucien would walk off with his head down.

Lucien stood there for a moment before he said anything. Looking squarely at Hogg. Hogg was more than a head shorter, but he was probably twenty pounds heavier. He was fat.

"Tell me, Hogg, is that your real name or do people just call you that because you look and smell like a pig. Come to think of it, pigs aren't as stupid as you," Lucien said, never raising his voice.

Everyone there was shocked; nobody had ever talked to Hogg like that. Hogg himself was the most surprised. Nobody had ever *dared* to talk to him like that. Weasel and Satchel were equally surprised.

"You son-of-a-bitch, you! I'll tear you apart and beat you to death with your arms."

"Well, you going to just stand there and talk or are you really going to do something stupid. Let me guess, you're not as smart as a pig, so you probably are going to do something stupid, right? Well come on you stinking pig."

Hogg was so mad now, he couldn't think or see straight. His face was red and fire was sleeting from his eyes. He bellowed and raised his right arm to throw a punch to Lucien's face. He charged at Lucien and swung at his head but Lucien blocked his swing and at the same instant he grabbed Hogg by his trouser belt and his shirt and using Hogg's forward movement, Lucien picked Hogg up and turned him upside down and threw him over two tables and he landed on the third table and it crashed to the floor.

About now Weasel and Satchel came to Hogg's defense and charged at Lucien. Weasel threw a right hand punch at Lucien's head and Lucien caught his fist in midair and gave Weasel's arm a snap and everybody heard the bones snap in his arm. His hand was also crushed. Satchel sucker punched Lucien beside the head with little effect and Lucien back handed him to the head and sent Satchel against a table. He recovered and came at Lucien again and again. Lucien caught his fist in midair stopping the punch. And he kicked Satchel's left knee breaking it. He went down screaming. Satchel was out of it, but Hogg was now madder than hell.

Chester heard a disturbance from down the hallway and he came running to see what was happening. He stood in the entrance way just as Hogg stood up and charged towards Lucien. Lucien blocked his swing and grabbed Hogg by the face and began to squeeze. He pushed him back against the wall, still squeezing Hogg's face. "There'll be no more trouble, will there, Hogg."

"Nooo—no more trouble."

Lucien released his grip and saw Chester walking towards him. "Someone go to the infirmary and get the doctor."

"He went home."

"Then go tell one of the other duty guards to send someone after Doctor Mallard."

Satchel was still screaming about his knee. "Someone go to the infirmary and get me two long splint boards and several cloth cravats," Lucien said and then knelt down beside Satchel. Chester walked by to the kitchen to talk with the help.

"Satchel, I can help you and relieve the pain. Do you want me to help you?"

"Yes, damn it!" Satchel screamed.

Lucien sat on the floor facing Satchel and put his left

foot against Satchel's crotch and then he placed both hands on Satchel's foot and started to pull slowly. When Satchel stopped screaming Lucien stopped pulling.

"Who started this fight?" Chester asked the kitchen help.

They all said Hogg did and then Weasel and Satchel came charging at Lucien. Then they told Chester everything that had happened.

Chester then talked with each inmate there and got the same answers. He looked at Lucien rendering aid and comfort to Satchel, who he had just beaten the hell out of. As if nothing at all had happened.

When the inmate was back with the splint boards and cravats, Lucien said, "Johnny come here and take my place. Put your foot where mine is and I'll slide mine out. Get comfortable and take his foot and hold steady pressure." Satchel only winced slightly.

"Do you know what you're doing, Lucien?" Chester asked.
"Yes!"

The boards were too long so he held one by the side and marked it with his thumb nail even with his shoe and did the same with the outside board. "I don't suppose you have a knife or saw blade or anything, Chester."

"You're kidding right?"

Lucien held one board in his hands and broke it on the line and then the other board. Everyone was impressed but no one said anything. He next tied the cravats on. Two above the knee and two just below and then several along his leg and foot to immobilize it. "Where did you learn this stuff, Lucian?" Chester asked.

"There are always accidents working in the woods."

When he had finished, Satchel was comfortable and he was carried to the infirmary, as were Hogg and Weasel.

"Okay, the rest of you back to your cells. Shows over. Lucien you stay; we need to talk."

"Who started this, Lucien?"

"Hogg did."

"Did you hit him or the other two with your fist?"

"I back handed Satchel after he sucker punched me."

"Let me see your hands."

Lucien held out his hands and turned them over. Neither hand looked as if he had just been in a fight and beaten the hell out of three guys.

"This wasn't your fault, but I don't know how Warden Farrar is going to look at it. You go back to your cell and in the morning after breakfast you report to the warden's office."

* * * *

Chester walked over to the warden's office to talk with Warden Farrar while they waited for Lucien. "Come in, Chester. What in hell went on here last night? There are three men badly beaten in the infirmary. How many were there that attacked these three men and why aren't any of *them* in the infirmary? You have a lot of explaining to do, Chester. Who or what men attacked those in the infirmary?"

"Warden Farrar—just one man and he was not injured. Although he did receive one punch to the side of his head, but it didn't seem to bother him."

"Who in the hell did this to this bunch? Everyone is afraid of Hogg and his two friends."

"Lucien Jandreau, Sir."

"Lucien did all that damage? I always thought of him as nothing more than a tall drink of water. And you say he wasn't injured at all? That's just frigging unbelievable."

"You want to hear something even more unbelievable?" Chester asked.

Warden Farrar didn't say anything. He just waited for Chester to continue. "He never hit anyone with a closed fist. He did back hand Satchel after he sucker-punched Lucien. And more unbelievable than that, Sir, after the fight was over Lucien took charge of the other inmates and sent one to the infirmary to get splinting material to immobilize Satchel's broken knee. This act of kindness even surprised Satchel."

"I talked with Dr. Mallard already this morning and he said whoever set Satchel's knee and splinted it did a very good job, so good in fact that he was going to leave the splint just as it is for a couple of days to allow the bones to start mending before he puts a cast on his leg. So you're telling me Lucien did this after he broke his knee?"

"Yes Sir, I was there and watched him."

"What started this fight?"

"I questioned everyone that was there and saw the fight and they all said the same thing. Lucien was mopping the floor and Hogg started bullying him like he has been doing since Lucien's arrival. Well this time Lucien stood up to him and called him a stinking pig and this made Hogg really mad. He charged towards Lucien and Lucien blocked Hogg's swing at him and somehow he managed to snap Hogg's arm and broke the bones. Everyone said the same thing. They all heard the bones snap. Then Lucien picked Hogg up and turned him upside down and threw him across two tables and he landed on the third table and it crumbled to the floor. Weasel and Satchel had been standing at the entrance, so that tells me they had gone there purposely to beat up Lucien. When Hogg landed on the table, Weasel and Satchel charged in at Lucien. Weasel swung at Lucien's head and Lucien caught his fist in midair like he had done with Hogg and he squeezed so hard he crushed Weasel's hand and then he snapped his arm like he had done with Hogg and everyone heard the bones in his arm snap.

"About now Satchel sucker-punched Lucien in the head, which didn't seem to bother him much, and Lucien back handed him, sending him sprawling again and this is when Lucien kicked him in the knee breaking it. This is when I enter the scene. Hogg staggered to his feet bellowing he was going to kill Lucien. He swung at Lucien with his good arm and Lucien blocked it and grabbed Hogg's face in his hand and began to squeeze. Lucien said, 'There'll be no more trouble will there, Hogg.' Hogg said, 'Nooo—no more trouble.'

"Lucien let go of Hogg's face and he fell to the floor."

"You're telling me Lucien did all this to those three inmates without a scratch?" Farrar asked.

"Yes, Sir."

"I think we have underestimated Lucien."

"Sir, it wasn't Lucien's fault. He was defending himself."

"I understand that, but what do we do with him now?" Farrar asked.

"I don't understand you, Sir."

"Hogg and his two cronies ruled the roost, sort of. They had everyone afraid of them. Now Lucien could be king if he wanted to and what if he gets a following and they decide to break out. We could have a serious situation here, Chester."

"You could be correct, Sir, and I understand your concerns, but I don't think Lucien is the type to start trouble." Chester laughed then and added, "He stops them."

"Well anyhow, I want you to watch Lucien closely."

There was a knock on Farrar's outer office door. "That'll be Lucien now, Sir."

"Have him come in," Farrar said.

"I understand you had some trouble last night, son."

"A little, Sir."

"Show me your hands."

Lucien held his hands out for Warden Farrar to inspect. "Turn them over." Lucien did. "There is no sign that you hit any of them with a closed fist."

"No Sir, I didn't."

"Why do you think Hogg singled you out to beat up on?"

"I'm not sure, but he and his two friends have been trying to roust me and insult me ever since I arrived. I have no idea why. When I saw Weasel and Satchel standing guard at the entrance, I knew Hogg was intending to beat on me."

"Chester has done a very thorough investigation and it is clear you were only defending yourself. And Hogg and his two friends have had this beating coming to them for a long time now.

"Normally both parties in a fight would be sent to isolation for a while, but the circumstances here are different. I will have to write this in your file Lucien, so don't let this sort of thing happen too often. You're free to resume your duties."

"Thank you, Sir," and Lucien left and walked back to the kitchen.

"You know Chester, I still find it difficult to understand how he did so much damage to those three without getting hurt."

Yes Sir, but you know it's my thinking that Lucien should never have been sent here."

* * * *

Lucien went back to work and word about him beating the hell out of Hogg and his two friends spread throughout the prison like a fire fueled with gasoline. Even the hardcore inmates in Block A were impressed and glad Hogg had finally gotten the beating he deserved. For two days everyone treated Lucien like an untouchable novelty. No one knew how they should react to what Lucien had done. And they were a little afraid of him.

After Lucien left the warden's office, Farrar walked over to the infirmary. "Hello Doc. How's our three causalities coming?"

"Well, I finally have them all bandaged up. Hogg has a crushed hand and both bones are broken in that arm and the bones in his face were almost crushed also. He'll be okay, but his face is swollen and sore. His hand and arm, though, will take longer to heal.

"Weasel also had a crushed hand and broken bones in that arm. He'll heal but it will take a while like Hogg.

"Satchel has a broken jaw which I wired together so it'll

heal. He'll be sipping water and soup broth through a straw for six weeks. Once I put his leg and knee in a cast, he'll wear it for two months before I can take it off. When his knee heals, he'll limp for the rest of his life. If I didn't know better, Warden, I'd say a steam roller rolled over these three and not the man who didn't have any injuries. To tell you the truth, Henry, I'm impressed. And this Lucien—well *I* couldn't have done a better job setting Satchel's knee and immobilizing it.

"Henry, just who is this Lucien guy. I have never seen injuries inflicted to three brutes by one man before. It should have been the other way around," Doctor Mallard said.

"I'm working on it, Doc."

Little by little, attitudes, fear and a new found respect were getting back to normal. Except for the inmates and the kitchen crew who witnessed Lucien handle himself against the three. But this wasn't the only change occurring. All the guards and Chester included and Warden Farrar were noticing a subtle change happening at the prison. The earlier apprehensions and fear were gone. Of course Hogg, Satchel and Weasel were lounging in the infirmary. But Hogg and Weasel were soon scheduled to be released back to the yard. Warden Farrar was concerned about what might happen then. *Would Hogg try to reclaim his position as king, or would he submit?*

One afternoon Lucien had his duties finished at the kitchen and he went over to the infirmary. "Hello, Doctor Mallard. How are Hogg, Weasel and Satchel progressing?"

"I'm surprised to see you here, Lucien. They are doing quite well."

"Any chance I could talk with them for a moment?"

"Nothing physical, okay? You are only to talk with them." Dr. Mallard motioned with the tilt of his head towards the recovery room.

Lucien walked into the room and Hogg turned to look at him. At first there was fear and panic etched in the lines on his face and in his eyes. "Hello Hogg, I'm not here to fight with

31

you." Lucien could see Hogg relax somewhat. "I only came by to see how you are, and that I have no ill feelings towards you."

"Thanks, Lucien. It is still difficult to talk much," Hogg replied.

"Sure thing. I understand you and Weasel will soon be released back into the yard." Hogg only nodded his head.

Lucien turned to look at Weasel and Satchel and they were obviously too upset seeing Lucien there to say anything. Lucien nodded his head and left. Doctor Mallard had been standing in the doorway watching. He was dumbfounded watching Lucien.

* * * *

Hogg and Weasel returned to the yard the following week. They still each had a cast on their arm, wrist and hand, and the visible bruises on Hogg's face were gone.

Chester watched them all that day with great interest. Before, when Hogg and his entourage walked near other inmates, the inmates would walk away. Now they seemed not to be afraid of them as they stood their ground and didn't walk away. Hogg also noticed the change and slowly he understood he had lost the hold of fear he had had over the other inmates, and he knew things would never be the same.

* * * *

Eventually the casts came off all three and Satchel had to use crutches for a while. His knee had healed but it was still sore and stiff. They all avoided Lucien like a plague and they were not in any shape to try and bully their way around the other inmates. Chester was the first to see and understand the change among the inmates. *Lucien is good for the prison and the other inmates*, he was thinking to himself. There was even a change in behavior and attitudes with the hardcore inmates. Without knowing it, Lucien had become the kingpin of the entire prison, but there were still a few who were afraid of him because of his strength. Warden Farrar was one among them.

"Excuse me, Chester."

Chester stopped and turned around, "Yes, what is it Lucien:"

"Is there any possibility of changing my work duties?"

"There might be. Are you getting tired of kitchen duty. It's the easiest work in the prison."

"It has nothing to do with the kitchen actually. The kitchen crew are a great group of men. I would like something more physical."

"What have you in mind Lucien?"

"I would like to be assigned to the quarry making gravel and small rocks from big rocks."

Chester almost choked and his breathing stopped for a moment. "Did I hear you right Lucien, you actually want to work in the quarry?"

"All of my life, Chester, I have had to do hard, heavy work. I need to do something that'll make me feel a little bit normal here. Yes, I want to work in the quarry."

"Okay, I'll see what I can do. You understand you'll need Warden Farrar's approval."

"If the kitchen crew ever need extra help for whatever reason, I'd be more than happy to help out."

"You must understand, Lucien, the inmates working in the quarry aren't there by choice. Some are there for discipline reasons. Some were sentenced to hard time by the courts. These are some of the hardcore inmates in Block A. No one is there because they want to be, Lucien."

"Maybe, but I would still like to be reassigned," Lucien said.

"You will be paid. You'll be paid ten cents for every hundred pounds of gravel you crush and make. This of course is held on account for you. It can be used in the prison store or you can save it for when you are released. I'll talk with Warden Farrar, but I can't guarantee anything."

"That's all I ask Chester."

After lunch that day Chester went to see Warden Farrar.

"Come in, Chester, sit down."

"No thanks, Sir."

"Are the inmates still behaving?"

"Yes, Sir."

"Are the other inmates looking towards Lucien as their savior?"

"No, Sir, but the inmates are quieter because of him. Sir, Lucien would like his duty transferred to the quarry. He says he needs the physical work to help him adjust to prison life."

"That's an unusual request. Usually the inmates are asking to get transferred out. If he wants to swing a sledgehammer all day making gravel from big rocks, I'll okay his transfer effective tomorrow morning."

The next morning Chester escorted Lucien out to the quarry. "Lucien, this is guard Larry Thomas. He will be in charge of you from now on."

"Follow me, Lucien," Larry said.

Lucien followed him down into the quarry. "This is your work station here. At the end of the day your gravel will be weighed and put on your account. You cause any trouble out here and I'll send you to isolation. Are we clear on that?"

"Yes Sir."

"At the end of each day you must turn in your sledge-hammer and shovel. Your name is on each and you are responsible to see that they are not stolen."

Lucien took his tools and turned away to start work. Larry went back to his observation post where he could watch all the inmates. Ten now including Lucien.

Lucien swung the sledge blow after blow, cracking open huge rocks with one blow. Blow after blow. Rock after rock and day after day Lucien swung his sledge making gravel. He was tired after each day and he was beginning to sleep better. He was tired each night and he no longer lay awake thinking about things. His appetite was growing with each day and he was beginning to fill out around his shoulders and arms and he was putting on weight. Not fat, but muscle. Because of his friendship with the kitchen crew, he had all he wanted to eat.

Days that were too cold or snowing or raining the inmates did not have to work in the quarry, but Lucien did. He swung his sledge blow after blow, day after day. He was tired at the end of each day but he was happy. He was making two hundred pounds of gravel each day. That was twenty cents a day. He kept it on his account and only using it at the prison store for necessities. He stopped counting the days of his incarceration. One day while they were eating, the inmate sitting beside him said, "Lucien, why are you so happy all the time? And why in the hell are you working in the quarry when you don't have to?"

"Well, living in my father's lumber camp and working for him was more like prison than this. I was always hungry and now I'm not. I had to work from sun-up to sun-down and now I don't. Working in the woods is really more dangerous and strenuous than working in the quarry. Each night in the lumber camp I had to sleep with snoring, smelly men on each side of me. If I rolled over during the night my face would be next to another man. My bunk here is by far more comfortable than the lumber camp bed. I'm here because I accidentally killed someone. But my life here is more like a vacation than my life before."

No one spoke. There were some somber looking faces on the men at his table. They were almost feeling sorry for Lucien.

Christmas and the New Year came and passed without anyone noticing. There wasn't any celebration in prison. Only when one of them was released.

One year had passed for Lucien and he was never aware of it. He had stopped counting the days. One night as he laid in bed thinking about his life in prison, he was beginning to wonder if there might be something psychologically wrong with him. To be that content about his life in prison. He was always in a happy mood and this happiness had begun to affect other inmates as well, since the confrontation with the prison bully, Owen Hogg.

Warden Farrar began to realize that there was an aura of happiness amongst the inmates and he like Chester knew it was because of Lucien Jandreau. And he began to feel more at ease with Lucien, as he now understood that all Lucien wanted was to do his time.

During that first year Lucien had read every book and magazine in the library; albeit it was a small library and collection of books.

"Chester, I have read every book and magazine in the library, is there any possibility of getting more reading material?"

"I could look around—anything in particular?"

"I would like some science and college level math books."

"I know the Warden won't approve the purchase of any books, but I'll look around and see what I can come up with. I know a couple of people who may be able to help out."

Warden Farrar was a very private man and one day he asked Lucien to come to his office. "Sit down, Lucien. Because of that incident with Owen Hogg and his friends, things and attitudes have changed in the prison. The inmates don't walk around always afraid and some even seem to be happy. I have put all this in your personal file. But the reason I asked you here —I understand you enjoy reading."

"Yes Sir, I've read everything in the library, and Chester thinks he can find me some science and mathematic books," Lucien replied.

"Lucien have you ever read the Bible? You know there are many interesting stories in the Bible."

"I tried to read my mother's Bible once."

"Well what happened?" the Warden asked.

"Well, isn't everything in the Bible supposed to be true, God's words?" Lucien asked.

"Yes that's correct, Lucien."

"And we're not supposed to question it. Right?"

"Yes, that also is correct."

"I couldn't get beyond where Noah built his ark."

"What was the problem, Lucien?"

"Well, according to the Book Genesis, which we are not suppose to question, God opened the windows of heaven and it rained for forty days and forty nights. And God let the water cover the earth, even the mountains. I don't believe it could rain enough in forty days and forty nights to cover the mountains. And if it did, where did the water drain off to, because everything was supposed to be flooded. I could never find an answer and I decided that maybe the stories in the Bible were just that. I suppose there's a lot of good in the Bible, but I just couldn't get past Noah and his ark," Lucien said.

"I never heard it put just like that before. That's all I wanted to say, Lucien. You're free to leave."

"Yes, Sir."

After Lucien left, Warden Farrar pulled out his Bible from his desk drawer and turned to the book of Genesis and read it. After he had finished he could see Lucien's point. It's funny to think why he had never questioned the same thing himself.

He replaced his Bible and stared out the window into the open yard thinking about Lucien. He surely wasn't the typical prisoner who comes through here. With everything that he knew about Lucien, he couldn't help but think that there was something special about him.

The next day Chester brought two thick books for Lucien. One was mathematics and the other was college level science. "And I brought you two dime novels, Lucien. These two are about a guy who leads a party across the Canadian Great Plains to the Rocky Mountains, written by Eugene Terrill and printed in Toronto."

Lucien accepted the books graciously and quietly thumbed through the dime novels. "These two look interesting."

"You owe me twenty cents, Lucien, for those two," Chester said.

"The only money I have, Chester, is on account through the prison. I suppose you could buy something at the prison store through my account."

"I could use some tobacco," Chester said.

Chester left and Lucien put the new books on the only shelf there was in the cell and he sat on his bunk and began reading the first dime novel, *An Encounter with a Bear*. There wasn't time to finish it so he laid it on the shelf with the others. It was time for breakfast and he mustn't be late.

* * * *

"Chester, I'd like to see you in my office please," Warden Farrar said.

"Come in and sit down. I have a very peculiar request from Harvey Bradford, New Hampshire Prison Warden. It seems he has a prisoner he would like to get rid of. He's a fighter, a trouble maker, and keeps things stirred up in New Hampshire's State Prison. What do you think about taking him and putting him in with Lucien?"

Chester was silent, thinking about that. Then, "Well, I think Lucien could handle himself okay. There might be trouble at first, but I think Lucien, with time, could straighten him out. Do we tell Lucien or let things unfold naturally?" Chester asked.

"We might tell Lucien he'll be getting a cell mate soon but nothing more. Let Lucien work on this new inmate on his own."

"What's this new inmate's name?"

"Alvie Jones. He has twenty years to do for murder. "

"By all rights Alvie should be in Ward A, but —"

Warden Farrar interrupted then. "Yeah, but this is a different set of circumstances. We'll put him to work in the quarry beside Lucien."

* * * *

Two weeks later the New Hampshire prison wagon rolled through the main entrance and everyone stopped what they were doing to see who was arriving. Alvie was five foot eleven, rugged built with square shoulders and weighed two hundred pounds.

"Lucien, a new prisoner has arrived from New Hampshire and is in isolation now. When that is over he is going to be in your cell with you." Lucien made no comment.

Lucien was asked to help out in the kitchen that evening as two men were sick. He ended up working for two weeks in the kitchen before the two were well enough to come back. Lucien didn't mind at all. When the kitchen was finally clean in the evening, he would return to his cell and read the two dime novels. He was fascinated with Eben McNinch. And he wasn't sure if he was a real man or just a story made up by Eugene Terrill. There was part of him that wanted to believe that Eben McNinch really existed.

Alvie's isolation had ended he was escorted to Lucien's cell. "Your cell mate is Lucien Jandreau. He is currently working in the quarry," Chester said. He opened the cell door and Alvie dropped his things on the bottom bunk, Lucien's bunk.

"That bunk is Lucien's. You'll have to take the top bunk."

Well, it's mine now," Alvie said.

"Okay, you'll remain here, until you're called for supper," that's all Chester said and he walked off smiling, knowing Lucien in his own way will take care of things. But he would like to be here and watch.

When Lucien returned to his cell after work, Alvie was lying on his bunk and his two dime novels were on the floor. The guard Larry unlocked the cell and then closed it and locked it and left.

Lucien picked up the two novels and put them back on the shelf and said, "You leave my things alone, Alvie, and that is my bunk."

"Not any longer, pal. It's mine now and I like it."

"I said that is my bunk, Alvie."

"And I said it is mine now."

The next thing Alvie knew he was hanging upside down. Lucien had grabbed his left leg with one hand and hauled him off the bunk and was holding him upside down. "Let me down you son-of-a-bitch!"Alvie screamed.

Everyone on Ward B could hear Alvie screaming, but no one knew what was happening.

"I said that is my bunk, Alvie."

"If you don't let me down you son-of-a-bitch, I'll pound your head into hamburger!" he yelled.

Lucien lifted him as high as he could and then he dropped Alvie on to the floor, on his head.

Alvie stood, wobbling and rubbing his head. "You stupid son-of-a-bitch! I'll teach you who's boss here!" He yelled and swung at Lucien's head with his right fist.

Lucien side-stepped and grabbed Alvie's wrist and pulled him forward and slammed him into the end wall and toilet. And Alvie bellowed some more. He stood up, sizing Lucien up. He wasn't that much taller. He swung at Lucien again and this time Lucien grabbed his fist like he had done with Hogg. And he held Alvie's fist and began to squeeze and he slowly lowered his arm. Alvie had no choice but to go down on his knees and almost in tears, he said, "You son-of-a-bitch, if you don't let go of my hand I'll beat the living hell out of you!"

Everyone in Ward B now knew what was going on and everyone was being quiet so they could listen.

Alvie was beginning to be a little afraid, as no one had ever done this to him before. He had never been beaten. He tried to stand so he could grab Lucien. As he tried to stand Lucien began to squeeze harder and bend his arm down almost to the breaking point.

"How long are we going to do this, Alvie? I could crush your hand and break your arm. Whatever I decide to do is entirely up to you. So how's it going to be?"

"All right, all right, damn it! Just let go of my hand!" Alvie screamed.

"Are we going to fight over my bunk again?"

"No!"

"Am I going to have any trouble with you?"

"No, damn it! Let go!"

Lucien let go of his hand and said, very calmly, "Next time, Alvie, I'll crush your hand until you can never use it again." He relaxed his grip and then he let go and stepped back. Alvie stood rubbing his hand and thinking that someday he'd make Lucien pay for what he had just done.

Chester walked down the cell corridor checking out each cell. He stopped at Lucien and Alvie's cell and asked, "How's it going here boys? You getting acquainted all right?"

"Sure thing, Chester, no problems here," Lucien said.

When it was time for supper and their cell door was unlocked and opened, Alvie actually walked behind Lucien to the mess hall. Alvie's hand wasn't broken, but he still had to eat with his left hand and he was having a difficult time of it. But what surprised him the most, no one asked why and no mention was made about his earlier screaming and bellowing. This puzzled him. But he still held contempt for Lucien and when the time was right he intended to square things.

* * * *

In the weeks that followed Alvie would get an inmate off by himself so he could bully him, and without question other inmates would come to his rescue and Alvie would have to bug off. Alvie soon realized that there was no leader among the inmates, no gangs. But they seemed to come to each other's needs or rescue.

One day while in the laundry Alvie was trying to browbeat another little mousy inmate when Lucien walked up behind him and kicked him so hard in the ass it lifted him off the floor and the he fell to the floor, madder than hell.

"You son-of-a-bitch, I'll teach you to kick me in the ass!" then he realized it was Lucien standing there.

"What is this all about, Alvie?" Lucien asked.

"Nothing," he replied gruffly and left the laundry.

One day he saw Hogg and his two friends walking around the compound and he hurried to catch up with them. Hogg saw him coming and he stopped and waited for him to catch up, then all four walked together around the compound.

"Hogg, I'd like to speak with you without your pals."

"Anything you have to say, you can say it in front of them," Hogg replied.

"I've been watching you and I think if we work together, the four of us, we can own this prison and all the inmates and have them work for us."

"And why should I believe a word you have to say," Hogg said.

"Listen man, the four of us could run things around here."

"Yeah, but you have over looked one important factor."

"What's that?"

"Your cellmate, Lucien Jandreau."

"The four of us could take him," Alvie said.

"Don't count on it."

"What's the matter with you, man. This is a chance of a lifetime. To be someone, to be king. We could do it."

"No we couldn't do it. We tried once. The three of us all took on Lucien at the same time and he maimed all three of us for life. He damn near crushed my skull, squeezing it with one hand. No we ain't going up against him again and I'd advise you to forget it. Besides, we sort of like how the prison runs from the inside now, if you know what I'm saying. Besides, all the other inmates wouldn't let you do it. Not even Ward A. Forget it, Alvie. Now leave us alone and don't bother us again."

The truth be known, Owen Hogg had the stuffing scared out of him with his encounter with Lucien and he didn't want any more to do with him. Every time Hogg saw Lucien somewhere the same old cold fear would return.

Alvie walked away feeling all alone. Things were different here than in the New Hampshire prison. Here the inmates seemed to be policing themselves and somehow Lucien sat at the top of that policing, but he wasn't taking much of any credit for it or overseeing any of the policing. "This is strange," Alvie said to himself.

* * * *

Little by little, Alvie's attitude began to change and he was even beginning to make some friends. "Remarkable change with Alvie, wouldn't you agree, Chester?" Warden Farrar asked.

"Yes, certainly. He learned he couldn't bully his way around here. The other inmates wouldn't allow it."

"You know, Chester, I've said before, Lucien doesn't belong here. But I'm glad he is. Look at the difference in attitudes of all the inmates."

"I understand what you're saying Warden. He is more like us than he is an inmate," Chester replied.

"For the sake of argument, left's say Lucien has to leave here, leaving Hogg and his gang and Alvie. How long would this peaceful atmosphere last?"

"Probably not long. Lucien is, without even trying, the rock for all the prisoners, and because of him, that we have this easy-going atmosphere," Chester said. "To tell you the truth Warden, I hate to see the day when Lucien leaves. He has made guarding the inmates so much easier."

* * * *

Lucien was fascinated with the science book. He had never heard of electricity, but now after studying this science book, he understood it fully. And the new experiments that scientists were conducting. He found particularly intriguing how electrons, as small as they were—not visible by the naked eye—were able to make motors and machines work.

He would work out math problems on the pages of old newspapers. He had never heard of algebra but he now understood it and had conquered most of the equations and was able to solve most of the problems set forth in the book.

Lucien had spent almost two years in prison now, and still each night he went to sleep feeling good about himself and content. As much as he would like to be on the outside and free to go where he wished, he was never allowed that freedom working for his old man. So for the time being, life here in prison was better than living on the outside at home.

Alvie had finally adjusted to prison life there at Thomaston and no longer tried to bully his way around the other inmates. He even had made a few friends. Lucien and Alvie shared a cell but their relationship was only an amiable existence. They tolerated each other and each other's privacy. They were not friends.

Word had spread to other prisons about the easy-going atmosphere at Thomaston and a few had requested transfers to Thomaston. But unless they had extenuating reasons for the transfer to Thomaston they were denied.

Things couldn't be better at the Thomaston prison, for Warden Farrar and the prisoners. Henry sat back in his chair and lit the tobacco in his pipe and put his feet up on his desk, looking out the window at the prison yard. "Yes Sir, things are good here."

Then one day a Captain Manfred Scott from the United States Army arrived at the front gate of the prison and requested to see the Warden. The guard at the main gate escorted the Captain to the Warden's office. "Warden Henry Farrar, my name is Captain Manfred Scott, U.S. Army, and I am here by the authorization of the Secretary of Defense and President James Buchanan." The Captain showed Farrar his documents.

"The U.S. Army is in need of soldiers in the West, to

protect American settlers from the Indians. Enlistments are low."

"How can *I* help you, Captain Scott?"

"The United States is offering amnesty for inmates who take the offer and enlist. There are of course some conditions."

"What are they?" Farrar asked.

"No hard time inmates. Inmates must have no more than three years left on their sentence. And they must have a good record here in prison. I don't want any malcontents, or troublemakers."

"Certainly, Captain."

"Could you have a list of inmates for me that have no more than three years left to serve by noon? No hard-timers though."

"Certainly. Would you like breakfast, Captain?"

"Already had my breakfast. I need to find the Western Union Office. I'm expecting a telegram and I need to send one. I'll be back at noon, Warden Farrar."

Captain Scott left and Warden Farrar resumed to finish his morning coffee before compiling the list for Scott. "Boy, he sure was brisk," Farrar said aloud.

With his coffee finished, Farrar worked on the list, and finally finished shortly before Captain Scott returned. He had compiled a list of twenty-three names. Lucien Jandreau was one of them.

Lucien had seen the Captain walking across the yard towards Warden Farrar's earlier and at the time he wondered what was going on. Others also had seen the Captain and all were wondering the same thing.

"Come in, Captain Scott. I have that list for you. Would you like some coffee or a drink perhaps?"

"Coffee would be fine, thank you," Scott replied.

Farrar poured the cups while Scott perused the list. "This inmate, Jandreau, he was sentenced to five years for involuntary manslaughter and has served just over two years. My orders are no murderers."

"If you would read his file, Captain, maybe you would

have a different opinion. Lucien does not belong here. He never did. Even the judge who sentenced him said the same thing. It's all in his file."

Scott sipped his coffee while he read Lucien's file. When he had finished reading he finished his coffee and set the cup and file down and said, "He sounds like an extraordinary man. Under these circumstances I can waiver the manslaughter charge. But I have some questions for him."

"I can have one of the guards go get him. He is working in the quarry."

"No, that's okay. I'll want to see all of these inmates in the dining hall right after breakfast tomorrow. I'll talk with Jandreau then. Why is he working in the quarry? Isn't that usually for the hard timers and for punishment?"

"It's all in his file, Captain."

"Yes of course. I'd like to take all the files with me so that I may peruse them all."

"Sorry, Captain, those files don't leave my office. Tomorrow you'll be free to have them with you when you talk with the inmates," Warden Farrar said.

"That's okay; tomorrow then."

Lucien and the others saw Captain Scott entering the Warden's office again, and again they were wondering why. Soon the whole prison knew about Scott's visit and everyone was wondering if they would be on the Captain's list. A chance to end their imprisonment.

* * * *

During breakfast the next morning Warden Farrar entered the dining hall, which he rarely did. "May I have your attention. I have a list of names here and I'll read them off for you. Those on the list will remain here in the dining hall after breakfast. If I do not read your name, you are to resume your regular duty. Thank you," and Warden Farrar left and went back to his office.

Lucien's name was read off, but not his cellmate, Alvie, and this made Alvie angry. There were several names from Ward B but none from the hard-timers.

Lucien sat with three other inmates sipping coffee, waiting for Captain Scott. Everyone was talking and the noise level in the room was more than Lucien could stand. He opened the door to leave and met Captain Scott. "Going somewhere, Lucien?" Scott asked.

"Sir, I needed some fresh air and away from this hum of conversations," Lucien said.

Scott didn't reply, but he smiled and liked the way Lucien answered. More of a scholar than an idiot. He had read and reread Lucien's file many times. He was impressed with the man.

"Men if you would sit down and be quiet we can get started." He waited for everyone to stop talking. "My name is Captain Manfred Scott and I am here looking to enlist new recruits into the Army. The United States Government has seen fit to offer each one of you amnesty if you enlist. There is a catch though. If you are accepted, and I will make that final decision, you will have to serve in the Army equal the time you have left on your sentence. If you screw up before the end of your sentence, you will be put back in prison to serve the time you have left as of this moment. You will not be credited with the time you have served in the Army. Your training will commence with your arrival at the post you will be stationed at."

"Captain," one inmate asked, "if we do enlist, where will we be sent?"

"I'm glad you asked that. As soon as we can we'll start our trek to the West. We'll go to St. Louis, Missouri, cross the Mississippi and then overland to Fort Kearny, Nebraska. There are other groups of inmates from other prisons, like yourselves, who will be going to other forts in the West.

"Now if there are any of you who think you cannot abide to these conditions you are free to leave now."

Three inmates got up and left.

"Now when I call your name, come forward and sit here." Scott called the first name and went through his file and the inmates agreed to the conditions and enlisted. When he came to Lucien, he said, "Mr. Jandreau, I would prefer if you would wait until I have interviewed these other men." Lucien sat back down wondering why.

Three men were rejected because of earlier infractions in their files and five men were short-timers and had no interest to serve in the Army. That left twelve inmates. "Okay men, we will talk some more tomorrow morning after breakfast. You are excused."

"Lucien, come up and sit down. I have gone through your file many times. We don't usually take men convicted of murder. But you were convicted of involuntary murder and sentenced to only five years. There is a letter from Judge Butler in your file. He states that you should never have been sent to prison, that the accident was just that. But the law stated he had to find you guilty. Warden Farrar has also stated that you should never have been sentenced to prison. And you have proven yourself to be the ideal prisoner. In spite of that incident with Owen Hogg. The Warden also has stated that the attitude of all the inmates changed for the better after the Hogg incident and how the inmates started to look after and help each other. And this was all because of you.

"I'm going to make an exception to military rule and accept your enlistment, if that is what you want?"

"Yes Sir, I do want to enlist," Lucien replied. "I was sent here for a reason. Because I lost my temper and my action resulted in the death of Fred Jenkins. I will have to live with that for the rest of my life. The life I found here in prison was a little better than living and working for my father. I have learned a lot while here, but I like the idea of helping American settlers. It's time I moved on."

"I understand, Lucien, that you have recently taught yourself college level math and you have been studying science also."

Yes Sir, I like to read and use my mind," Lucien replied, still feeling nervous and ill-at-ease.

"You are free to leave now, Lucien. We leave tomorrow morning."

"Yes Sir."

Out of twenty-three possible candidates the Captain was able to enlist twelve. Some were short-timers, the Captain rejected a few and a few decided, for whatever reason, not to enlist.

* * * *

"Lucien," the Warden said, "please come to my office for a moment before Captain Scott arrives."

Lucien finished his coffee and walked over to Warden Farrar's office, "Lucien, you have some money coming to you for the gravel you made in the quarry." And Warden Farrar gave Lucien $30.00. "Doesn't seem like much for two years work, but that is the prison rule. I wish you luck, Lucien."

"Thank you, Sir. You have been most kind during my stay here," Lucien said.

The next morning the twelve inmates who had enlisted stayed in the dining hall after breakfast and Captain Scott and a Sergeant entered the room. "Gentlemen, I must leave you now in the hands of Master Sergeant Cedric Quinlin. Sergeant Quinlin will be in charge of you until we meet in Illinois."

Master Sergeant Quinlin stood just under six feet and he had broad shoulders like Lucien's, but not as strong.

"Sergeant, you have your orders and you know our time table. I leave you in command."

With that the Captain turned and left the dining hall.

"Men, today you will sign your enlistment papers and get sworn in. You will also be issued uniforms. Your training will not commence until we reach Fort Kearny in Nebraska. Once you sign your enlistment papers, you'll no longer be inmates, but U.S. soldiers and you will conduct yourselves accordingly. If not, your enlistment will be terminated and you'll return to your locked cells. You, from here on, are no longer animals and you will not act like one. If at any time one of you commits an act which would incarcerate you again, you all will be sent back immediately to finish your sentence. So, my word to you is, you'd better police yourselves.

"Now, knowing what your punishment will be if anyone of you screws up is there any of you who have second thoughts about enlisting?" No one spoke up or left.

"Good, then one by one come up to my table and sign your enlistment papers and then I'll swear you in as a unit."

When Lucien walked up to the table Quinlin was surprised with his size. He silently hoped he was good-natured.

Once everyone had signed their enlistments and were sworn in Quinlin said, "Corporal Dan Evers is outside with a wagon, with your new uniforms. I'll need three of you to help carry them in." Lucien was the first to stand up.

Warden Farrar had discussed with Captain Scott about the real possibility that Lucien would want to enlist. And he told the Captain he would need an extra-large uniform to fit Lucien. Lucien pulled on his pants and then the shirt and they fit very good. He buttoned his shirt and hooked his belt. And he was smiling radiantly. He was happy.

"Okay men, if I may have your attention. We aren't due to leave for three more days. So we will stay here. Although your cell doors will no longer be locked. If any of you want to go to your homes to take care of any unfinished business, you can leave now. But—and I say this very sternly—if you desert and are not here by 0700 Thursday morning, you will be considered a deserter and you will be chased down and shot. And the rest of you—well you know what your fate will be."

Only a few left to take care of things or say good-bye to loved ones. Lucien left and boarded a train for Skowhegan. The train had to go to Augusta and then he reboarded another train for Skowhegan. He was home in Skowhegan in time for supper.

* * * *

When Lucien walked into his mother's house, she turned expecting to see her husband Maurice. "Oh my God, Lucien, is that really you!" And she dropped the pan she was holding.

Lucien hugged her and she began to cry. "What are you doing in this uniform? You still have three years to serve," she said between crying.

He told her all about enlisting and she cried again, because her son would be going away forever now. But she was also happy he was out of prison. She also knew he couldn't ever stay around here.

"I'm just glad you're out of that awful prison, son," and she dried her tears.

"It wasn't that bad, Ma. In fact I kinda enjoyed it. It was a lot better than living under his rule and working for him."

Lucien's sister Becky, six and the youngest, didn't know anything about prison, but she was glad to see her big brother. Laurence, nine, was a bit stand-offish at first, but he soon mellowed and he too was glad to see his really big brother.

Bertha had made a chicken stew and biscuits during the day. "Sure can't beat home cooking, Ma."

Lucien slept in the barn that night on a bed of hay. This brought back fond memories when he was a little boy. Just before daylight the rooster started crowing and then the hens started clucking and soon all the barn animals were wanting their morning feed. Lucian got up and fed all the animals and then washed up before going in the house. "What would you like for breakfast, son?"

"Eggs... any way you want to cook 'em. I haven't eaten an egg since leaving here two years ago."

Bertha fried up a slab of bacon and scrambled the eggs with homemade bread and butter.

Lucien helped clean up the kitchen and dry the dishes. "Ma, I need to talk with you serious-like. When I get to Fort Kearny in Nebraska I'll write and give you my address. I'll write often to you, and Becky and Laurence. And if Pa does anything to hurt you, Ma, or Becky or Laurence, I want you to tell me. I want you to promise me, Ma. Pa can't keep going on bullying people like he done to me. I won't stand for it, if he starts in on Becky and Laurence. Promise me, Ma."

"I will, son."

Lucien reached into his pocket and gave his $30.00 to his mother. "Ma I want you to have this and buy yourself a new dress and bonnet and something special for Becky and Laurence."

"How did you get $30.00 son?" Bertha asked.

"I was making gravel in the prison quarry and I got paid for it. You take the money, Ma, and use it.

"I have to get my things in the barn, Ma, and then I have to leave."

"Okay, son."

Lucien walked out to the barn and just as he was going to lift the anvil and block of wood to get his money, his father walked in behind him. He heard the barn door creak and he turned around.

"What in the hell are you doing here!" Maurice bellowed, walking towards Lucien. "What, did you escape? You never were any good."

Lucien squared off to face him and he said, "I created the accident that killed Jenkins, but it was you who should have gone to jail. I'd had all I could take of your bullying and fault finding and I lost my temper, causing Fred to die. You're nothing but a bully and you should have gone to prison."

"Nobody talks to me like that. Especially my own blood, you whelp. I'll teach you to talk to me like that," and he took two quick steps toward Lucien and was about to throw a punch to Lucien's head when Lucien grabbed him by his belt and his shirt and using Maurice's momentum, he lifted his father off his feet and turned him upside down and threw him into the tie-up wall. Maurice bounced off the wall and started to stand when Lucien grabbed him by the throat under the chin and lifted him up. His feet swinging in the air.

"Now you listen to me, old man. I enjoyed prison life after living under your rule and shadow. I was happy there and now I've been given amnesty and enlisted into the Army and I'm leaving for Nebraska.

"All my life you bullied me and found fault with everything I did. All I ever wanted from you was a little recognition. That's not love, but that would have been enough. I could never understand why you acted as if you hated me and you took that hatred out on me by bullying me.

"I'm going to write Ma and Becky and Laurence often. And if they ever tell me that you are doing the same to them as you did to me—I'll dessert the Army if I have to, but I'll come back and take care of you for good." He squeezed Maurice's throat a little more. For the first time in his life Maurice was scared. Terrified because he never expected his son to react like this.

"Do you understand me old man?"

Maurice couldn't speak but he tried to nod his head that he did. Lucien turned, still holding on to Maurice's throat and threw him across the barn into the opposite wall. Maurice collapsed, gasping for air and rubbing his throat.

Lucien picked up the anvil and block of wood and set it aside and dug into the dirt where the block had been setting and he pulled out of the dirt a small leather pouch, counting $400.00 dollars. He put the pouch inside his shirt and walked over to Maurice. "I had $85.00 hidden away upstairs in the house. It isn't there now. I assume you stole that. That makes you a thief. Remember what I said, old man. Don't you ever start bullying my family."

With that said Lucien left the barn, "Ma, remember what I said, if he starts up on you."

"I will, son. You be careful."

"Good-bye, Ma. Good-bye, Becky—Laurence.

* * * *

Lucien had to wait for two hours for the train to Augusta. There was nothing to do but walk around the terminal or sit on one of the wooden benches. He had left his family behind and he was not thinking about them or his father. He had finally said to him what he had wanted to for a long time. It was done and now he had other things to think about.

It was evening by the time he arrived back at the prison. As odd as it might seem, this seemed more like returning home, than when he had actually returned to his home only yesterday. *How things do change in one's life.*

Alvie was locked in his cell so Lucien had to have one of the guards unlock it so he could lay down and go to sleep. Alvie was surprised to see Lucien back. He thought he had seen the last of him.

The next day, for something to do, Lucien went out to the quarry to break rocks. The troop wasn't scheduled to leave for another day yet.

CHAPTER 3

1858

When the twelve ex-inmates left the prison they all said good-bye to Warden Farrar and a few of the guards, but as they walked to the train station no one looked back. All of the passenger cars were full so they had to ride in an empty freight car. They sat on the floor and leaned back against the walls. For some reason they were subdued, quiet. No one felt like talking. They were all deep in thought about where they were going and what they would be doing. It was too late now to turn back.

They changed trains in Augusta and again in Lewiston. In Portland there was a delay while the train was coupling new cars, so supper was brought out for the men. Lucien went back for seconds.

"We'll be travelling all night, men, so you'll be able to sleep, this time in the passenger car. We'll be stopping in Portsmouth, New Hampshire for a few men from Vermont State Prison and a few from New Hampshire State Prison. From Portsmouth we go to Leominster, Massachusetts, then on to Albany, New York and Buffalo, New York. Our last passenger for this group will be in Leominster. Other groups will also be forming much as this one. As soon as the engineer is finished coupling we can board the last passenger car.

Six more ex-inmates joined them in Portsmouth. Four from New Hampshire and two from Vermont. Near Leominster, Massachusetts they picked up six more. They had to couple another passenger car for the men. The train went near Worcester,

Massachusetts, then through Albany, New York to Buffalo. Lucien and others were sick of all this train riding and sleeping in the uncomfortable seats. The food was plentiful and good. Some of the guys were beginning to complain.

"Men, when we reach Buffalo we'll board a train with a much larger locomotive engine and we will be coupling a freight car for us. And we'll have to stand guard in the car twenty four hours a day. I have a schedule worked up and I'll post it on the wall of this car. I'll explain more when we reach Buffalo."

At Leominster they were joined by six more inmate enlistees, one of them being a black man. He wasn't six feet tall, but he had square shoulders and he was well built. It was obvious he had seen a lot of hard work. Samuel boarded the car with the others and when he started to sit beside one of them: "Hey, what in the hell are you doing? Just because you have papers declaring that your master had to set you free doesn't give you the right to associate with us white folks; go sit in the back," John Adams said.

Samuel stood back up, not wanting to offend anyone or start any trouble. He looked towards the back and all he saw were white folks. Lucien saw the look on his face and he stood up and said, "Hey you! You looking for a seat? You can sit with me."

"Hey boys, we have a nigger-lover among us," John laughed.

Lucien waited until Samuel had walked to the back. "Hello, I'm Lucien Jandreau," he shook Samuel's hand. He had a firm grip. Samuel was impressed with Lucien's grip also.

"I'm called Samuel, Samuel Freeman. Thank you for sharing your seat."

John was still talking and laughing. "Sit down, Samuel. I'll be right back."

"What are you going to do, Lucien?" Lucien nodded his head towards John. "Forget it, Lucien."

"No, we can't forget it. We are a unit and we must act like

a unit, looking out for each other. He could ruin this freedom for all of us; you just stay here, Samuel."

Lucien walked to the head of the car and stopped where John was sitting. Without saying anything he reached down and grabbed John by his throat under his chin and lifted him out of his seat. His feet were swinging in the air.

"Look you," in an even calm voice, "we are a unit. What happens to one happens to us all. I lived my whole life with a bully like you. I would strongly advise you to change your ways. Do you understand me, John? We are a unit. Got it?"

Just as Lucien was setting John back in his seat, Sergeant Quinlin entered the car, "What's going on here?"

"I was just explaining to John, here, that we are a unit," Lucien said.

"Okay, go take your seat now; we are about to move out."

After Quinlin had taken his seat he looked at John, one of the last men to board in the group from Leominster. He also saw John rubbing his neck and the red mark on his neck. He looked up at Lucien and guessed what had taken place. He would keep an eye on John and Lucien. He didn't figure Lucien for a troublemaker though. He smiled to himself and sat back and his head was soon on his chest and snoring slightly.

They were on a straight route to Buffalo. They didn't have to change trains again until Buffalo. They stopped long enough to take on water and more food supplies for the men.

The next morning, "Private Jandreau come here!" Sergeant Quinlin bellowed. It took Lucien a few moments to understand he was wanted. He rushed to the head of the car.

"Yes, Sergeant."

"Private, from your prison records, you spent some time helping in the kitchen."

"Yes, Sergeant."

"Well, our cook needs help to feed all of these men."

"Yes, Sergeant."

"Two cars down."

Lucien walked through the next car to the mess car. Lucien was happy to help out. He worked all day with the kitchen crew, cleaning up and preparing for the next meal. His day ended about 8 p.m. that evening.

There was still a little daylight left and he sat next to the window watching the countryside as it passed by. As interesting as rail travel was he had actually thought that the train would travel faster. At the pace they were going a good horse could run faster. But the train didn't tire, although it had to stop regularly for water.

In Buffalo they changed trains and Lucien had time to walk around and stretch his legs. He walked up to look at the locomotive. It was huge. So much bigger than any of the other engines, so far.

From Buffalo, New York, they traveled to Detroit, Michigan. "We'll be here for twelve hours while we load some special cargo that we will be taking with us to Fort Kearny." After all of the wooden boxes were loaded Sergeant Quinlin had worked up a security guard schedule. "There will be a security watch of four men at all times. You'll have fours on guard and eight off. Everyone is scheduled," Sgt. Quinlin said.

Lucien and Samuel had the midnight to 4 a.m. watch. Sergeant Quinlin decided to pair them two together, as they seemed to get along well. And Quinlin had no reservations that Lucien would look after Freeman.

From Buffalo they headed towards Erie, Pennsylvania. This locomotive was large enough so it carried a water tank car behind the coal car. It was plumbed directly into the boiler. This was a long stretch of tracks and they only stopped at Erie for water, which took a long time to fill the tanker car.

From Erie they headed towards Cleveland, Ohio. There they replenished their food supplies also.

Lucien was traveling across a lot of country, but besides what he could see from the passenger window, were the train stations. He was disappointed. He was hoping to see much of the country that he was traveling through.

From Cleveland they headed southwest towards Fort Wayne, Indiana. The tanker car was almost on empty when they rolled to a stop under the water tower.

Everyone had settled into a normal routine with their guard duty. There was no bickering or complaining. Not even from John Adams. The men learned from the attendants at the water tower that the two other trains had stopped there with ex-inmates, now soldiers, and they had taken different rails when leaving Fort Wayne, than they were heading.

Before leaving Fort Wayne, the train picked up two more freight cars. "What else are we hauling, Sergeant Quinlin?" Lucien asked.

"Horses. We'll pick up more once we cross the river." Meaning the Mississippi River.

They went straight across Illinois, stopping only for water and food. They were making good time according to the relief engineer. They were traveling about 25 miles per hour.

They crossed Illinois and stopped across the river from Fort Madison, Iowa, "This is as far as we can travel by train. From here to Fort Kearny we go by horseback and pulling three freight wagons. The third wagon will be our chuck wagon. And since Lucien is the nearest thing we have for a cook, you have the job, Lucien. The others will have guard duty. You won't. Samuel."

"Yes, Sergeant," Samuel replied.

"Do you want to be Lucien's helper? You two seem to get along pretty well."

"Yes, Sergeant."

The crates were off-loaded into the wagons and the horses: fourteen were led off and put into a holding corral near the tracks. These were well fed with hay, grain and water.

With all the cars off-loaded, the train backed through and switched onto another set of rails. "Men, it's late, too late to cross the river tonight on ferries. We'll do it after we eat in the morning. Your guard duty still continues tonight. Except Lucien. From this moment until we arrive at Fort Kearny, you are cook."

Before turning in that night Lucien went for a walk down to the river. It sure was wide. As he was looking across to the other shore, somehow he began to sense or feel that he was being guided to the west. He loved his mother and brother and sister, but thi— Whatever it was that was guiding him, was much stronger than the memories of home.

Whatever it was that was causing this sensation about the west was suddenly making him feel very happy. As he began to smile, his earlier excitement about going west was now renewed and he couldn't wait to cross the river and be on their way to Fort Kearny.

Lucien and Samuel were up at 4 a.m. the next morning to start preparing breakfast.

Lucien was becoming a talented cook. This is with eggs, bacon, stews and pan bread. He noticed that there were a lot of baked beans on board the chuck wagon and he wasn't sure how his beans would turn out.

His coffee was black and strong and no one complained.

"Come on men, stop your molly-lagging. All this freight and horses aren't going to get across on their own. Let's go, men," Sergeant Quinlin said.

The horses were boarded first on the ferry and taken across. The ferry had to make three trips and then two more for the three wagons.

"When are we going to learn what is in the crates, Sergeant? What's so secretive?" one of the men asked.

"You'll know when I say so," Quinlin said.

Once everything was on the west side of the river Quinlin said, "We'll have to take everything inside the fort and we have two days here for those of you who may not be able to ride. We only have two days to teach those of you who can't."

The horses were all corralled and the freight wagons secured. "Lucien, you and Samuel will not be cooking breakfast in the morning. Everyone will be eating in the mess hall," Quinlin said.

After breakfast the men who couldn't ride were told to wait for Quinlin at the corrals and the other men were making sure the three wagons were fit for a long trip. The axels were greased and all wheels were tightened. They checked and repaired the harnesses, and helped to put new shoes on the draft horses who would be pulling the wagons.

"Lucien, you want to help me with the non-riders?" Quinlin asked.

"Sure thing."

The horses already saddled, the men started out by leading them around the corral by the reins so the horse could get used to its rider.

"Okay, unsaddle your horses now and brush them down and then saddle them again. Let them get use to you saddling and unsaddling them. Then lead them around the corral some more."

"When you sit in the saddle don't grip your horse so tight with your legs. If you do he will think something is wrong or about to happen. Your horse will read your body actions," Lucien said.

"That's very good, Private. Where did you learn that?" Quinlin asked.

"My Pa beat it into me."

After a half hour of leading their horses around the corral, John and the others mounted up. At first they just sat still, letting the horse get use to having them on his back.

They let their horse walk around the corral at first, so both the horse and rider could get use to each other. Then little by little they let their horse run.

At the end of the day they were quite saddle sore. Quinlin had already decided that these six men would drive wagons. Two to a wagon so they could relieve each other.

After breakfast the next day Quinlin said, "Men, meet me over by the two freight wagons."

"It's time you knew what we're carrying. These crates contain three hundred new .45 caliber Sharps rifles. Plus three hundred of the new Remington revolvers, percussion capped cylinders. There is also powder and bullets. Now open one of the rifle crates and each of you take a new rifle. Open up the powder and bullet crate and load your rifle."

Each man was busy looking at his new Sharps rifle. It was like receiving an early Christmas gift. When the rifles were all loaded, they opened another crate with the new revolvers. These were already loaded except for caps. There were also belts and holsters for each man. "Put a cap on each cylinder and put the hammer on safety. Once we reach Fort Kearny you'll be trained with the revolvers. I am issuing you men these firearms now because it is a long trip to Fort Kearny from here. If robbers or Indians learn what we are carrying they might try to steal them. So be vigilant, stay awake in the saddle and always know what is around you. If you see something, don't holler out. Come tell me.

"Now, let's mount up and head out. Lucien, you ride up front with me. The rest follow in columns of twos, then the wagons."

"Sergeant Quinlin?"

"Yes, Lucien."

"If we are eventually going to connect up with the Oregon Trail, doesn't that trail start west from St. Louis?" Lucien asked.

"Yes it does."

"Then why did we come to Fort Madison?"

"People trying to get to Oregon have to leave early in the season or they're likely to get snow bound crossing the Rockys. There'll be so many people, wagons and horses in St. Louis right now we wouldn't have a chance of crossing the river. All we have to do is keep heading west and eventually we'll hook up with the Oregon Trail."

The day was hot and dry and they were kicking up so much dust. Those in the rear were covered with it. They traveled across huge grassy plains where you couldn't see the other side. The soil looked to be dark and rich, good for growing crops.

Every once in a while they would maneuver through gullies and wash outs. They saw small herds of buffalo. One night at supper one of the men said, "Sarg, why don't we get us a buffalo tomorrow so we can eat some fresh meat?"

Another man spoke up, "Yeah, a thick steak would chew up awfully good."

"Okay, tomorrow morning just before we start to head out, Lucien, you, John and Bill ride out in front and shoot something. A buffalo would be nice. Don't go too far astray. There might be an Indian hunting party out looking for fresh meat also. Only one buffalo," Quinlin said.

* * * *

Bill and John helped Lucien and Samuel clean up and pick up after breakfast the next morning. They each were excited about the hunt. "I'm putting you in charge, Lucien. I figure you have had more experience with hunting."

John Adams attitude had certainly changed since he boarded the train in Leominster. Quinlin was quite observant of the change and how he was helping out. He no longer tried to bully Samuel or anyone else. And Samuel was becoming a better cook than Lucien.

"Samuel."

"Yes Sir."

"Don't call me Sir, Private."

"No, it's a habit from my days as a slave," Samuel said.

"Samuel, do you like cooking?"

"Yes I do. I use to watch my ma back home."

"Would you like to be our regular cook and take over for Lucien?"

"Yes, Sarg. I could do that. But I'll be needing me a helper."

"I want Lucien mounted and ready to act if we should get ambushed, and not with his hands in the flour barrel. You can have Paul help you. He isn't so sure of himself on horseback."

Lucien, John and Bill had traveled a long way ahead. "Aren't we getting too far ahead of them?" John asked.

"Yeah, we are, but let's see what's on the other side of that knoll first."

The three of them rode up the knoll and on the other side was a herd of buffalo that stretched west for miles. There was a small group not far away. They eased their horses back down behind the knoll out of sight. Lucien and John handed their reins to Bill. "Hold the horses here, Bill, until we shoot," Lucien said.

"You're more used to hunting probably than either Bill or I, Lucien. You shoot the buffalo," John said.

"Okay." Lucien pulled his Sharps rifle out of its scabbard and stepped down out of the saddle. The buffalo weren't at all nervous. In fact they kept coming closer as they grazed. Lucien looked for a lone buffalo and took a fine bead right behind the head and fired. The buffalo dropped dead and the others ran off for a short distance and then stopped and continued grazing. Lucien reloaded his rifle.

"Nice shooting, Lucien," John said.

"I hope you know what to do now, Lucien, I have never been hunting and I don't think John knows how to butcher an animal," Bill said.

"Well, I'll show you. First though we make sure he is dead so we don't get hurt."

They walked up slowly to the buffalo. The ribcage wasn't moving. Its legs were still.

"I guess we're okay. You two take the front leg and the

back leg and roll it onto its back." Lucien had sharpened his knife as sharp as a razor and he wasn't long making a slit from the rump up the belly, chest and neck to the head. Then he began skinning. Fleshing the hide as he went.

"I just thought you split the belly and took the guts out, Lucien," John said.

"This way is cleaner."

They watched as Lucien expertly skun and fleshed the hide. When he was done Lucien said, "We need to make a travois to haul this meat back. We'll do that so we'll have something to put the quarters on, and off the ground.

They found the poles they needed and lashed them together with rope.

After the quarters and back straps were loaded onto the travois Lucien said, "Let's make a small fire and roast some of the heart and liver before we head back. I'm hungry enough to eat my horse."

While John and Bill gathered wood and chips enough for a small fire, Lucien opened the chest cavity and removed the heart and liver and put those on the travois. Then he folded up the hide to take with them. Bill also brought back several long stem branches to stick the meat pieces on to roast over the fire. It didn't take long to roast small pieces of meat.

"Wow, is this good," Bill said.

"Yeah, a little like moose."

John looked up and when he did he dropped his roasting stick. "We have company boys. Indians. Six of them."

Lucien and Bill turned to look." They outnumber us two-to-one Lucien," Bill said.

"We can't out run them dragging this travois loaded with meat, Lucien," John said.

Bill and John grabbed for their rifles and started to get up. "Sit down. Both of you, and let go of your rifles. We're outnumbered alright and we can't outrun them. Maybe we can befriend them."

"Are you crazy, Lucien?" John said.

"Have you a better suggestion? It's possible they are scouting for buffalo or they could only be a hunting party. I say we invite them down to join us."

"Okay," John said, "but I still think you're crazy."

"Me too, Lucien," Bill added.

Lucien stood up and waved his arm welcoming them to come in. He had to wave his arm several times before they started to come down slowly off the knoll towards them. "Keep roasting meat fellas, so they can see what we are doing."

They rode up to thirty feet from Lucien and just sat on their ponies talking among themselves.

Lucien kept using his hands and arms motioning and beckoning them to sit and join them and roast meat.

The Indian in the middle was probably the leader, as he was doing most of the talking amongst them. Finally he nodded his head at Lucien and he dismounted and he apparently told the others to do so as they too now stood on the ground.

Lucien motioned for them to joint them and sit. He sat down and motioned for them to sit across the fire from him. Surprisingly enough they did.

John handed each a roasting stick and Bill a piece of meat. They knew what to do with it and they all soon were roasting and eating meat. From the moment the Indians were eating, Lucien thought perhaps it had been sometime since they had eaten.

Finally when everyone had finished Lucien pointed toward their leader and asked, "Lakota?" He shook his head no.

"Dakota?" Again no.

"Sioux?" Again no.

"Cheyenne?" Again no.

The leader patted his chest with his hand and said, "Pawnee!" Apparently very proudly. Lucien, John and Bill all nodded their heads that they understood and they said, "Pawnee."

To help seal their friendship Lucien had an idea. He

stood up and motioned for the leader to stand and then to follow Lucien away from the fire. Lucien kneeled on the ground and scrapped together some dry dead grass and sticks and removed the magnesium fire starter from his shirt pocket. Lucien showed him how when he scratched the pieces together the magnesium made sparks. Then he put the magnesium bar into the bundle of dry grass and scratched the bar several times before the grass caught fire.

The leader wanted to look at it, so Lucien handed it to him. The leader looked it all over and he scratched the two together like he had seen Lucien do and sparks jumped out.

He handed it back to Lucien and Lucien shook his head no and gave it back to the leader. "I Lucien." And he said his name slow and several times before the leader understood the meaning and then repeated—"Lucien."

The leader patted his chest and said slowly, "Cetan" (*hawk*).

Lucien said his name slowly several times until Cetan smiled broadly.

He patted his chest again and said, "Cetan." Then pointed to Lucien and said, "Lucien." And he grinned again.

"John, Bill, do you think it would be a good idea to give our new friends a hind quarter of the buffalo and the hide. After all we are probably on their hunting grounds."

"Just so long as we can leave peacefully," John said.

"Yeah, me also," Bill added.

"Okay, get a hind quarter and the hide then and give it to them."

Cetan and his friends accepted the gift willingly and then mounted their ponies and rode off. At the top of the knoll Cetan stopped and turned around and raised his arm above his head and hollered "L-U-C-I-E-N!" Then he rode off.

"I think we'd better be leaving also and find the unit," Lucien said.

It was afternoon, and they followed their own trail back until it intersected with the main body. Then they followed that trail and caught up with them just as they were making camp for the night.

* * * *

Samuel and Paul took the meat and started slicing it up for steaks that night and steak and biscuits in the morning. All the men were happy to be eating fresh meat.

"Before you three eat I want to speak with you three over here," and Quinlin walked away from the others.

"Okay, what in the hell took you three all day. I had expected you by mid-afternoon waiting for us. Not riding in on our trail. You talk first, Jandreau."

"After we had the buffalo meat loaded on the travois we decided to build a small fire and roast us some meat. We were hungry. Before we had finished eating, six Indians rode up. They outnumbered us two to one. We might be able to get two or three of them and then they would have gotten two or three of us. We talked it over and decided to invite them to share our fire." Lucien went on to tell Quinlin all about the event.

"And you're telling me you made friends with six Indians and they weren't hostile? Which tribe were they from or didn't you know?"

"Pawnee, Sarg. And we made a friend out of them," Lucien said.

"It just doesn't figure."

"What's that, Sarg?" John asked.

"The three of you go off hunting, and none of you have any experience in the west or the Indians out here and you invite a party—probably either a scouting parting or hunting party—and you make friends of them. It just don't figure. Did you get how any of them are called?"

"Yes, Sarg. The leader is called Cetan," Lucien replied.

"I'm going to have to write up a report tonight about this and when we get to Fort Kearny I'll have to report this to

Captain Scott. He was a couple of trains ahead of us and he is probably already at the Fort. You're dismissed." As the three walked off Quinlin watched them leave and scratched his head and said, "If that doesn't beat all." But he expected Lucien was responsible for the entire event.

Fresh buffalo steaks with their usual beans and biscuits was a delicious treat.

* * * *

As they traveled across the grassy plains of Nebraska, Quinlin kept thinking about Lucien and making friends with six Pawnee Indians. Lucien had done the correct thing in that situation, of course, but what worried Quinlin was would Lucien ever be able to submit to Army procedures and authority.

The men ate fresh buffalo meat for two days. And because of the high protein content, everybody, Quinlin included, had more energy and were happier.

The wagons were loaded heavy and their progress across the endless plains was slow. One day while Lucien and John were out front scouting, they saw four men on horseback at a great distance. They appeared to be sitting there watching them. "The way those four are dressed I'd say they are white men. Hiders or miners maybe," Lucien said.

"Or they want what we have in the wagons," John said.

"I think you're closer to the truth on that, John. We'll slow our progress, so we won't be that far from the others."

When they stopped for the day Lucien and John told Quinlin about the four riders. "Lucien, eat and get some rest. I want you, John and Bill on guard duty at 10 p.m. to 2 a.m. One of you three with the horses and the other two out front away from camp a bit. Pick a good location."

Lucien, John and Bill ate first and managed three hours of sleep. Quinlin woke them and then he turned in. Bill stayed with the horses.

They were camped behind a bushy knoll and they climbed to the top and decided this was as good of a spot as any. Just ahead and a little to the left Lucien could see their camp fire. "John, you stay here and keep a sharp watch out. I'm going to get close enough to their camp to see if they are there or the camp fire is only a decoy."

"All right, Lucien, but be careful."

Lucien left carrying his rifle in one hand while walking bent over and parting the tall grass with his other hand. He was afraid that as tall as he was he'd silhouette above the grass. Occasionally he would scare out a rabbit or fox, but at least they ran off without signaling an alarm.

He was close enough to see four men sitting around the fire and their horses were close by, and he could hear what they were saying. They were planning to attack on foot after mid-night and they knew about the firearms and shot and powder and how much it was worth. They were planning to kill everyone, so there would be no witnesses. He crawled in behind one of the four and then he stood up and pointed his rifle at the one sitting across the fire. When he saw Lucien he jumped to his feet and hollered, "Holy shit! Where in the hell did you come from and what do you want? We ain't got no money!" The others stood up also.

"Hold it! Stay away from your rifles and throw your handguns over by the horses." When they hesitated Lucien said, "Now, damn you." They did.

"You four have been following us, looking for an opportunity to ambush us while we were asleep and kill everyone so there'd be no witnesses."

"We had no such intentions!" one of them said.

"I was here long enough to hear you talking. Now we're going to walk back to our campsite."

Just then the one closest to Lucien grabbed for Lucien's rifle but Lucien was quicker. He saw the man coming and he hit the man beside his head with the rifle barrel knocking him to the ground. Another rushed in and Lucien hit him on the bridge of

70

his nose with the rifle butt breaking his nose. He let the screams out of him. "You son-of-a-bitch, you broke my nose!" He got up to have at Lucien again. Lucien dropped his rifle and took two steps closer to another of the four who was charging in at Lucien and swinging his right fist to hit Lucien beside the head. Lucien grabbed his trouser belt and his shirt and using the man's forward momentum he picked him up and threw him over by the horses on his back.

Another stepped in and Lucien back-handed him breaking his jaw, but he wasn't through yet. He came at Lucien again and Lucien grabbed his right arm and twisted it and dislodging his shoulder and then he snapped the forearm. He went down screaming.

Another came at Lucien and he grabbed his arm and brought his iron like fist down on his collarbone breaking it. He was done. There was one left, the one Lucien had thrown. This one put his head down and charged towards Lucien and Lucien stepped to one side and brought his fist down on the back of the man's neck. His collarbone was also broken and Lucien also broke his right arm. The fight was all out of them.

The leader said, "No more, Mister—no more."

He helped them to their feet and said, "You boys can walk all right. There's nothing wrong with your legs." Lucien untied their horses and leading them, he ushered the four beaten men back to camp. He left their dunnage and firearms. Their horses were already saddled. Probably for the night attack they had been planning.

Even though the four men could walk, the progress was slow, with broken bones and all. "Hey! John!" Lucien hollered.

"Yeah, over here Lucien. And why in the hell are you hollering?"

"Go wake up Sergeant Quinlin. I have a surprise for him." John ran off and shook Quinlin awake.

"What is it? What in the hell are you doing waking me now?" Quinlin spouted.

"I'm not sure, Sarg. Only Lucien told me to wake you," John said.

Quinlin got up and waited by the fire for Lucien when he saw Lucien bringing in the four men who had been following them he bellowed, "What in hell is all this, Lucien? These men look as if they have been through a meat grinder. What in hell happened out there?"

Very calmly and coherently Lucien said, "These four men were planning to attack us sometime after midnight and kill us all and leave no witnesses."

"Okay, but what in hell happened to them? They're all beat to hell. Broken bones and a bloody mess. Who did this to them, Private?" Quinlin asked.

"I did, Sarg."

"You? There's not a scratch on you. You sure don't look like you've been in a fight. Particularly with four outlaws. Let me see your hands, Private."

Lucien held out his hands and turned them over. "There's not a mark on your hands or you, Private. What in hell is going on here, Private?"

"I don't know what else I can say, Sarg. They attacked me first," Lucien answered.

"Okay for now, but Captain Scott is going to want to talk with both of us when we get to the Fort."

"Sergeant, those men need their wounds attended to."

"Yeah, but we don't have a doctor with us."

"I can help some. At least stop the pain. But they need attention now and not in the morning, Sarg. I need Samuel. I think he has seen these types of wounds before."

"Okay, go wake him."

Lucien went to awaken Samuel. Sergeant Quinlin stood there watching Lucien walk away and wondering who in the hell this man was. He gets into a fight with four outlaws who would wish to kill him and he doesn't even get a scratch, torn clothes or dirt on his clothes. "God help us if he ever turns on the Army."

But then, he never turned on the prison guards.

It took Lucien and Samuel until daylight to apply splints to broken body parts and bandage wounds. The one with the broken jaw, Lucien had to wrap a bandage around the top of his head and the bottom of his jaw. "We have to keep your jaw immobile until the bone mends."

"How am I gonna eat?" he mumbled.

"You'll have to sip broth through a hollow reed."

The only thing Lucien could do for the broken nose was to pull his nose away from his head enough to reset the bone. He hollered with pain.

"What are your names?" he asked the leader.

When the guy didn't reply, Lucien said, "I asked you a question—or do you want me to toss you around some more?"

"I'm Jessy Smith and these two here are my brothers, Ralph and Claude. The one with the broken jaw is Gil Rawlings."

"Are you four wanted by the law anywhere?"

"Nah." But Lucien didn't believe him.

Gil Rawlings' head was swollen bad where Lucien had hit him beside his head with his rifle barrel. Lucien had given him a cool wet cloth and told him to keep the cool compress on the swelling on the side of his head. Luckily no one had any broken legs so they could ride horseback, as uncomfortable as that was going to be.

"This is all we can do for them, Samuel. Just in time for you to start breakfast. Do you need any help, Samuel, since you were helping me?"

"Sure. You can make the coffee and put more wood on the fire. Then you can find a hollow reed for Rawlings and fix him a cup of broth. I need to set the beans on the fire to warm up and start more soaking for tomorrow. Sure would like another buffalo, Lucien."

Once they were on their way, the Smith brothers complained all day. But there was nothing anyone could do to make the ride any more comfortable. Gil just couldn't speak.

At night Quinlin insisted that their legs be bound. He wasn't taking any chance of losing them. Two days later, while Lucien, John and Bill were on point about two miles ahead they came onto another buffalo herd. This time John made the shot and they didn't stop to roast the meat. As soon as the travois was loaded they headed back to meet the unit.

They all ate well that night, except Gil. He sipped meaty broth through his hollow reed. Everybody was happy again. The earlier bickering among the men had stopped and they were all feeling energized.

As Lucien lay on his bedroll that night while looking up at the stars, he was thinking that this Army life was not bad. Better than prison life and so much better than life back home.

When a rain storm blew in from the south with strong wind, Quinlin told the unit to make camp early. They had very little waterproof gear. The wind blew and it rained for two days. Everybody was irritable and soaking wet. It was also difficult to keep the cook-fire going. The only thing anyone wanted was coffee. Their only protection was under the wagons.

When the wind and rain stopped they didn't move for another day. They took the time to dry out, but most of the food supplies were ruined. They would have to depend on the buffalo now or starve.

These plains would make for excellent farming and grazing for beef cattle. But the Indians considered these plains as theirs. There was a wagon train moving westward. People from the east looking for a better way of life, free homestead land and the adventure of building a new life and community.

But along with the good people looking only for a better life there were those seeking riches. Gold seemed to be a bad fever in most people. Just the mention of gold would start people dreaming, planning and lusting for the yellow dust which would lead to riches.

It was probably the lust for and searching for gold that caused the most problem for the Indians that were already living on this land.

And the most infuriating guise of the influx of the white man were the hide hunters. They never asked for permission to hunt on land belonging to the Indians. They simply pushed their way into their land regardless that the Indian tribes depended on the buffalo for their livelihood. Buffalo were food, clothing, tools and shelter. They depended on the buffalo for their existence. So when the natives saw the slaughter of hundreds of their buffalo when only the hides were taken and the meat left to rot, the natives were furious and some waged war against the white man expansion. And this is why the Army was in the west: to insure the safe passage of the white settlers. Not peace, but only to safeguard the settlers.

Each night as Lucien lay on his back watching the stars and then sometimes while on patrol out ahead, he'd stop on top of a knoll and look out across the plains wondering what would eventually become of the native Indians with the increase of settlers coming west.

He had only been in the west a very short time now and already he was beginning to question his role and duties.

* * * *

One day out from joining the Oregon Trail where the trail came close to the Little Blue River, the unit was attacked in the daylight by six white men; all wearing bandanas covering their faces. Even though none of these new recruits had had any professional training other than the time they had been on the trail to Fort Kearny, these men—soldiers—were reacting like they had been in the Army for some time. Two of the riders were shot and dehorsed on the first volley of shots. The remaining four pulled back to think about another attack.

"Burchel, damn you, you told us these soldiers would not even be carrying weapons. That they had not been trained and that they were right out of prison. We lost a third of the men and now it's four against twenty-five of them. You led us into a trap,

Burchel. I'm out of here and I have had enough of you and living off scraps," Neils said and he turned his mount and rode off.

Burchel knew what the reward would be if they could get their hands on those wagons. Thousands of dollars. But what could he do with only three men against twenty-five. Nothing. Sadly he and his two remaining cohorts rode off also.

"Looks as if they have given up, Sarg," John said.

"I hope so. Check and see if anyone was injured, Private."

None of the men had been hit. "How do you suppose they knew what we have in the wagons?" Lucien asked.

"What makes you so sure they know?"

"Then why would six riders attack twenty-five soldiers, if they didn't know."

"Good point, Private."

"How many days out of Fort Kearny are we?" Lucien asked.

"We have maybe one day to the Little Blue River, then two days north to Fort Kearny and we'll have to cross the Platte River."

"Sergeant, do you think that there might be a chance that information about these guns was leaked out of the Fort?" Lucien asked.

"It's possible. I just don't know, but I'll make some inquiries."

"Come on, men, saddle up and move out. Let's put some distance from here. Good job."

That night Quinlin doubled the guard in case the riders tried a night attack.

* * * *

They finally reached the Little Blue River. They were all thirsty, even the horses, and they all were dirty and smelling. They washed in the river and then their clothes. Feeling better now, their dispositions were more cheerful also.

Two days later they reached the Platte River but waited for morning to cross in the daylight. They had pushed themselves and the horses hard for two days and now; they needed a break.

Lucien stayed awake long into the night looking across the river at Fort Kearny. His new home. For how long he had no idea. He wasn't apprehensive, only his mind was wondering.

Sergeant Quinlin was also awake sitting by the fire. Staring at the flames. Something Lucien had said about the riders after their attack—was there a leak from Fort Kearny. If there was, he would keep his suspicions to himself for now. He looked and saw Lucien sitting up; he too was still awake. There was something peculiar about Lucien he couldn't understand. *On the face or his appearance, behavior and manners, he seems to be a quiet, thoughtful man. But somewhere there is hidden a terrible exact opposite that when released he is a like a raging bull in a china closet. And then when it is over he resumes into his quiet, respectful demeanor.*

They all crossed the Platte the next morning without incident. Captain Scott was waiting for them at the river.

Sergeant Quinlin stopped and saluted. "Any problems Sergeant?" Scott asked.

"A few, Captain. We brought a few of those problems with us." And he pointed toward the four men still on their horses.

"What happened, Sergeant?"

"They were planning to attack us and leave no witnesses and steal the firearms." That's all Quinlin wanted to say about the encounter now. When he wrote up his report he would be more enlightening.

"Anything else, Sergeant?" Scott asked.

"Yes, one day out from the Little Blue River we were attacked by six riders. Two were killed when they attacked and the remaining four I guess decided against losing any more men and they rode off."

"It was my order, Sergeant, that these men were not to be armed until after their training here."

"Yes Sir, that is correct, but I decided considering what we were carrying, to arm the men. And it turned out I was correct. To a man they fought like any seasoned soldier and I'm proud of them all," Quinlin replied.

"I'll want your written report, Sergeant, as soon as you can," Captain Scott turned and left.

The firearm wagons were taken immediately to the arms and ammunition bunker. As they crossed the compound Lucien noticed that the so called fort was made mostly of sod and adobe and there were a few wooden buildings. But most shocking, were the fortifications around the fort. But Fort Kearny had been built to help safeguard the passage of the many setters traveling the Oregon Trail westward. Kearny provided escorts for the many wagon trains to Fort Laramie.

Then Fort Laramie would provide escort further west. They were fighting against the different tribes there. There were fortifications around the fort as they were occasionally attacked by Indians.

Since 1848 there had been several homesteads and farms built within the shadow of Fort Kearny and so far the only problems the settlers have had were the frequent visits by an Indian or two looking for something to eat. To keep peace the settlers had always willingly provided a hot meal or something cool to drink in the heat. The Indian was also fascinated with the farmer's tools. He had never seen such things. At Fort Kearny the natives were more curious.

Lucien noticed a few Indians wandering aimlessly around Kearny, and he thought this a little strange. Maybe they were here to provide escort against outlaws such as the riders they had encountered and not so much because of Indians. He had a lot to learn. He also saw a trading post that dealt in hides and furs. There were two stores, a place to eat and another large two story building that was a saloon and hotel upstairs.

When the wagons were offloaded, Sergeant Quinlin showed them their barracks. It too was made from sod and adobe but it was clean, cool and comfortable. Quinlin had his quarters at the end of the barracks. "Men, we have had a tiring two and half months of traveling to get here. Take the rest of this day and tomorrow off. You'll be expected to report for Reveille Wednesday morning."

The first thing Lucien wanted was a bath and then he went to see if he could purchase some civilian clothes. Feeling more human now he also bought some writing papers, envelopes and some pencils, so he could write his mother and tell them where he was and that he was fine.

He walked about Kearny looking at everything. Some of the men went first to the saloon for a drink. At supper that first night Quinlin asked, or rather delegated, "Private Jandreau, after you have eaten, you will write a report about your capture of the four riders. I need this report before you go to sleep tonight."

"Yes, Sergeant, you will have it. When I have finished the report what do I do with it?"

"Take it to Captain Scott's office. I'll be there."

There were now two hundred soldiers at Fort Kearny and for that many men it took a lot of food to feed them. And Lucien kept going back for seconds. The other soldiers there who knew nothing about Lucien couldn't believe how much food he could eat.

Lucien finished his report at 2100 hours and took it directly to Captain Scott's office. "Come in, Private," Scott said. "How do you like the west so far?"

"Well, it is better than prison, Sir. But I haven't seen much of it yet."

"How do you like being in the Army?" Scott asked.

"I do, Sir."

"You're excused, Private. Thank you," Scott said.

After Lucien had left Scott asked Quinlin, "What's your personal opinion of Lucien Jandreau, Sergeant?"

"He is an enigma."

"How so, Sergeant?"

"Well, he has no formal training, yet he performed better in the attack than any one of the older regulars. I think with our training and he getting used to the military chain of command, I think he might make a fine officer. He surely has already demonstrated his natural leadership abilities."

"I was impressed with him when I questioned him in prison. I saw an unusual person. If only we can harness those abilities, Sergeant. That'll be all, Sergeant, until I have read these reports."

It was late, but the Nebraska sky in August still had an aura around the horizon. The air was dry, not humid like the air in New England or central United States. Lightning bugs were real active. Like tiny sparks. He was tired so he decided to return to his quarters when he saw Lucien out enjoying he night sky like himself, he walked over. "Aren't you tired, Lucien? I mean we have had long days and short nights since leaving Madison."

"No, I'm not sleepy at all, Sarg. I'm not use to such a big sky. At home the forest closed everything in so all you ever saw of the night sky was a narrow gap through the trees. I'm seeing star clusters that I have never seen before. How about you, Sarg?"

"I've been talking with the Captain about the men and I was on my way to my quarters when I saw you. If you're not sleepy, how come you aren't with the others at the saloon having a few?"

"I have nothing against having a drink, but just to have one drink after another I think is rather pointless.

"I also have been doing some thinking, Sarg. Out here where it's quiet and a man can think."

Quinlin waited for him to continue.

"There's something that doesn't set right with me with those last riders.

"We traveled pretty steady once we left Madison and I don't believe those riders rode fast enough to get ahead of us and wait for us to come along. And no one saw any riders following us after we captured the Smith brothers and Rawlings. So I think they came out of Fort Kearny or somewhere around here, and then they must have known what we were carrying. That means someone from inside had to tell them. Someone who is in cohort with them. And probably the leader," Lucien said.

Quinlin thought about that for quite a while before answering. "Okay, let's say you're right. Any idea who we should be looking for?"

"I don't know, Sarg. You know people around here better than I do."

"Major Merrill, Captain Scott, Lieutenants Rolfe and Lane; they would have been the only personnel who would have known about the firearms. Rolfe and Lane may have known. I'm not sure. I don't think they knew. I didn't know anything about the firearms until I received a telegram from Captain Scott in Leominster, so I say only the Major and Captain knew," Quinlin said.

"Then one of them on purpose or accidentally leaked the information," Lucien said.

"Or one of them set up the robbery. Both Merrill and Scott knew the new people would not be armed. I had orders to that affect."

"Then that would explain why only six riders attacked twenty-five soldiers," Lucien said.

"Because as far as anyone would know, I would be the only one armed. This is really beginning to piss me off. I wish we had some concrete evidence of this."

"Then let's keep this between us for now and watch what comes and goes."

Sergeant Quinlin walked off towards his quarters and Lucien strolled to the other end of the village. This was the seedy part of the settlement with noisy, cheap saloons and cheap girls. He was beginning to think he'd rather have duty than a couple of days off in this village. There was very little to do.

Then something caught his eye at the seedy looking saloon. This in itself was suspicious, but one of the horses, a big bay with a white sock on its right front leg. He remembered this horse as one ridden by one of the six thieves.

He left and walked over to Quinlin's quarters. He knocked on the door. "Come in."

"Sarg, I was just down by the last saloon at the edge of town and I saw one of the horses that was ridden by one of the thieves that attacked us."

"How can you be sure?" Quinlin asked.

"His rider wore a ragged black and white checkered shirt. I thought maybe the two of us would go in and haul him out of there and over to Captain Scott's office."

"I don't think so, Lucien. He is probably here to see whoever gave him the information about us. We haul him out of there and his boss is gone. I say we wait until he leaves and follow him or perhaps his boss will come see him. We have no idea who his boss might be. It could be the Major, the Captain or one of the soldiers. We'll have to wait and see.

"If you want to do something, go in and have a drink and see if the checkered shirt is there. They're not so apt to recognize you and that saloon is off limits to the men. You wear your civilian clothes and have a drink."

He walked in and it took him several moments for his eyes to adjust to the dim lighting. Everyone was watching him as he walked up to the bar and ordered a drink. "Do you have any cold beer?"

"I don't know about cold, but it's cool and it goes down good," the barkeep said.

"I'll have one." He could see the man he wanted by looking in the mirror behind the bar. And he was wearing a black and white checkered shirt. Lucien guessed that he wasn't as tall as himself and he had a big gut on him. There were three other men seated at the same table near the back wall. These were undoubtedly his companions.

The barkeep set a mug of beer down and said, "That'll be two bits."

Lucien gave him the two bits and said, "This is an expensive beer."

"You said you wanted a cool beer. Well that costs a little more out here."

Lucien drank half of the mug before stopping. It was a good mug of beer.

"Hey, stranger," the guy in the checkered shirt said. "You looking for work. I just lost a couple of good men."

"Me, work? Oh no, I just stopped for a cool drink and my horse threw a shoe a while back. I'm on my way to meet up with my brother near Fort Laramie. Thanks just the same." Lucien finished the beer and set the mug on the bar and left.

Lucien left and walked over to Quinlin's quarters. "It's him alright, and he is with the other three men. It looked like he was waiting for someone. He offered me a job. The boss said he had just lost two good men. So now what do we do, Sarg?" Lucien asked.

"We wait and see who goes in. If they leave we follow them. We can see the saloon from inside the mess hall."

It was almost supper time now. They chose a seat where they could watch. Soon others began to sit down at the same table with trays of food. "Go ahead and get a tray Lucien. I'll stay here and watch and then I'll get mine."

No one had come or gone from the saloon and supper here was over and most of the men had left. Then just before sunset, "Here they come, Sarg. All four of them," Lucien said.

"And they're getting on their horses. As soon as they are out of sight we follow their trail. It should be easy enough to follow in this twilight and the full moon will be out soon."

Lucien noticed that the four men rode out quietly and not fast as if they were suspicious of anything. After about a mile the four left the well-used trail they had been following. "I know where they're going now. This trail that they're on goes to the Old Creek River. They'll probably bed down there for the night."

They kept following at a distance so the four riders wouldn't get spooked. After some distance Quinlin said, "We'd better leave our horses tied up in those trees over there and go in on foot from here."

They set out for the river, but not following the trail. "This close to the river they might have guards out."

Lucien liked how Quinlin was thinking. They climbed up a small knoll and the river was below them and the four men were setting up camp. They had just started a fire and some were gathering wood. "As soon as all four men are back, so we know where they are, we'll get a little closer so we can hear them talk."

They didn't have long to wait before all four men were back and sitting around the fire and drinking whisky. "Okay, Lucien, let's crawl down closer. No talking from here."

Lucien and Quinlin crawled through the grass side by each. They found some bushes for cover only about fifty feet behind the four men.

"He'd better get here soon, Burchel, I'm tired and I want to go to sleep," one of them said. Well, now they knew the leader's name, 'Burchel.'

"We were told, Burch," another one was saying, "that those new soldier boys wouldn't be armed. What happened anyhow? If we had known maybe we would have been better prepared. We lost two good men for nothing. He'd better have some good answers when he gets here."

"What are we going to do now, Burch, now that that raid was a flop?" Doug asked.

"I don't know Doug. Maybe we could rob a bank somewhere. We'll first have to wait and see what he has to say about all this."

The whisky was making them very talkative. Now they were talking apparently about a previous job that had rendered them plenty of money.

Both Lucien and Quinlin felt someone kick their boot

and say, "You two lay right where you are and unbuckle your handguns and slide them out from under you."

They did as they were told and the stranger took them and slung the belts over his shoulder. "Now get up and remember I'm holding a gun on you, so don't go doing something stupid.

"Now turn around."

When they had turned around and were now facing their captor. "You! Captain Scott. I never would have guessed it. Why, Captain?" Quinlin asked. Lucien was dumb-struck to think Captain Scott was behind this whole robbery.

"The money these firearms would bring. I was depending on them for my retirement. Until you two messed everything up for me. Now walk down to the fire."

"Burchel!" Captain Scott hollered, "I'm coming in with two hostages." They all stood up around the fire.

When they could see who the two were by the fire light, Burchel said, "You two! I never would have figured."

"You didn't, huh, Burchel. They were laying in the bushes not more than fifty feet away, listening to everything you idiots have been saying. Now they know the whole story, Thanks to you," Scott was upset.

"Sergeant Quinlin? And you stranger, I guessed you won't be looking for your brother?"

"You know Lucien, do you Burchel? How?"

"He came into the saloon today for a drink and I asked him if he was looking for work. That's all, Captain."

Scott pushed his handgun into Quinlin's side and said, "You two over there," and he pointed to the other side of the fire.

They moved and Burchel was standing about five feet away from Lucien. Scott was right behind Quinlin with his gun still poking him in the side.

"Too bad, sonny, you didn't take me up on the job offer. But I guess you won't be needing the job after tonight," Burchel said.

"Hey, you sloppy looking pig, if you're going to talk with

me, how about you step back a little more. Your breath smells like a used outhouse." This comment really made Burchel mad.

Quinlin was also shocked to hear Lucien talking like that to one of their captors.

Burchel took a step closer. His fist were doubled up and the blood vessels in his neck standing out. "When was the last time you took a bath, you fat pig. You smell worse than what comes out of the back end of a buffalo." The other three worked their way around and behind Quinlin and Lucien. "You dress and look like a slob, you filthy pig, and you stink," Lucien had raised his voice a notch.

And he saw Burchel take out his handgun and was coming at Lucien. Lucien took two steps towards him and this surprised everyone. Burchel swung his gun towards Lucien's head just as Lucien grabbed him and lifted him up off the ground and turned slightly and threw him at the other three knocking them off their feet.

Quinlin understood now what Lucien was doing and for a fleeting second Scott took his attention off Quinlin to see Burchel being thrown through the air. Quinlin quickly hit Scott's gun hand and knocking the gun free then he hit Scott in the face with his fist with everything he had. Scott was knocked backward, but not down. Quinlin moved in quick and punched him in the stomach and when he doubled over Quinlin delivered another blow to his face knocking him back and down.

Lucien moved in and grabbed Burchel again before he knew what had happened. He twisted his gun hand and squeezed his hand and crushed it and then twisted his arm behind him dislocating the shoulder. All Burchel could do was scream. Lucien grabbed him around the neck and picked him up then and with his palm, he hit Burchel on the nose, breaking it, and blood blew out in his eyes and over his face, soaking his shirt. He was done with.

Just then the other three rushed at Lucien and Lucien backhanded the one on the right sending him backwards and into

Quinlin. He hit the next fella on both sides of his ribcage with both fist and broke ribs on both sides. He let out screams and he was done for. The next guy punched Lucien on the side of his head and it hurt and clouded his vision for a moment or two. He swung again at Lucien and this time Lucien caught his fist in midair and squeezed so hard bones in his hand were crushed. He too was now screaming. Then Lucien grabbed the same arm and pulled it backwards and dislocated the shoulder. He was out of the fight. Now the one he had backhanded was back on his feet and coming at Lucien. Lucien picked him up and threw him about thirty feet through the air and he landed on his side and broke some ribs. Those four were all done in and Lucien looked at Quinlin. He and Scott were still going at it. Trading blow for blow. "Want some help, Sarg?"

"I almost got him now," he was just able to say.

Quinlin hit Scott in the ribs and this hurt Scott. Then Quinlin hit him in the face while he was doubled over. This sent Scott backwards on the ground on his back. Quinlin walked over to him and asked, "You had enough or do you want some more?" Quinlin said.

Scott was just able to speak. "No—no more, Quinlin. No more."

Quinlin looked around and saw the other four men lying on the ground all beat to hell. "You did all this to those four?"

"Yeah."

"I didn't know what you were doing at first talking to Burchel like that. Not until you grabbed for his gun. Look at you, you're no worse for the wear. You don't look like you have been in a fight." Then he laughed and said, "Look at me!" They both laughed. "I look like I lost."

"Let's tie these guys up for the night and take them in in the morning. I'm too damned tired to take them in now."

They used some rope they found on the horses and secured all five of them. Lucien's four were still screaming with pain.

87

Then Quinlin and Lucien stretched out by the fire and tried to sleep.

Burchel and his partners were hurting so much from their injuries they screamed and moaned all night and no one was able to sleep. At sun up Lucien finally got up and put more wood on the fire so he could make some hot coffee. That's all there was in the outlaw's saddle bags. But hot black coffee made he and Quinlin feel better. Captain Scott was too worried about what would happen to him now.

Lucien and Quinlin had to help the four mount their horses. "I don't think any of you is in any condition to run off, except you, Scott. You'll ride your horse with your hands tied behind you and I'll lead your horse with your reins."

Lucien put the fire out and mounted up. "Let's go. I'll take the lead, you follow behind me and Lucien will take up the rear," Quinlin said.

They rode slow so not to inflict more discomfort for the four than what was necessary. At Fort Kearny everybody stopped to watch the group pass by. No one recognized the four, only Quinlin, Lucien and Captain Scott. "But why are his hands tied behind him—and all beat up?"

They rode right up to Major Merrill's office. He saw them coming and went outside to greet them. When he saw Sergeant Quinlin he said, "Where in hell have you been, Sergeant? You never made roll call this morning, nor you, Private Jandreau, and why is Captain Scott's hands tied behind him?"

"Major, the Captain was responsible, along with these four men, for the attack on us near the Little Blue River."

"Why does everybody look all beaten to hell, even you Sergeant Quinlin, except Private Jandreau?" Major Merrill asked.

"We'll tell you, Sir, but I think we'd better lock these guys up first," Sergeant Quinlin replied.

"Certainly, certainly, Sergeant. Take them all to the holding cells and then report back here directly."

"Yes Sir."

Sergeant Quinlin and Lucien escorted the five prisoners to the holding cells. As Lucien closed and locked Burchel's cell, Burchel said, "You did a pretty good job on me, Private, after I'd been drinking all day. When I get out I'm coming after you."

"I'll be looking for you, Burch. I'm not worried about you," Lucien said.

The others weren't saying anything. They knew what was in store for them. Leavenworth Prison in Kansas.

"Come in gentlemen and have a seat. I've been reading your reports about being attacked at the Little Blue River. And your prison record, Mr. Jandreau. Warden Farrar speaks very highly of you. But I'm more interested how you handled yourself when a prisoner. Quite impressive. Where did you learn to fight like that?"

"I didn't learn to fight anywhere, Sir. I was never in a fight until I was in prison."

"Hum, so this style of yours just came naturally, Private?"

"I would have to say so, yes, Major. I'm as strong as four men, Sir, and if I ever hit anyone with a closed fist, I'm afraid I'd kill them, Sir."

"Fascinating, Private, that you can discipline yourself like this during the heat of a battle. I'm going to give you a job, Private. I understand you and the other new enlistees have not had any training; is that correct, Sergeant?"

"Yes Sir."

"Then Private Jandreau, it will be your duty to teach these soldiers to fight like you do.

"Now to get to this robbery situation. When did you first suspect Captain Scott and the others?" Major Merrill asked.

"Right after we arrived here, Sir. Private Jandreau and I were talking about the attack at the Little Blue River and because of the way it took place we both believed that someone from Fort Kearny was giving these outlaws information about the firearms and ammunition we were freighting."

"Why didn't you come forward at that time with your suspicions?"

"Because we weren't sure until last night when we apprehended all of them who else was involved," Quinlin said.

"That was very forthright of you, Sergeant."

Sergeant Quinlin went on to describe for Major Merrill from Lucien recognizing the bay horse, what they heard the men talking about and when Captain Scott had walked up behind them and had captured them at this point, and how Lucien verbally assaulted Burchel purposely to get him mad and how this caused Scott to take his attention away from his prisoners at this time.

When he had finished Major Merrill said, "That is simply fascinating. It is obvious that you two work well together, so Private Jandreau, I'm going to break the rule and promote you to Corporal and assign you to Sergeant Quinlin."

"Thank you, Sir." Lucien said.

"Now I'm going to need a complete written report from both of you starting with why you decided to arm the new enlistees when you left Fort Madison and then pick it up again when the attack started at the Little Blue River. The prisoners and Captain Scott included will be taken to Fort Leavenworth and then to the Leavenworth Prison. And your reports will be sent with them. That way you will not be required to travel to Kansas.

"That's all I have gentlemen and you're free to leave." Quinlin and Lucien stood up to leave and Major Merrill added, "Oh one more thing: because of your actions I am recommending a citation be added to both of your personal records. Thank you."

Quinlin and Lucien had not slept at all and had not eaten for almost twenty four hours. The mess hall was closed but the chief cook said he would fix them some bacon and eggs. "How many eggs, gentlemen?"

Quinlin said, "Three for me."

Lucien said, "I'll take six." Quinlin just looked at him surprisingly.

Later, sure enough Lucien ate all six eggs, plus bacon and a biscuit.

They went back to their barracks and laid down and were sound asleep. While they slept the news about Captain Scott and Burchel and his men spread through the Fort and that's all anyone wanted to talk about.

CHAPTER 4

Lucien was a natural teacher. He was very precise with his instructions and patient when one of the men was not progressing. "Remember you don't have to hit an opponent with a closed fist. If you do you're going to hurt your own hand. Possibly breaking it, then you're finished in the fight. Use the palm of hand and hit your opponent on the end of his nose as hard as you can. This will break the nose, drive him backwards and for a few moments he'll be disoriented. This will give you the upper hand. And it makes no difference if your opponent is bigger than you. He is going to have his own blood all over him and in his eyes.

Lucien had only a week to teach the men self defense. Then was firearms training. Even though all the men were quite familiar with firearms they were also taught attack procedures, close quarters and hand to hand combat. This is where their self defense training helped them. After two weeks they were now beginning to feel like soldiers.

Once their training had ended Quinlin took the men out on daily patrols, so the men could get use to the country. Occasionally they would find a small band of Pawnee braves watching them from a far or on the top of a knoll. They would make wide arcs around Fort Kearny until they had seen all of the country side within a five mile radius of the fort.

When their indoctrination of the surrounding country side was finished, Quinlin received orders to take his troop out for an extended stay visiting all of the settlers along the Oregon Trail to Lewellen, including Lexington, Guthenburg and North

Platte, then they were to turn north and hit the Niobrara River and follow that to the junction with the Missouri River, then turn south for the Oregon Trail and back to Fort Kearny. Major Merrill gave Quinlin a rough map where all the settlers and farms could be found that laid outside of the established settlements.

"I'm sending Private Samuel with you, as he volunteered since he came out here with you and your troop. He is bringing along a helper. Here are orders to pick up supplies at each settlement and or farms and a voucher to be given to each for the supplies.

"Oh, did I mention you'll be taking along Lieutenant John Sanford. He has a few years out here, so he'll fit in okay I'm sure."

That didn't make Quinlin feel any better about this assignment. He would rather go with his men, and not have to drag along Lt. John Sanford. "He has been here a while and not experienced yet the problems with the Indians, settlers or the Nebraska countryside. I have instructed him to give you a free hand, that he is there more as an observer to learn. I have told Lieutenant Sanford not to engage the enemy if at all possible.

"You'll be on your own out there, Sergeant Quinlin, so don't take any unnecessary chances. If you are not back here before November, I will assume you have met up with trouble some where and I'll send out a regiment and work backwards on your map. Now you have the rest of today to get your men equipped and draw your necessary supplies, and as of this moment Samuel Freeman and his helper Bruce Burns are assigned to you. Dismissed Sergeant."

This is the opportunity, Master Sergeant Cedric Quinlin had been wanting for. Only he'd prefer to leave the lieutenant behind. As he crossed the compound to supplies he was having bad feelings about taking along a neophyte commanding officer. But then again if someone with experience didn't instruct the men then they would remain neophytes.

Two days later the troop left. Everyone was excited about the detail, especially since it would take them several weeks. Sergeant Quinlin certainly was happy and as they rode along he kept trying to read the lieutenant's demeanor from the expressions on his face. He usually was pretty good at this, but with this lieutenant, he wasn't sure.

There was one farm between the fort and the Oregon Trail. A Mr. and Mrs. Kermit Herring. They eked out a living supplying food supplies and feed for the animals for the forts. They had two sons and a daughter, and they were second generation from Germany.

Being so close to the fort they obviously would not have had sightings or problems with the Indians. They watered their horses and left.

A large wagon train had passed through the day before escorted by an attachment from Fort Laramie, who had escorted a stage coach and fright wagons east and waited for the wagon train going west. Quinlin knew that if they continued their quick pace they would catch up to the train in less than a day. And he didn't want to be on the back end of a dusty wagon train.

They caught up with the train two hours before sunset the second day out. They followed in a dusty wake for two hours and that night after supper: "Lieutenant Sanford, I would recommend that we leave at least two hours before sunrise tomorrow to get ahead of the train and the dust and so we don't leave the train in our dust. These people have a long, tiresome and dusty journey ahead of them. It would be a good token not to make it any more dusty or tiresome than necessary."

"Schedule the security as such. And thanks, Sergeant, for bringing this to my attention."

That evening Lloyd Briggs, the wagon master, and Lieutenant James Rioux came to pay their respects to Lieutenant Sanford and Sergeant Quinlin. "What are your orders, Lieutenant?

I know we don't require two detachments to escort a wagon train." Rioux said.

"We're observing the Indian activity around Fort Kearny and talking with the settlers."

"Mr. Briggs," Quinlin inquired, "isn't it late in the season to have just left Missouri?"

"You're not new to escort duty are you Sergeant Quinlin? If we were going all the way to the Pacific Coast, then yes. But these folks are Mormons and they'll take the Salt Lake Trail at Fort Briggs. I figure on getting them there in another month."

"Then what will you do, Mr. Briggs, stay in Utah for the winter?" Quinlin asked.

"Not at all. I'll start out on my own and maybe catch up with a detachment heading east."

"We'll be leaving early, Mr. Briggs," Lieutenant Sanford said. "We'd like to get ahead of your dust. We won't make as much of course."

"Do you mind me asking, Lieutenant? Your detail of new recruits, but all these men, to me don't act like pilgrims to the west."

"Thank you, Mr. Briggs."

That night as Quinlin laid on his bedroll and looking up at the night sky and stars he had noticed the lieutenant's expression change slightly when Mr. Briggs told the lieutenant that he thought the troops were anything but pilgrims to the west. Why had this seemed to have bothered the lieutenant? Quinlin's take on the lieutenant was that he wanted to be known as an Indian fighter. He knew he would have to be careful with him. He lay awake long into the morning hours still watching the stars over head. It seemed as he had just fallen asleep when Samuel's helper was awakening him.

They were very quiet, trying not to disturb the others. Their breakfast was eaten in a hurry and just as they were leaving the wagon train, the rest of detachment were just getting up.

* * * *

They visited the settlements at Lexington, Guthenburgh and Lewellen. They made camp for two days to rest and resupply with provisions for the long trek ahead. There wouldn't be any more settlements. Only the occasional farm.

"Lieutenant Sanford?" Quinlin inquired.

"Yes, Sergeant, what is it?"

"I'd like your permission to take one man and visit a couple of farms in the area."

"Permission granted, Sergeant."

Quinlin walked off to find Lucien. He was helping to grease the wagon axels and repair the harnesses. "Lucien, saddle your horse. You're coming with me." Quinlin saddled his own horse.

"Where are we going, Sergeant?" Lucien asked.

"I needed an excuse to get away for a few hours and the lieutenant gave me permission to take one man with me and talk with a couple of farmers in the area."

There was a nice spread just west of the settlement and they pulled up at the hitching rail near the barn. A man was just walking out. "Hello. You're two weeks early."

"Maybe you have us confused with someone else. I'm Sergeant Quinlin and this is Corporal Jandreau."

"If you not after wagon, then yes you aren't the ones I am expecting in two weeks. I am Olaf Suenson. People call me Swede. I build wagons for Army. Come, too hot to talk outside. Come inside."

They followed the Swede across the yard into the house "Ola!" Swede hollered, "Ola, we've got company."

"Well, come in old man. Don't make them stand in the hot air listening to you call me."

"Sergeant, Corporal, this is Ola my wife."

"Sergeant, Corporal, would you like a cool drink?" Ola asked.

"My Ola, she makes lemonade from sumac that grows near the river. Makes good hot tea in the cold winter too.

"Now tell me, Sergeant, what do you and Corporal do just two of you?"

"We are with a small detachment that's on patrol talking with settlers and observing Indian activity," Quinlin said.

"We have no problems with Indians."

"How long have you and your family been out here Swede?" Lucien asked.

"We come out right after the Army forts were built along the trail to protect the wagons. Ola, how long we been here?"

"This is 1858 and we settled on this land in 1846. Twelve years."

"You have a very nice house and buildings, Swede."

"It takes a lot of work. When Ola and I and our two sons left Pennsylvania we had only clothes we wore and my tools," Swede said.

"We had so many beautiful things back home," Ola said.

"Ola, she still all over me because I made her leave everything. I tell her I can make new things once we get settled." The Swede began laughing and then said, "She hasn't let me stop yet making these things."

"How old are your boys, Swede?" Lucien asked.

"Ollie, he oldest. Nineteen now. I think. Svend is only fifteen. They out getting me wood to make into wagons and wheels."

"Living out here as you do I would think it would be lonely for your boys out here. I mean no girls or social life," Quinlin said.

Swede almost choked on his drink. "Hum, two years ago a wagon train come through here. This one wagon needed a lot of work, so I trade for new wagon and repaired his. Ollie met the man's daughter and told his Ma and me he was going to Oregon with her and her family. I had to hit him twice behind his head 'fore he decided he maybe better stay. How am I going to make wagons, fix wagons and wheels without any help? I took Ollie to Indian village and told the chief my Ollie needed a wife. He lives in the other house now with his own family and he works here still.

"There's more and more people going west every year. That means more and more wagons need to be fixed. And wheels. People forget they suppose to grease wheel every day. I make new wagons for Army also."

"You have a nice place here, Mr. Suenson and thank you, Ola, for the cool drink," Lucien said as he and Quinlin mounted up.

That afternoon they talked with another settler who supplied beef to the Army forts. "Those red devils take a few head of cows each year. Only a few, so I don't get too worked up about it.

"If you soldier boys leave this country my livelihood— well I might as well give my land back to the Indians. It wouldn't be safe to live out here without the Army's constant presence. I make my living almost exclusively by selling my beef to the Army.

"With the forts where they are, you boys keep the Indians in check, so life out here is tolerable."

Quinlin thanked him and he and Lucien rode on. They circled the little village and back to their camp.

The next morning they headed north to the Niobrara River, leaving Lewellen behind. So far they had encountered a variety of mixed feelings towards the Indians. Where the Suenson's lived comfortably with them, the beef ranchers tolerated the Indians as long as there was the constant Army presence.

The air was clear and smelled of grass and flowers gone by. The days were still warm, but at night the temperature would drop and the men slept closer to the fires. Sergeant Quinlin knew they still had a long journey ahead of them and he was certain that they would return to Fort Kearny before the cold weather had settled in. He watched each man separately, even Lieutenant Sanford, and also as a working organized group of soldiers, and he was happy.

Even the lieutenant was beginning to show signs that he was also enjoying the country. But two days after reaching the Niobrara River and following it east, Sergeant Quinlin noticed that a small band of Indians, probably Pawnee and probably only a curious hunting party of maybe four or six braves, could often be seen watching them from the tops of the knolls at a distance.

"I wonder if they're planning to attack us?" Lieutenant Sanford said.

"I would sooner expect that they are only a scouting party for a larger hunting party looking for buffalo," Quinlin said.

"Then why do they stalk us?"

"Curious, probably. This is their land and they may be wondering what we are doing so far from Kearny."

"Maybe, Sergeant, but I still don't like them watching us. It's time, Sergeant, that we show these redskins that we are not afraid of them."

The next day about mid-morning the same small band of Indians could be seen on top of another knoll. Just sitting on their horses and watching them. Sanford halted the troop and said, "Sergeant Quinlin, it is time we showed those redskins something. You continue on, Sergeant, following the river. I shall take five men with me and run those troublemakers off."

The lieutenant picked five soldiers at the front of their small column. "Follow me men. We'll have a little fun." And they rode off and Sergeant Quinlin and Lucien formed up the rest of the men into a smaller column and moved out.

"What does he think he is doing, Sergeant?" Lucien asked.

Quinlin shook his head and said, "He wants to be an Indian fighter, Corporal. Let's move out."

"He'll get himself and those five men killed," Lucien said.

The lieutenant and his men rode directly at the scouting party at a slow gallop. The Indians sat their horses and watched the six men advancing. Before the lieutenant had reached the bottom of the knoll, the scouting party turned their horses and galloped off. When the lieutenant reached the top of the knoll, the Indians were nowhere to be seen. Not even a trail of dust. It was as if they had never been on the knoll at all. The lieutenant turned around and rode back to rejoin the troop.

* * * *

When Lieutenant Sanford returned to the troop, they had progressed two miles down river. As upset as he was with the lieutenant going off like that, Quinlin didn't say anything. All the men were jubilant, thinking they had chased off a band of renegades.

A wind storm blew in from the west and for two days they had to hunker down in a thicket next to the river. For two days the wind blew with hurricane strength, with only an occasional rain shower. The storm was mostly wind and for two days the horses were spooked. They wouldn't eat or drink and with a constant restlessness. When the storm finally broke the men had to shake out their bedding and equipment from the sand.

Nothing more was said about the lieutenant's recklessness, chasing off the band of Indians. But Quinlin had formed an opinion about Lieutenant Sanford, that he really didn't care about the welfare of the men or their mission. He was more convinced now than ever that Sanford wanted to become an infamous Indian fighter. Up until now the command at Fort Kearny had enjoyed a peaceful relationship with the Pawnee tribe. But Quinlin suspected that that was about to change because of Lieutenant Sanford's callous disregard for his men, the mission and the Army's relationship with the natives. It was obvious to Quinlin now that Sanford's objectives were clearly his own and not the Army's.

They saw a herd of buffalo and a Sioux hunting party. "This might create some hard feelings," Quinlin said.

"Why is that, Sarg?" Lucien asked.

"This side of the Niobrara River is Pawnee land and if they knew the Sioux were hunting buffalo on this side of the river, there would be hell to pay."

"I don't understand, Sarg. Isn't there enough buffalo in that one herd for both the Sioux and the Pawnee?"

"Sure there is, but Indians don't like even other Indians from a different tribe hunting on their land. When it comes to hunting, the tribes are very protective. It's their survival. Food, clothes, tools and bedding. When they butcher a buffalo, or any animal as a matter of fact, there is very little waste."

"This party is serious about hunting, Lieutenant. They are not paying any attention to us at all. The whole tribe will not be far away. Even the women and kids come out on the hunt to help take care of the meat. We need to take a wide berth around them."

"Move your men closer to the river, Sergeant. We'll use the tree cover to shield us," the lieutenant said.

Along the river they found many buck deer and four were shot. The temperature at night was cooling off and the daylight hours were not as warm and the fresh meat would not spoil as quickly. All were glad to have fresh meat. The troops ate steaks and venison stew. They ate well for several days.

Lieutenant Sanford secretly wished that they would encounter a hostile band of Indians. He had no personal knowledge about his men's abilities to fight. He wanted to see what they were capable of and not have to take Sargeant Quinlin's word that they were able. He had pushed his orders once with Quinlin, but he doubted very much if he would let him get away with it again.

They didn't find anymore white settlers until they had reached the confluence of the Missouri River. There was a group of trappers looking to canoe as far up the Missouri River as they could before cold weather.

"They won't make it," Quinlin said.

"How do you know that, Sarg?" Lucien asked.

"This is their first time in this country and they started too late. They should already have their camp set up and trapping the fall fur. I sure wouldn't want to be one of them come January when the artic winds blow out of the north and they don't even have a shelter up yet."

Six weeks after leaving Fort Kearny they rode into Freemont. Freemont existed because of the Mormons traveling through to Utah and pilgrims looking for a better life. The town existed to cater to the westward travelers. They made camp just outside of the town and for two days they rested and resupplied their provisions.

There were two families who arrived too late to join the last train west, so they had no choice but to spend the winter in Freemont and the two men actually found work. Life in the back of the covered wagon during winter wouldn't be easy, but they had no choice.

From Omaha they only had another two weeks before they would return to Fort Kearny. They had been on patrol for nine weeks, and their return was just before cold weather. Everyone was tired from the constant on-the-move, even the over-energetic and overzealous Lieutenant Sanford. Major Merrill gave everyone a two-day leave. Of course there was nowhere they could go in only two days. So they stayed at the Fort and took care of personal affairs.

Lucien had received a letter from home and he wrote one letter to his mom and one for his brother and sister. All was well at home and Lucien's father had actually changed his ways, some. Lucien smiled when he read that.

There were reports to write for Sergeant Quinlin and Lieutenant Sanford and there was no mention of the lieutenant chasing off the Indian hunting scouts.

The second day off John, Bill, Lucien and Quinlin stopped at the better saloon in the afternoon for a cold beer. They were in civilian attire and none of them were wearing sidearms. Lucien bought a round for everyone and they found a table against the back wall. Lucien was beginning to feel too good about this new life as a soldier, and he had closer friends here than at any time in his previous life.

There was a group of four men at the center table who were drinking and playing poker. Two of them were friends, it appeared, and it was too difficult to tell about the other two. They were talking loud, too loud, and it was obvious they each had had too much to drink. Whiskey and then beer.

Another round of beer was drunk and then another and another. The poker players were getting louder and louder. Apparently the two friends were doing okay but from the conversation it seemed as the other two were losing a lot. Lucien kept looking over at the poker players in disgust at their bawdy behavior. The biggest of the four, who was also doing most of the winning noticed Lucien looking over at their table and said, "You got a problem, mister?" he said loudly.

Before Lucien could answer one of the players who had been losing a lot of money lost again. He began wondering out loud if the two that were winning were cheating somehow. But he didn't come right out and accuse anyone. The four continued playing and he leaned back in his chair talking socially with his friends and occasionally looking over at the card players.

The big fellow noticed Lucien looking at him again and said, "Hey, mister, why don't you mind your own business before I teach you some western manners and throw your ass out of here," the big-ass card player said.

"Mister, my friend didn't mean anything," John said. "Lucien, you'd better mind your own business."

"I never said a word, John."

"You going to hide behind your friends, mister? Or are you going to act like a man."

"Mister," John said. "If I were you I'd leave now, before you really piss off my friend."

103

"You're a coward, you know that, mister. You going to let this whet do your talking? You going to let your friends do your fighting?"

"Mister, he doesn't need us. As I said before, you'd better leave."

"Shut up, you whet."

"I warned you," John said.

Lucien finished his beer and said, "You know, loud-ass, I've been watching you and you are cheating. And you know something? You're not a good cheater, either. Your friend has been helping you. I've noticed every time your friend deals, he passes you the card you need under the table. Therefore, the cards are probably marked also.

"You know, loud-ass, I wish you and your friend would just leave. There's a breeze blowing the stink from you two over to this table and frankly I've smelt cleaner pigs."

Quinlin choked on his beer and spit up. John and Bill were smiling.

The two losers backed away from the table and the loud-ass and his friend were getting madder and madder. The loud-ass sat there fuming. Lucien got up and picked up his beer mug and said, "Guess I'd like another cold beer, barkeep," and he took two, maybe three steps and the loud-ass backed away from his table and drew his handgun. But before he could bring it up level on Lucien, Lucien threw his beer mug at the loud-ass's head.

The glass mug broke cutting his forehead and he fell over backward. The friend stood up and before he cleared leather with his gun, Lucien backhanded him sending him unconscious into the corner of the room.

The loud-ass was trying to compose himself and wipe the blood from his face. When he reached for his gun Lucien stomped on his wrist with his boot. Loud-ass screamed with pain as his wrist broke. Lucien picked his gun up and tossed it to his friends. Then he took the gun from the unconscious fellow and tossed that to his friends. He turned to the other two card players and said, "Take what money is yours. Only your money and if I were you I'd be more careful who I played poker with. Now you two get out of here." They picked up their money and left without saying a word.

The barkeep stood behind the bar with a sawed off double-barreled shotgun. He looked at Lucien and said, "Just in case." He unloaded it and put it back under the bar.

"Sarg, how about these two spending a couple of days in the brig and then sent out of town."

"Might be a good idea. But I think those two are going to have to be patched up by the Doc first. That guy," and he motioned with the tilt of his head, "has a broken jaw and loud-ass there won't ever be able to draw a gun with his gun hand now, unless he learns to draw and shoot left-handed."

John threw a mug of beer in the face of the unconscious fellow and then they both were taken to the infirmary and then the brig.

When they left town they were pretty meek and quiet.

* * * *

Cold windy weather was coming and almost the entire enrollment at the fort were assigned to firewood detail. The only forests were along the water ways. There was also an occasional stand of timber in the low lying ravines and gullies. Lucien was glad for the exercise. The time spend touring Nebraska was interesting, but at the same time it was boring. Lucien seemed to excel during periods of heavy activity.

With no wagon trains moving along the Oregon Trail during the winter months much of the soldiers time was spent in training. This gave Lucien and the others in his group time to meet and talk with members of the other groups.

Christmas at home usually meant disappointment for Lucien. There was a meager exchange of gifts and a nice roast chicken dinner, but the rest of the day was spent working at chores around the house and sometimes even at the crew camps in the woods. Here at Fort Kearny, Christmas was a day of feasting, comradery and relaxation. Tears filled Lucien's eyes when he thought of his brother, sister and mother. He hoped they were all fine and that his father had taken his threats literally.

* * * *

Captain Scott's position still had not been filled since his arrest the previous summer. Lieutenant Sanford was looking to fill that position. He was secretly planning maneuvers which would, he hoped, put his name at the top for promotion.

"Major Merrill, I'd like your permission to take my unit out for winter maneuvers," Sanford said.

"Why on earth, Lieutenant. There won't be any westward traffic until spring and the natives are too busy trying to survive the cold and snow to be of any consequence," Major Merrill said. "If you are looking for something to do I'll assign your unit to repair the buildings in the fort."

"Yes Sir. I'll start immediately." That wasn't the detail he was wanting but if his unit did a good job then the Major might be impressed and remember him when the time came to fill the Captain's position.

So for the rest of that winter Lieutenant Sanford and his men worked on one building at a time until all repairs were finished. The roof on each building was leaking and the wind blowing through cracks and holes in the walls would blow a candle out.

New tables, chairs and winter doors were made and the kitchens dismantled, cleaned and rebuilt. When there was warmer weather some of the men built new corrals and hitching rails.

Mail and small freight was transported out to Fort Kearny from Independence, Missouri once a week. There were copies of the Independence newspaper and once a month a newspaper from New York arrived. In each issue were articles about the southern states threatening to secede from the Union. While blaming President Lincoln for wanting to abolish slavery once and for all.

The unit Lucien was in were all from the northeast and many of the other soldiers were also from the north. But there were a few who were staunch believers in the south and their way of life. Lucien knew that someday things would blow up here also.

In early April Major Merrill sent his aide to tell Lieutenant Sanford to come to his office. "Come in, Lieutenant. Sit down. You and your men did a fabulous job this winter repairing the fort. Everyone is commenting about it. I won't forget this, Lieutenant. Now the reason I asked you to stop by, Lieutenant, you are to meet a wagon train at Independence, Missouri on April 30th. That means you'll have to leave tomorrow and make it a fast trip to Independence. Take the rest of today to put your supplies together. Dismissed, Lieutenant, and godspeed."

The entire unit was happy to have the escort detail and it showed in their demeanor along the trail. Although the lieutenant was pushing them to reach Independence on time, no one was grumbling because of the fast pace and long hours.

They were still jubilant two weeks later when they arrived in Independence.

Last year's wagon master, Lloyd Briggs, met Lieutenant Sanford and the unit outside the city where the wagons were gathering. "Lieutenant, Sergeant, we have a hundred wagons making this first trek this year. Everyone is expecting war to break out soon, and many folks, like many of these nice people, are trying to get away from the fighting. No wagon master has ever tried to take across a hundred wagons at the same time. It has been unheard of until now. I hired another good master, John Harris, and four riders to help out. This of course had to cost these people more money. But no one complained. They simply wanted to get as far away from the east as possible before the fighting starts."

"Are all the wagons here, Mr. Briggs?" Sergeant Quinlin asked.

"We are still waiting on two. If they don't arrive before sunrise day after tomorrow, we leave without them and they lose their deposits."

"Once we get started, Lieutenant, what I'll want from you and your soldiers—well first, I plan to space out the wagons in the middle. Fifty in front and fifty following up. I'd like half of your people, Lieutenant, to ride up front with me and the rest to bring up the rear with Mr. Harris. He'll be working back and forth along the second group. The four extra riders will flank at the midway of the two groups. Two riders to either side to watch for Indians.

"I have already been told that at Fort Laramie I'll pick up another escort unit and you'll return to Kearny. "

When Lucien was free for the evening he picked up a newspaper from a local merchant. The front page was covered with articles about the South's intention if President Lincoln freed the slaves. They would secede. As much as he loved this country, that would be one fight he would not want to be in. Americans killing Americans. The news in the paper of course, was already a month old.

According to the paper, Missouri was considered a slave state, but Lucien wasn't seeing any negative acts or hostility here from the many Negro workers. Everyone seemed to be happy. He was really confused about the issue now.

That evening just before dark the other two wagons arrived and Lucien and Quinlin showed each to their place in the train and Mr. Briggs arrived to collect the final payment and explain the rules.

Shortly after sunrise the next morning, the teams were harnessed and the wagons were secured. That first day was a learning day. The entire day was made up with mistakes. Some wagon in the middle of the first group stopped so his wife could rest and this caused every wagon behind them to stop. At the end of the day when they were circling in formation for the night, half the wagons turned in the wrong directions and those behind naturally followed.

After three days everyone was getting the hang of it and there were fewer screw-ups. Both Briggs and Harris had seen the same problems before with almost every train they had taken west.

One night while sitting and talking around the fire, Briggs said, "There are Christians here, Jews, Mormons here, almost every ethnic group that makes up this country, and the one thing they all have in common is they all are escaping the pending war that is sure to come. There are folks from the North as well as some folks from the South."

One thing everyone was learning, was to help others and learn to ask for help when your own reserves were depleted. The one hundred wagons, comprising about four hundred people, were working as a team. Even Lieutenant Sanford seemed to be fitting in very naturally, which really surprised Quinlin. Maye he had grown out of the idea of being an Indian fighter.

The hundred-wagon train stretched out so long that those in the rear could not see the front even when crossing a flat plain. The only problems they were experiencing was at night when they tried to circle a hundred wagons. After the first week Mr. Harris suggested, "Why don't we make two circles. One encompassing an inner circle of wagons. The front column circle up first inside and the rear encircle them."

After that there were no more problems. Some of the folks were even disappointed that they were not seeing any Indians.

By the time they had reached Lewellen several of the wagons needed some repair, so they made camp for two days between town and the Suenson's, where the Swede and his sons repaired the wagons. "You must remember grease these axels every day in this dry heat and wind blown sand." While the wagons were being repaired, horses were groomed and harnesses cleaned and repaired. The women took this time to wash clothes and do some cooking. Everyone was helping another. Lucien was particularly interested how everybody, no matter where they were from or religion, they came together as a unit. *The North and South could take a lesson from these people,* he thought.

On the morning that they were to depart everyone was anxious to get going again. They still were looking at two months of travel. If all went well.

With each passing day the wagon train was able to travel a few miles more than the day before, as they now were doing a good job at the close of the day corralling the wagons and then getting started in the morning. The young boys and girls had to gather firewood and buffalo chips along the way while they walked beside the wagons. Consequently the wagons in the last group found fewer sticks of wood or buffalo chips. But each night the firewood and chips gathered by the front group were shared with the rear group. "This is the first time in all my years ram-rodding wagon trains, that the folks shared their firewood and buffalo chips with the rest of the wagons. These people are special."

This was a good time of year to be on the Oregon Trail. While the days were warm, the nights were cool which made for good sleeping. The air, even though it was warm, was not humid. The plains looked like a green velvet carpet. The oxen and horses had excellent grazing and water was bountiful in the streams that flowed in many of the ravines.

A day out from Fort Laramie a courier riding to meet them, met them at their night camp. "I need to see Lieutenant Sanford, Private," the courier said.

Private Jones said, "Follow me, it'll be easier than trying to give you directions."

"Lieutenant Sanford, Sir, Private Harris has ridden from Fort Laramie to see you."

"Thank you, Private. You may go back to your sentry duty."

Private Harris handed a dispatch from Major Daniel at Fort Laramie:

Lieutenant Sanford.

You have been directed by Colonel Albert at Council Bluffs to proceed to Freemont. I have received information that a band of Cheyenne Indians have followed the Niobrara River from Wyoming and are attacking small Pawnee villages, killing many of the braves, taking their young women and girls. It is also believed they have done the same to the white settlers.
You are directed to the nearest Pawnee village on the Missouri. Get what information you can from there and then check out the white settlers. When you reach Freemont there will be a map of settlers available for you. You need to stop these attacks Lieutenant and drive them or any survivors back into Wyoming.

Colonel Albert
Council Bluffs

"Private Harris, you can inform Major Daniels that we will proceed to Freemont at sunrise. You're dismissed, Private."

"Gentlemen, we have new orders. We are to proceed to Freemont as soon as possible at sunrise." He read the dispatch out loud so there would be no question.

"Sergeant Quinlin, you and Corporal Jandreau spread the word we'll be pulling out at daybreak. And we will still maintain the usual watch."

CHAPTER 5

They traveled as fast as the chuck wagon would go, oftentimes not stopping until after sunset; light conditions permitting.

Lieutenant Sanford had informed the troop why they were going to Freemont, and now why they were traveling so fast, and no one complained. The men were all tired as were their horses, but the Lieutenant pushed on regardless.

Less than two weeks later the troop arrived at Freemont and they were met by Colonel Harris' aide. "Lieutenant and Sergeant, if you'll follow me I'll take you directly to Colonel Harris' quarters."

"Come in, gentlemen, have a seat. Would you prefer coffee or whiskey?"

"Coffee would be fine, Sir," Lieutenant Sanford replied.

Harris didn't say anything more until he handed them a cup of steaming coffee. He had a shot of whiskey. "A band of Cheyenne Indians led by Temni came out of the Wyoming Territory and followed the Niobrara River where it intersects with the Missouri River. There he raided a Pawnee Village and the Pawnee have asked for our help. Your unit, Lieutenant, is the only one available to respond.

"This Temni supposedly has brought women along, although they are left behind somewhere when he raids a village. He has killed several of the Pawnee braves without receiving any causalities. He took women and young girls and what horses he didn't run off, he took.

"Here's a map of the homestead settlers along the Missouri

112

and the Niobrara Rivers. I think you should go first to the Pawnee village and see firsthand what the Cheyenne did and maybe you'll pick up some information. The chief's name is Mato.

"I can only assume the Cheyenne are doing the same to the settlers. Find the Cheyenne and exterminate them, Lieutenant, and bring back any hostages

"The Pawnee leave us in peace, Lieutenant, so I feel obligated to help them. Make an example out of this band of Cheyenne. Teach them to stay in the Wyoming Territory.

"Here's a copy of my orders, Lieutenant. Draw enough supplies for a long detail. Are your men up to this, Lieutenant?" Then in a second thought, "Of course they are or they would not be out here in this God-forsaken country. That's all, Lieutenant. You have your orders."

Once outside of Harris' quarters, Sanford said, "Sergeant, we'll draw the supplies we need tonight then have the men get a good night rest."

Secretly Lieutenant Sanford was in his glory. Now he had a chance to show his superiors that he was a seasoned Indian fighter. And better yet, he was to answer to a superior who seemed to dislike all Indians. He had a free hand how he was to execute Colonel Harris' orders.

That night while Lieutenant Sanford was studying the map Colonel Harris had given him, he began to wonder if the Cheyenne party came out of the Wyoming Territory and hit the Niobrara River and raided the few settler's homesteads along the way. *Would a seasoned fighting tactician go back the same way? Particularly since the Niobrara River comes close to white settlements and Fort Lamarie?* He doubted it very much.

If he was running from the Army he'd travel further to the north along the Missouri River and then turn west and hit the Cheyenne River before encountering the Lakota tribes. He didn't know in how much of a hurry this Cheyenne band would be, returning to their lands. If they were traveling fast, then there would not be any way in hell he'd ever catch up to them.

He had an idea and went to see Sergeant Quinlin. He was cleaning his firearms. "Sergeant Quinlin."

"Yes, Lieutenant?"

"I'd like to speak with you and Corporal Jandreau in private." They followed the lieutenant to his quarters.

"Sit down, men. I have a special detail for you two, to scout ahead for this Cheyenne party. We'll have to stop and talk with the Pawnees and settlers along the rivers. This will make us so far behind the Cheyenne we may never catch up to them. And Colonel Harris' direct orders were to find them and stop them and rescue the hostages. I want you to beeline it to the confluence of the Niobrara and the Missouri Rivers. I want you to follow the Niobrara west and find where the Cheyenne crossed. I believe they'll cross the Niobrara and head northwest for the Cheyenne River, well away from the Lakota tribes. I think they'll then follow the Cheyenne west to the Wyoming Territory.

"I don't think they'll cross the Niobrara near the confluence with the Missouri River because the water there will be too deep. They'll need shallow water to cross safely with women along.

"When you find them, one stay with them and watch. Follow at a distance and leave a marked trail. The other one ride hard leather back to the unit. We'll be following the river.

"Draw what you need for supplies tonight, so you'll get off early in the morning."

The lieutenant unfolded his map again and explained what he had been thinking about the Cheyenne.

"That's pretty good work, Lieutenant. I think you're right with everything. You can count on us, Lieutenant. We'll find where they crossed and one of us will bring the information back to you," Quinlin said.

He was genuinely impressed with the lieutenant's ability to strategize the Cheyenne's movements with so little information. *Maybe there was hope for him yet.*

Quinlin and Lucien were awake and up before the rest

of the camp had awakened. Samuel and his helper were both up and starting to cook breakfast. "Here, I'll serve you two now. We have the last of the fresh eggs and beef with biscuits. Eat up, the coffee is almost ready."

* * * *

Shortly after Quinlin and Lucien were on their way, Lieutenant Sanford said, "Mount up, men. We have ground to cover. Private Adams, you ride point with me. Private, I'm making a field promotion. You are now a Corporal. When we return to Fort Kearny, I'll make the promotion permanent."

"Yes Sir, thank you."

"We need to pick up the pace, Corporal. Go back and spread the word. We'll stop at noon to water and rest the horses."

They had to ride one day in the rain and eat soggy biscuits with a watery stew. The next two days the weather cleared and just before sunset of the third day they rode into the Pawnee village. "Corporal, take care of the men and horses. I'll be with Chief Mato."

"Yes Sir," John replied, happy to have some responsibility now.

No one, not even the Lieutenant, knew what to expect once they started to investigate the complaint. In order for the Pawnee Chief Mato to complain to the U.S. Army and ask for help against another tribe, then there had to be some validity to the information. But the Cheyenne were not raiding only the Pawnee, they were also supposedly going after the white settlers.

Lieutenant Sanford was led to Mato's lodge. The young man opened the flap and indicated that Sanford should enter. Mato was sitting on a fur robe and leaning against a wooden support. "Lieutenant...good you have come. Sit and we talk." Mato started to fill his pipe.

"Mato, we don't have time to smoke. The longer we wait the further away the Cheyenne are apt to be."

"Sit down, Lieutenant. First we smoke the pipe, then we talk. The tobacco makes body feel good and loosens the tongue," Mato lit his pipe and handed it to the Lieutenant. Sanford sat and accepted the pipe.

Almost a half hour had passed before the last ember in the pipe went out. Mato tapped the ashes out and put the pipe back with a few more articles.

"My people woke up and women began to make food to eat and Cheyenne rode in fast on ponies."

"How many Cheyenne, Mato?"

"You have more soldiers, Lieutenant. My warriors were not armed. First wave of Cheyenne kept my warriors from weapons. After them Cheyenne men picked up two young girls and two woman who had no man. Two my warriors died, four ponies. They took some ponies and let loose more. They rode off yelling and women and girls screaming."

"Why take two girls, two women and a few ponies and only two of your men died?"

"They look for new blood for their people. This happen before. Sometimes we need new blood for my people. Then young brave goes by himself to another village and takes a girl for his woman."

"Cheyenne killed two my warriors, took ponies and made it so we no able to follow them. Pawnee people wish to live in peace with white settlers and soldiers, so I ask for help," Mato had finished.

"Mato, have you heard that the Cheyenne were also raiding white settlers?"

"Lakota runner stopped here and said Cheyenne raided two settlers near Niobrara River. Took children, ponies and beef for food."

"Did any white settlers die?"

"Lakota runner say nothing about whites dying.

"What you do when find Cheyenne party?" Mato asked.

"Free the girls and women they captured. I have orders

to run them out of Nebraska Territories and punish those responsible," Lt. Sanford said.

"One Cheyenne brave come to steal one of our girls or woman for his woman, this is our way. All tribes have been doing it for long time, for new blood, not whole party and take so many girls and women, kill two of my people, steal and run off our ponies. This was not Indian way. Leader of Cheyenne party big trouble. Bring trouble for all Indian tribes."

"We'll stay here tonight, Mato, if that is okay with you."

"What you do come sunrise?"

"We'll try to find their trail and follow it. It shouldn't be that difficult to find and with women and girls and stolen horses along they won't be able to move fast. I have two more men ahead of me to see if they cross the Niobrara River. We believe the Cheyenne will cross the Niobrara River and head north to the Cheyenne River and then follow that back to the Wyoming Territory."

"You think like an Indian. This is good," Mato said.

* * * *

Sergeant Quinlin and Lucien rode fast and hard for the Niobrara River just west of its confluence with the Missouri River. They would ride hard for a while and then walk their horses and let them stop to drink from streams they crossed. At noon they rested their horses for a half an hour and then continued their ride.

The second day out just before sunset they found where many horses had passed through a few days ago. At sunset they followed the trail to water's edge of the Niobrara River. "I'll be damned," Quinlin said.

"What's the matter, Sarg?"

"The Lieutenant was right on about the Cheyenne crossing the Niobrara River heading for the Cheyenne River."

Before turning in on that side of the river for the night

they built a marker for the lieutenant of rocks piled up in a three foot high mount and made an arrow with rocks pointing to the river. Quinlin was sure the lieutenant would understand that they had crossed here.

They crossed the river at sunrise the next morning. The water was really shallow. "I wonder if those Cheyenne knew about this shallow crossing. If they did, then we can assume they have made many raids before in the Nebraska Territory and the land of the Pawnee," Quinlin said. "These aren't the run of the mill Indians, Lucien. At least one of them, probably the leader, is very smart. That'll make catching him difficult."

"I don't understand, Sarg, why they took girls and women hostages. From what we know they didn't take anything of substance. Maybe a few horses, but they can't be worth all the risks," Lucien said.

"They certainly took something more valuable than horses. They took future breeding stock."

"I don't understand, Sarg."

"As primitive or backwards as the native Indians are perceived, they know enough not to allow incest among their people. It could be very likely that everyone in a tribe or village could be related to everyone else." Mato explained what the Cheyenne did was simply getting new blood for their people. To improve their own bloodline.

"Sometimes they'll take a white boy or girl thinking that when they mate with someone in the tribe that the newborn will possess some of the strength or knowledge of the whites.

"I have never seen such a large scale of taking new breeding stock as this. Usually if a young buck wants a woman not of his tribe, he'll sneak into a neighboring village and take one woman. Usually about his own age that he could take back as his own woman. For a Cheyenne party to do this on a larger scale—well, I have never heard of it before."

"Maybe they plan on selling the girls and women."

"Yeah, but the Indian doesn't do anything for payment.

But you may be on the right tack, Lucien. We won't know until we catch up with them. Now that they have crossed the river they may travel even slower. If they don't, then we may not catch up with them."

The next morning they made another rock marker and an arrow pointing in the direction. The ground was different on this side of the river and it was a whole lot easier to follow their trail. "A good rain would wash away all these tracks," Quinlin said.

As long as the trail was easy to see and follow they rode at a fast pace. The second day after crossing the river, early in the morning they found where the Cheyenne had camped for the night. The fire pit was still warm. "They're not far in front of us now." They led the horses for a while for a closer look at the trail signs.

"They still seem to be traveling slow. The horses are walking as are the women and the girls."

"How many would you say, Sarg?" Lucien asked.

"It's hard to say. But some of these women tracks are not all made from the hostages. That tells me they brought along some of their own women."

"Maybe to help with the girls and women hostages," Lucien said.

"Maybe—good point."

"It's time for you to high-tail it back and find the lieutenant. I have spent all my life in the woods and I know how to take care of myself. Besides you are better on a horse than me and you'll be able to travel faster," Lucien said.

"You're right and there is no sense in arguing. If the trail changes direction leave another marker. Be careful, Lucien."

That's all that was said and Quinlin turned his mount and rode off. Now at a fast pace. He had no idea where he would find the lieutenant. He wasn't worried at all about Lucien. He knew Lucien could take care of himself.

* * * *

Sergeant Quinlin rode hard and fast. During the warmer hours, he slowed his horse to a walk and at times he would get off and walk beside it. This was no time to run his horse into the ground or stumble in a hole because it was exhausted.

He ate while his horse ate and rested and rode fast and hard as long as there was enough light to see. He recrossed the Niobrara River after a half day of riding and after another day and a half he found Lieutenant Sanford and the unit following his trail.

The men rested and watered their horses while Sergeant Quinlin debriefed the lieutenant. "And why did you not stay with the Cheyenne and have Corporal Jandreau ride back to find us?"

"I am a better horseman, Sir, and Corporal Jandreau is better in the wilderness than I."

They mounted up and moved out. But not at such a fast pace as Quinlin had been riding.

* * * *

A half day after Sergeant Quinlin left, the band of Cheyenne turned a little to the west, directly towards the Cheyenne River. Lucien built another rock marker and a stone arrow indicating another change in direction.

That evening when Lucien stopped for the day, he saw to his mount first and then he ate sparingly and rested for two hours. When the full moon rose above the horizon, he led his horse and was able to walk along in the moonlight and follow the Cheyenne trail. After two hours, from the top of the forested knoll, he could look down and see the fires of their camp.

He tied off his horse and took the saddle and bridle off and began crawling his way down to the camp. To see what they were up against.

The air was still, no breeze at all, and the temperature had dropped enough so he could see his breath in the moonlight. He was still a long ways from the camp and he stopped to look for a good vantage point where he could see into the camp. About fifty yards off to his left he saw a boulder about four feet high sticking out of the side hill.

He cautiously made his way there and once there he lay on his back looking up at the night sky, catching his breath.

There was no movement in the camp. The only sounds were that of the crackling fires. He could see one sentry where the ponies were corralled. Other than that everything was quiet.

There was nothing more to gain by staying awake all night, so he relaxed and took catnaps. Shortly after sunrise the camp came alive. But no one seemed to be in any particular hurry. The Cheyenne women, four of them, seemed to be in charge of the captives. They wore their hair straight and on their backs. The Pawnee women wore their hair in long braids and there seemed to be three women, maybe in their teens. There was also one white woman, also in her teens, and two smaller children. Boy and girl. None of the captives appeared to have been abused. But they were made to help within the camp.

About two hours after sunrise two braves came walking into the camp dragging a mule deer. *Maybe this is why they are not in a hurry this morning. They took the time to hunt for food.*

The deer was left in the center of the camp and one Cheyenne woman and one Pawnee woman took care of the deer. It was skun and the hide rolled up and packed and the meat was cut into chunks and secured in packs which the women carried on their backs.

It was a little past mid-morning before the Cheyenne broke camp and continued in the same direction. Lucian waited until the Cheyenne band was out of sight then he made another rock marker on top of the knoll and then he began following them. Their camp site would be obvious but he left an arrow in the direction they had taken. Just in case a rain storm was to wash out their tracks.

* * * *

What had taken Sgt. Quinlin two days to find the lieutenant now took the unit three days to get where Sergeant Quinlin had left Lucien. It was late so they made camp there. Not knowing how close they were to the Cheyenne, only one smokeless fire was allowed and that had to be extinguished at dark.

Sgt. Quinlin found the marker and the arrow. At daylight the next morning they changed directions, following the trail.

* * * *

Even though the Cheyenne had gotten off to a slow start they kept traveling until after sunset and finally came to the Cheyenne River. The women began immediately to cook some food.

Lucien stayed where he could watch them all night and in the morning they made no attempt to break camp. Two men went hunting and three women brought in boughs for beds. *So they plan to stay awhile. Good.*

Like the other camp, the captives when not working were kept together in one area. So far it didn't appear as if any of them had been abused, only forced to walk. Which was probably only normal for native women.

Two women went foraging for herbs and the two hunters were back already, dragging another deer. And just like before it was the women who took care of it.

Lucien watched the Cheyenne camp from the knoll all day. Another deer was brought in and while the women took care of it, the men built a smoking rack to cure the meat. *They must be planning on a long trip.* He had no idea what the country was like to the west. By mid-afternoon another brave brought in a beaver which was eaten for supper that night.

As long as the meat was curing on the racks, Lucien knew

they would not move. Then he began wondering if the troop would be able to follow his trail. *Certainly Sergeant Quinlin would see his markers and arrows and be able to follow the trail. But what would the lieutenant do once they were here?* The Cheyenne camp seemed peaceful and so far none of the captives had tried to escape.

He lay back in the grass, looking up at the clear cloudless sky and wondering if what they were doing—recapturing the women and kids—was the right ethical and moral thing to do. *These native people have been on this land longer than I can even imagine. No one knows how long. Is the white man with all of our justices correct in telling the natives how they should live their lives? But what about the white captives. This certainly isn't part of the white man's culture. And all of the captives are just that, captives and not free to leave.*

What will Lieutenant Sanford do when he arrives here? This was worrying him.

That evening after everybody had eaten, more wood was put on the fire and dry logs carried into camp and placed around the fire and everyone sat around the fire. Someone was standing and talking, but Lucien didn't know the language and he couldn't see who was speaking.

* * * *

"The Cheyenne have slowed their trek, Lieutenant. They are traveling fewer miles each day now. I think we should make camp here for the night, Lieutenant, and in the morning I think I'll ride out ahead of you and locate Corporal Jandreau before the noise of the entire troop spooks them. I'm sure Corporal Jandreau is not far ahead of us now. I know the Cheyenne River is only a good day's ride from here," Sergeant Quinlin suggested.

"Point well taken, Sergeant. Make it so."

Quinlin was up before the others had even awakened and he grabbed some food and rode off. Just before sunrise a dark cloud blew in and he had to dismount and lead his horse as he followed the trail. Even in the dim lighting, occasionally, he could see a shoed-horse track and knew it was Lucien's. The sun was peaking up over the horizon, and because of the dark cloud Quinlin had to go slow. A half hour later the cloud blew away and the sky was clear. He rode hard to make up time.

Around 2 p.m. that day Quinlin was leading his horse through some brush when he topped out on a knoll and below him next to the Cheyenne River was the Cheyenne camp. He then saw Lucien behind a rock. He tossed a rock to get Lucien's attention.

Lucien crawled back to the top. "Sarg."

"How long have they been camped here?"

"Two days this evening. I think they are preparing for a long trek. They have been smoke-curing venison for two days."

"How have the women and kids been treated?" Quinlin asked.

"Very good. Four Cheyenne women safeguard the captives and they make them work along with themselves. The men never come near them."

"Do you think they'll be breaking camp tomorrow?"

"Not at daybreak, at least. They would have to pack the cured meat first and that is still curing."

Sergeant Quinlin was thinking, and Lucien asked, "Do you know what lies west of here, Sarg?"

"Yeah, been there only once. The Wyoming Territory badlands. That probably accounts for them smoke curing meat here."

"How far behind you is the lieutenant?"

"They could be here shortly after dark," Quinlin answered.

"Maybe the lieutenant should make camp a short way back from this knoll. In case more hunters go out and spot the unit. This is only a suggestion, Sarg."

"And a good one. I'll ride back and bring them up about a quarter of a mile back. There's a nice stand of trees where we can wait out of sight. You stay here, Lucien, and if you think they'll be breaking camp soon, you ride back. When we have the unit pulled up in the trees I'll come get you, and you, the lieutenant and I will make a plan.

"You hungry?"

"Does a beaver eat wood? Of course I'm hungry."

"Here, here's some dried jerky. That's all I have."

* * * *

Quinlin rode back and met the unit about five miles from the knoll. He briefed the lieutenant about what he had seen and what Corporal Jandreau had told him. "Lieutenant, there is a stand of trees we could camp in tonight out of sight, this side of the knoll where Corporal Jandreau is watching from the other side. It is about five miles from here," Quinlin said.

It was dark before they reached the shelter of the trees. Samuel and his helper fixed a meal of cold beans and bread and water. "No fires," Lieutenant Sanford said.

"Sergeant Quinlin, go fetch Corporal Jandreau. I want to talk with him myself."

"Yes Sir. I'll leave immediately." He walked up the knoll and crawled down the other side to Lucien.

"Lucien, the lieutenant wants you to come back with me."

Lucien followed Quinlin up and over the knoll and to their camp.

Back behind the chuck wagon and shaded from open view, Quinlin built a small fire so Lucien could draw a map of the Cheyenne camp. When Lucien had the camp outlined in the dry soil the lieutenant asked, "Do you think they'll be leaving tomorrow, Corporal?"

"I can't say for sure, Sir. The meat they are smoking is still on the racks. If it cures during the night, then they may leave."

"How many men?"

"Fifteen, Sir."

"Any kids besides the captives?"

"No Sir."

"Where do the men sleep?"

"There are some hide shelters tied up between trees near the river. Here." And he pointed.

"The captives?"

"Here, away from the river under another hide shelter."

"How is the best way to get to the camp from here, Corporal?"

"Around the right of this knoll. The land drops off a little before coming back up to the camp. If we're quiet, we should be able to sneak through there without being seen."

The lieutenant was silent for a while, thinking, then he said, "Good job, Corporal. We'll leave here at 3 a.m. and work our way up the draw and wait here," and he pointed to the map, "until first light. Then we strike. Corporal, you take John and Bill and you secure the captives and Cheyenne women. You protect the women and captives, Corporal.

"Sergeant Quinlin, you'll take half the squad and work your way through the camp circling to the right towards where the men are and I'll take the other half and go left."

"Any questions, men? Good. Corporal, that was some good work. Now get some chow and sleep," the lieutenant said.

Lieutenant Sanford was so excited he couldn't sleep at all that night. Here was his big chance to prove to his superiors that he was an Indian fighter. Quinlin talked with the men he would have, and after eating Lucien talked with John and Bill.

Lucien was exhausted. He sat on the ground with his back against a tree and was soon asleep.

* * * *

A little before 3 a.m., Sergeant Quinlin awoke Lucien. "It's time, Lucien."

Lucien, John and Bill led the way around the knoll and up through the draw. They stopped and waited for sunrise before entering the camp. "Remember what I said, John, Bill. We protect the captives."

The entire unit hunkered down just a few yards from the Cheyenne camp. No one made a sound. Not even heavy breathing. The only sounds were that of peeping frogs and the gentle sound of the river.

A few minutes before 4 a.m. a gentle breeze started to blow. The eastern horizon was a golden glow. It was still too dark to begin. They all had waited so long and now bored, still; they were actually eager for some action.

Finally the darkness was beginning to be pushed aside with the beginning of daylight. Some of the Cheyenne men were beginning to stir. Lieutenant Sanford looked at Corporal Jandreau and nodded his head to move out. He gave Sergeant Quinlin the same nod.

In complete silence the entire squad moved out into the camp. Lucien and his two men went directly towards the captives. The lieutenant and sergeant flanking the warriors. One of the Cheyenne woman saw Lucien and his men approaching and recognized the blue uniforms and screamed. The entire camp came alive. All four Cheyenne women were now screaming. The captives were surprised and huddled together.

With the first scream all of the Cheyenne warriors came alive with weapons in hands. Some with clubs, knifes and spears. Bows and arrows were useless at this close range. One warrior ran towards the captives and Lucien shot him. John and Bill both shot warriors running across the camp site. It only took a matter of minutes and every Cheyenne man and woman were dead.

The Cheyenne women had run towards their men screaming and were shot down. Mostly in the back.

As the commotion died and the gun smoke cleared, Lucien was sick to his stomach. He was afraid all along that something like this might happen. John and Bill felt the same as

Lucien. Some of the men were dancing around shouting, hoot and hollering and happy about what they had done there this day. The captives, all except for the whites, were afraid the same thing would happen to them.

Lucien talked with the two white captives and calmed them. "Can you talk with any of these women?"

"Yes, some," she replied.

"Tell her we will take them home and no harm will come of them. We'll take you and the boy and girl home also."

"Thank you," she replied. "You must know, Sir, they never abused us."

Lieutenant Sanford was very pleased with himself. He was as jubilant as if he had just won a great battle. He sent one of the privates back to bring up the chuck wagon.

"Sergeant Quinlin, we'll take this cured meat with us. We'll need more food than what we have to feed everyone now. It'll be a long trip home."

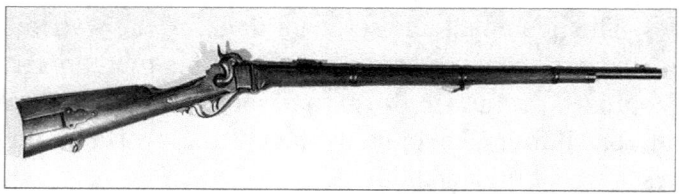

CHAPTER 6

It was the middle of June before Lieutenant Sanford and his men returned to Fort Kearny. Everyone was exhausted and Major Merrill gave everyone three days off to rest and recuperate. But where were they to go.

One day Quinlin and Lucien were drinking beer in one of the saloons and Lucien asked, "Sarg, why did we have to kill the four Cheyenne women? They were no threat to anyone."

"I can only explain it as, in the heat of the battle. I'm not saying it was right. There are some men who can be infected with the fever to kill, once a battle is underway. They shoot before thinking." They drank the rest of the beer in silence.

No one was doing much talking about the Cheyenne River Battle, as it was now being called. Maybe in retrospect everyone was feeling a little ashamed. All except for Lieutenant Sanford. He strutted around the fort as if he were really someone of importance.

Lucien went for a walk along the banks of the Platte River. He sat down under a shade tree and watched the cool water flow by. There were things going through his head that made him question what he was doing. He really enjoyed Army life, even out here so far away from home. He enjoyed helping people. But every time he thought of the Cheyenne River Battle, he became sick to his stomach. He didn't understand the natives as much as he wished he did. He understood what the Cheyenne party were doing. *But was it morally correct to kidnap young women and boys only to strengthen their own bloodline? Was is necessary to kill everyone? Even the women?* Surely the lieutenant could have tried talking with the Cheyenne first, before total extermination.

Lucien had another concern also: the increasing number of people heading west to escape what everyone says will happen; a war between the north and south. The country splitting up and fighting each other. Killing the natives was one thing, but killing fellow Americans was completely appalling.

Lucien walked back to the fort and met Quinlin and the two went to have a beer. He talked with Quinlin about his concerns, but unfortunately the Sarg couldn't help him much.

"I'm not saying, Lucien, that we were in the right killing everyone. But there's one thing I've learned in this here army, is to do what I am told and what is expected of me. I think it was as wrong to kill the women as you do, Lucien. But we already talked about that."

They sat in silence sipping beer.

After the three-day furlough the unit went back to escorting wagon trains from Council Bluffs and Independence to Fort Laramie. Because of a shortage of troops at Fort Laramie they had to escort a wagon train all the way to Independence Rock, west of Fort Laramie, where they met up with the returning escort and Lieutenant Sanford and his men returned to Fort Kearny.

This escort service for the many wagon trains kept up the pace all summer. When the last one left Council Bluffs it was only going as far as Salt Lake, a Mormon settlement. That was the last wagon train for the year.

The one topic most people traveling in the wagons west were talking about, was the war that was sure to come between the North and South. Increasing talk almost daily of the southern states seceding from the Union.

The soldiers at Fort Kearny were pretty much divided on their loyalty between the North and South. Sergeant Quinlin had the same beliefs as Lucien, that no man should own another. For Lucien, this kept reminding him of his father. They both had already made up their minds that if the war between the states did break out, they were going to stay out of it.

John Adams' field promotion to corporal remained in effect even after their return to Fort Kearny. Lucien had to laugh to himself about 'Corporal John Adams.' When they first met John was a bigot and a smartass. *How he has changed,* Lucien thought.

With the last train safely escorted to Fort Laramie the men at Fort Kearny turned their attention to preparing for the cold months ahead. It was only late August but Major Merrill didn't want the men sitting around with nothing to do. Some men were on firewood duty and some, in groups of two, were sent out to shoot buffalo and deer. Lucien, John, Bill and Sergeant Quinlin chose to work on firewood. They each needed some physical work in order to stretch some unused muscles.

The buffalo herds had moved to the north, just south of the Niobrara River. There were three groups of two men each and each group had a wagon to haul the meat back.

* * * *

A month after Lieutenant Sanford and his unit returned to Fort Kearny after seeing that all the captives had been returned to their families, a scouting party of Cheyenne had set out to look for the party that had left to find new blood for the tribe. They found the dead bodies next to the Cheyenne River.

Everyone, even the women, had been killed. Shot. Some in the back. There was only one conclusion. It had to be the work of the blue soldiers. The soldiers' trail could still be seen in places and this scouting party of four followed the trail to the Niobrara River. They stayed on the north side of the river as the south was the beginning of the land held by the Pawnee.

The scouting party returned to their village in the Wyoming Territory and the young chief was furious, and he was also a hot-head, and there were others in the tribe who had lost friends and family and they too wanted to show the blue coats who was the better warrior.

Cinksi (*son*), the chief, formed a party to go after these blue coats and teach them a lesson. As much as he wanted to go, he knew his place was to stay behind with his people and delegate a leader to pursue the blue coats. He chose his cousin Heton (*antelope*). All of the young men wanted to go, but Heton only chose a few of the very young. The others were seasoned fighters.

But Heton had overlooked a very important fact. This enemy he was after would have firearms. He and his braves had bow and arrows, spears, knives and clubs. Not a fair match. But he was eager for battle.

Heton and his party of thirty warriors rode out of the Wyoming Territory following the Cheyenne River. They carried very little food with them. They would hunt and harvest herbs for food. They were excellent horsemen and rode hard. They were at the Cheyenne River Battle site in two days. They made camp and hunted for food and herbs. Two days later they rode south towards the Niobrara River and the beginning of the Pawnee land. Pawnee were friends of the blue coats and this angered Heton.

* * * *

There were nine soldiers who left Fort Kearny and headed north towards the big prairie lands a mile south of the Niobrara River.

There they found a huge herd of buffalo. It was late in the day so they decided to camp in the trees and wait until morning. The air was cool and still that night and none of the soldiers realized that a short distance to the north was a Cheyenne war party looking for blue coats to retaliate against for the slaughter of their friends and family.

The buffalo bedded down where the soldiers had last seen them and at sunrise the next morning the soldiers rode quietly east only a short distance and began shooting. With only three wagons they decided not to kill more than six animals or they would not have room to haul all the meat back to the fort.

Heton and his braves were already on the move when they heard the first rifle shot. "Blue coats!" Heton yelled and they rode directly towards the sounds.

After the first shot, the buffalo stampeded and they were only able to bring down four animals.

Heton and his braves watched as the soldiers began dressing off the buffalo and quartering the animals. He only nodded to his companions and they spread out and rushed towards the soldiers. Their firearms now were useless to them. There were nine soldiers and eight were killed. Heton wanted one to survive, to send a message back to the fort. But first Heton removed the soldier's firearms and his shirt, hat and jacket and then he said, "Go tell your chief, we do this 'cause of Cheyenne massacre. You tell chief stay off Cheyenne land. Go!"

The lone soldier rode off and Heton's braves loaded the meat into the wagons. But they didn't know how to drive the wagons, so they walked beside the horses and led them.

* * * *

For Wilbur Dudley the ride alone back to Fort Kearny was agonizing. He was sorrowful about losing his friends, but the days were hot, blaring sun and the nights were cold. He had neither a shirt or a jacket to protect him from the sun burning his skin or keep him warm at night. He had no weapons nor any way to start a fire.

When Wilbur Dudley arrived back at Fort Kearny, he reported directly to Major Merrill. Dudley told the Major everything that had happened and what Heton had told him to tell the Major. "You're excused, Private. Report to the infirmary immediately."

Major Merrill was furious. This was the first he had heard about a massacre at Cheyenne River. It was obvious now that Lieutenant Sanford had not told him everything. He sent his aide to find Sargeant Quinlin and Corporal Jandreau and to report immediately to his office.

Lieutenant Sanford saw Quinlin and Lucien double-timing it to the major's office and wondered what was happening. "Come in, gentleman, and sit down. This is not a social meeting. I was just informed by Private Wilbur Dudley what actually happened at Cheyenne River. Now I want it from you two, without any exceptions." He was still so furious his face had turned to a deep red color.

When Quinlin and Lucien finished Major Merrill was even more furious. "You're excused. Go find Lieutenant Sanford immediately and tell him I want his ass in my office yesterday!"

Outside Quinlin and Lucien looked at each other. "We'd better split up. We'll cover more of the compound that way," Quinlin said.

Sergeant Quinlin found the lieutenant in his quarters. "Lieutenant, in Major Merrill's own words you are to get your ass over to his office yesterday, Sir!"

"Come in, Lieutenant, and you'll stand at attention! I have just been advised by Private Wilbur Dudley, Corporal Jandreau and Sergeant Quinlin about the massacre at the Cheyenne River!"

"Sir it wasn't—"

"Shut up, Lieutenant, and listen. Who in hell gave you the authority to kill everyone? Even the women! They were shot in the back!

"Well damn it, who gave you the authority to massacre everyone?"

"Colonel Harris, Sir."

"I did not tell you to kill the women or kill everyone! I told you to run the Cheyenne off Pawnee land and rescue the captives.

"You, Lieutenant, have ignited an Indian war that I doubt will ever stop. Damn you!

"We had a very peaceful existence here with the different tribes. You have made one hell of a mess here, Lieutenant, and I have no choice but to respond to the Cheyenne killing eight of my soldiers. The defense department will require that I do something. You, Lieutenant, will assemble your troops immediately and draw sufficient supplies and leave as soon as possible for the Cheyenne River and find this party that killed my soldiers. You've caused a mess here, Lieutenant, that I doubt if we'll ever be able to put behind us. As for Colonel Harris, I'll file a formal complaint with the defense department. Now get your troops together!"

Sanford tried to say something and Major Merrill cut him off, "Not one word, Lieutenant. Dismissed!"

* * * *

Sergeant Quinlin, Corporals Jandreau and Adams readied the troops as fast as possible and Private Samuel and his helper Bruce Burns loaded the chuck wagon with supplies and water. No one knew how long they would be gone. It was high noon when the troop left the compound at Fort Kearny, heading directly north toward the Cheyenne River and Cheyenne Territory. They covered twenty miles in that half day. Everyone was exhausted, even the mounts.

They crossed the Niobrara River and found where the Cheyenne had crossed with the wagons. It was the same place where the earlier Cheyennes had crossed. Apparently they were well acquainted with this shallow crossing and the countryside.

Lucien was scouting ahead of the troops and about five miles from the main body he found one wagon with a broken tongue. Not knowing how to repair it the Cheyenne left it and put the meat on the other two wagons. Now they were weighed down and would be moving slower.

Lucien rode back to advise the lieutenant and the troops rode as fast as they could. The chuck wagon would have to catch up when it could. He left two soldiers to accompany the chuck wagon.

* * * *

Heton wasn't upset that he had to leave one wagon behind. What did bother him though was the fact he didn't have the knowledge to fix it. But leaving the wagon would only be more bait for his trap.

They made camp at the sight of the massacre and were making plans to stay for a while. The meat was cut into strips and hung on curing racks over the fires.

While the meat was curing he sent out two groups of four braves each to scout the country behind them. Looking for the blue coats who would be following their trail.

After several days the meat was cured. Two groups of four still scouted around them and one day news was brought back that the blue coats were coming and would reach the Niobrara River crossing that day. That would give Heton about a day and a half to set his plan in motion.

The next morning while two scouting parties were watching the blue coats from a distance, he and another brave rode out to find a ravine and canyon he could use to trap the blue coats. Just south of his camp, maybe a half day ride and a little to the east he found just what he wanted. He would lure the blue coats into the canyon and then block their escape.

* * * *

Sergeant Quinlin rode up beside Lieutenant Sanford and said, "We have company, Lieutenant. There are four braves watching us from the high ground to our left. So far they have made no attempt to intervene. They may be only a scouting party watching to see what we are doing."

"I have seen them, Sergeant. Back to your position."

"Yes Sir."

Heton had figured to lure the blue coats into the narrow canyon in late afternoon. The next morning, figuring the blue coats would still be following his trail, he sent six braves out to let the blue coats chase them into the canyon. Eight more braves would be hidden along the canyon walls to prevent the blue coats from trying to escape over the walls. He would lead the rest and come in behind the blue coats when they entered the ravine.

He sat his mount smiling and happy with his plan.

When Lieutenant Sanford saw the six braves so close directly in front of him he ordered the entire troop to pursue. The six braves wheeled their tough ponies and ran off. The blue coats following. Samuel and Bruce tried to keep up, but they had fallen behind. Lieutenant Sanford was leading the chase and he did just as he was supposed to do. He followed the bait into the ravine and following it toward the canyon. When they had ridden beyond where Heton was hiding, he and his braves pulled out and followed them.

Samuel saw Heton and his braves turn and start to follow the troop. He stopped, not sure what he should do. After a moment he turned the horses to the left and found a secluded shelter to wait out the coming battle. It didn't look good when he saw maybe sixteen or eighteen Indians chasing the troops.

Lieutenant Sanford didn't know he was being chased either until he reached the dead end canyon wall. Somehow the six Indians he had been pursuing had disappeared.

When the arrows started flying the lieutenant hollered, "Take cover!"

Everyone ran for the rocks for shelter. Two soldiers were down with arrows sticking in their backs. "This was a trap, Lieutenant!" Quinlin said. He wasn't happy. They shot back when they had a target. Three Indians were killed right off. Then another soldier caught an arrow in his chest and he was dead.

They had a tremendous advantage with their rifles and handguns over the bow and arrow. They had managed to kill the Indians that had been above them on the canyon wall, but four more soldiers were dead and that many more were wounded.

"There was a lull in arrows and the lieutenant asked, "Sergeant Quinlin, what are the casualties?"

"We have six dead and three wounded."

"How serious are the wounded?"

"They can still shoot, but reloading is a problem for them."

Lucien was unscathed so far. He was worried what might have happened to Samuel and Bruce. The Cheyenne had them pinned down pretty good. As long as they stayed behind the rocks they were fairly well off. But their ammunitions were already running low and everyone needed water. This had been Heton's plan from the beginning. He had the blue coats in a corner without food and water.

"How many of the damned Indians have we killed, Sergeant?" Lieutenant Sanford asked.

"Not known, Sir, but I'd say they have lost more men than we have."

"We need that damn chuck wagon for supplies. Where in the hell is it?"

"Private Freeman and Burns were cut off when the Cheyenne followed or chased us in here. I'd say they have taken shelter somewhere," Quinlin replied.

Lieutenant Sanford was more worried about the captain bars he so wanted than the loss of his men, or that he had been so anxious to prove himself that he had let his entire squad get pinned down.

Just as he was thinking there'd be a lull in the fighting another volley of arrows were let loose. One striking the lieutenant in the left shoulder and seriously wounding him, but not fatally. For sure only one of Heton's braves were hit.

"Are you okay, Lieutenant?" Quinlin asked.

He broke the shaft of the arrow off before answering. "I'll be okay, but I don't know for how much longer we can hold out. Tell your men, Sergeant, not to waste their ammunition. Make every shot count.

"Sergeant Quinlin, you have more experience with the

Indians than I have. Will they attack at night?"

"I'm not sure. There are some soldiers who will say they won't. But I don't know myself."

"How much water do we have?"

"Only what each man has in his canteen, Sir."

The attacks had slowed. The only time an arrow would be shot at them would be if someone exposed himself above the rock cover. It was going to be an awful long night.

* * * *

Heton sat back at his position watching for one of the blue coats to expose himself. Even though he had lost about as many men as the blue coats, he was still pleased with himself. Bow and arrows matched against rifles and pistols. *What I could do if I had the rifles*, he thought.

He knew the blue coats would not attack in the dark. They were not that sure where he and his braves were concealed. He wished the moon to be bright, but instead there was no moon at all and a nighttime attack against the blue coats would be impossible. But he and his braves would rest more comfortable tonight than the blue coats.

As the hours passed Heton was satisfied that the blue coats would not move or attack until daylight. He had stationed two braves to watch the only exit, just in case. He leaned back against a rock and listened to a coyote howl off in the distance. He catnapped all night, which was probably more than the blue coats were doing.

* * * *

Lieutenant Sanford and his men kept a watchful eye all night. Even though there was total darkness, they were still afraid the Cheyenne might try an attack. No one slept during the night and all were thirsty and hungry.

Sgt. Quinlin sat listening. He, too, heard the lone coyote. At first he thought it might be a Cheyenne signaling his brethren. He was angry with himself for letting the lieutenant lead them into this canyon. He knew better than to go chasing after the Cheyenne riders.

Lucien sat behind his rock and wondered if the army life was indeed better than prison life or life with his old man. At the moment things were not looking so, now. But he like everyone else stayed awake all night, listening and watching.

* * * *

Privates Samuel Freeman and Bruce Burns cut brush to hide the chuck wagon and they secured the team behind a wall of branches they had erected. They were close enough to hear the gunshots, hollering and screams. "Samuel, what are we going to do?" Bruce asked.

"We sit here until the battle is over. Whoever wins will come back through the same ravine. If it is the Cheyenne, then we wait until they leave the area."

"I wish we could help them," Bruce said.

"If we tried to get this wagon through with supplies the Cheyenne probably would take it, and then our boys would even be worse off," Samuel said.

So they too stayed awake most of the night worrying about the troops and their friends.

The Cheyenne were the only ones who had had any sleep during the night.

* * * *

Lucien could see the eastern horizon getting lighter. He wondered how long after sunrise the Cheyenne would attack again. He was also wondering how the wounded men were doing. Lieutenant Sanford included. He was thirsty and hungry and he was sure they all were. He checked his pistol again. He was out of ammunition for his rifle.

About a half hour after sunrise Heton and his braves made a frontal attack on the troops. They came screaming and hollering and much to Lucien's surprise they were actually shooting as they ran and then nocking another arrow. Whenever any of the soldiers exposed himself to shoot at the advancing Cheyenne, the Cheyenne would let loose their arrows.

The Cheyenne lost three more braves and three soldiers died and the lieutenant was struck a glancing blow to his head and he was unconscious. Sergeant Quinlin had an arrow sticking out of his right shoulder, rendering his gun hand useless. John and Bill had both been wounded, also with an arrow in their shoulders.

There were two men left besides Lucien who had not been struck with an arrow. "Lucien, the lieutenant took a blow to the head and he is in and out of consciousness and I have an arrow in my right shoulder and I'm no help to you. You're in charge now, Lucien. Do what you can."

Lucien checked with everyone to see how much ammunition the surviving men had. They all had just a cylinder full of bullets. This was not good.

Lucien didn't have long to wait when the Cheyenne attacked again. But they too were running low with arrows and some of the remaining braves, eight, were actually throwing rocks at the soldiers. After the failed attempt the Cheyenne pulled back to their cover. No one on either side that time had been injured.

Heton's braves had only three arrows left between them. Soon they'd have to use their spears, knives and clubs. They had no idea how many blue coats were left.

He got his braves together and explained to them what he wanted to do. One archer would stay back ready to shoot his arrows when the blue coats exposed themselves. The rest were going to make another charge.

Heton nodded his head and he led the charge towards the blue coats. Lucien, John and Bill saw them coming and two of Heton's braves were cut down, and then the firing stopped. The troops had no more ammunition. Losing two more braves Heton retreated back. They too had no more arrows. One arrow struck Lucien in the left shoulder. But since the arrow had slowed from too great of a distance to be very effective it had done very little damage.

The arrow stuck in the fleshy part of his shoulder. Lucien broke off the shaft. Then he looked up and saw the remaining six Cheyenne proceeding on foot towards their position. They were carrying spears, knives and clubs. Apparently they had no more arrows. This gave Lucien the edge he needed. He picked up a dried piece of wood that had been under foot all this time. It was about six feet long and about three inches through. He hefted it and decided it would make a good weapon. He stood up and said, "John, you and Bill stay where you are. I'm going to give these men a little bit of hell," and he started walking towards them.

Lieutenant Sanford had regained consciousness and ordered the remaining soldiers to follow Lucien. "Just shut up, Lieutenant!" Lucien said.

Heton was uncertain what to do now. One blue coat willing to take on six Cheyenne and all he had was a club. This made Heton and all the others nervous. Before Heton could make a decision about what to do, Lucien hollered and ran toward the Cheyenne. This actually frightened the Cheyenne. They had never encountered an enemy like this before.

Lucien spun around while bringing his club up and hit Heton on the side of his chest. Lucien heard bones breaking. One of the braves lunged at Lucien and stuck a knife in his left arm. Lucien ignored the knife and pain. He grabbed that brave by the throat and squeezed his neck until he went unconscious and limp, then Lucien let go and dropped him.

Heton stepped up again and Lucien hit him in the face

with the flat of his hand smashing Heton's nose and blood spurted all over him. The others were coming at Lucien and he whirled his six foot club like a jiu-jitsu master. Even the lieutenant and Quinlin were impressed. Those four went down hard with broken limbs. Heton was back on his feet wielding a long knife. He took one step at a time towards Lucien. His face and the front of him a bloody mess.

The lieutenant was screaming for Lucien to kill the filthy son-of-a-bitch. "Quinlin!" Lucien hollered, "Shut the lieutenant up!"

"With pleasure," and Quinlin hit the lieutenant in the head with his good fist and knocked the lieutenant quiet.

Lucien stood looking at Heton and said, "You understand my words?"

Heton nodded his head that he did. "Good. No more killing. No one else needs to die today. We were wrong and you were wrong. What is done is done!" Lucien stood there with his club in his hands, a knife sticking in his arm and shaft protruding from his shoulder.

Lucien held high his club and threw it. This signified to Heton that Lucien meant what his words had said. Heton threw his knife. "Too many die here."

"Take your wounded and leave in peace and we will too.

"John, Bill can you two see to our wounded? Quinlin? How is the lieutenant?"

"Resting peacefully."

"Can you do anything for his wounds?"

"Already done."

"How about you?"

"I need a new bandage on my shoulder."

Lucien fixed a new bandage and checked on the lieutenant. He would be okay. John and Bill were taking care of the wounded. Two had died during the night from their wounds and three soldiers remained that they soon bandaged up.

Lucien walked over to check on the wounded Cheyenne.

He made splints for the broken limbs and helped Heton to bandage the open wounds.

The lieutenant had regained consciousness and he saw Lucien helping the Indians. "I'll have you court marshalled for this, Corporal."

* * * *

It had been several hours since Samuel and Bruce had heard any gun fire. "What do you think, Samuel?" Bruce asked.

"I don't know, but I think we should take the chuck wagon in and see."

Lucien heard something and looked up to see Samuel and Bruce coming in with the chuck wagon. "We need water, Samuel. Bruce, make room in the wagon for five wounded. The dead will have to be left here. There isn't enough room in one wagon for twenty-three dead bodies."

Heton and his men already had their wounded on travoises behind their ponies and were leaving the canyon. Before disappearing out of sight Heton stopped and turned his pony to look back. He had never seen such a fighting individual in all his life and one that was so concerned about his enemy's well-being and so obliging. He would remember this one. He rode off to join his men.

* * * *

The trip back to Fort Kearny was a quiet trip. The lieutenant kept drifting in and out for the first day and a half. Lucien's wounds were not hurting as much as were the other three wounded. Sergeant Quinlin probably was fairing the best. He rode horseback and the last day Lucien had to ride in the wagon.

"Don't worry about the lieutenant, Lucien, I think you did right. He's just pissed off because you had to take command."

144

CHAPTER 7

The wounded were hospitalized and their wounds treated. Luckily the wounds were not that serious. Not even the lieutenant's. "What happened to your jaw?" the doctor asked the lieutenant. "Looks like someone hit you."

Lucien's most serious wound was the arrow head and broken shaft sticking in his left shoulder. The doctor had to cut the flesh to get it out. The knife wound was healing nicely.

Sergeant Quinlin's wound, once the doctor removed the arrow head and cleaned it, began to heal nicely also.

Lucien laid on his cot next to Quinlin's and he asked, "What did we accomplish out there, Sarg? I mean the Cheyenne lost as many men as we did."

"It started when the lieutenant ordered everyone killed at the Cheyenne River. Then I suppose the Cheyenne had to avenge their men and women so they killed our eight buffalo hunters. In all honesty I don't think any of this would have happened if the lieutenant had just rescued the captives."

After a week Sergeant Quinlin and the other three wounded were released. The lieutenant had to spend two more days in the infirmary.

"Corporal Jandreau, Sergeant Quinlin, I'd like to see you both in my office, now."

Sit down, men. I want to know what happened out there. And I want to know everything, and not like last time."

Sergeant Quinlin started talking, telling the Major how he and Corporal Jandreau rode at the front of the column with the lieutenant and one at the rear. How the lieutenant allowed himself and his troops to be lured through the ravine and into the canyon.

When Quinlin came to the point where he had taken an arrow in his shoulder, Corporal Jandreau explained his actions and Sergeant Quinlin giving him command because he and the lieutenant were out of it.

Sergeant Quinlin told the major about how Corporal Jandreau took on by himself the last six Cheyenne braves with only a wooden club. "You see, Sir, we were out of ammunition and apparently the Cheyenne only had spears, knives and clubs left to fight with.

"Sir, Corporal Jandreau acted commendable. He fought like a jiu-jitsu master. At the end he said there was no sense in any more men dying. The Cheyenne leader agreed and Corporal Jandreau told him to take care of his wounded and leave. I believe, Sir, that if it had not been for that gesture, we all probably would have been killed. This way the Cheyenne leader will take this back to the tribe, his people."

"I'll need a full written report from you both and send Corporal Adams and Private Bill Anson to my office. I want to hear their version of the story. And last I'll hear from Lieutenant Sanford. Dismissed, men."

Corporal John Adams and Private Bill Anson told Major Merrill, almost verbatim, as that told by Sergeant Quinlin. In the end he thanked them and said, "Dismissed."

"Major if I may, I'd like to say one more thing," Corporal Adams said.

"Yes, Corporal, what is it?"

"In all due respect, Sir, but Private Anson and myself have talked a lot about this. In light of Corporal Jandreau's actions we both think he should receive some sort of an award, I mean, Sir, honored for his heroism, Sir."

"If that don't beat all gentleman, a corporal and a private recommending someone for a medal." The Major laughed and said, "Gentlemen, I'll consider it. Dismissed."

After Lieutenant Sanford was released from the hospital

he, too, had to report to the major's office. And he told a completely different story.

"I have written documents by Sergeant Quinlin and Corporal Jandreau and corroborated by Corporal John Adams and Private Bill Anson. All four of them gave me basically the same story, and it is completely different from what you are telling me. You want to try again?"

"You said you got a different story. Did any one of them tell you that someone, probably Sergeant Quinlin, hit me and knocked me out, so he and Jandreau could take my command?"

"Oh, Lieutenant, Sergeant Quinlin did indeed hit you. But to keep you quiet while Corporal Jandreau was trying to negotiate a truce and stop the killing. You were delirious, Lieutenant, and you wouldn't shut up.

"I sent a formal report about Colonel Harris to the Department of Defense. And as for you, Lieutenant, I have already made up my mind. You are not fit to command men. Maybe sometime in the future if you show positive changes you'll be given another chance. But until then you are immediately demoted to Staff Sergeant and you'll answer directly to Sergeant Quinlin. Now get out of my office before I lose my temper. You have caused too much trouble with the natives. Now get out!"

* * * *

Lucien wasn't sleeping good at night. Images of the first battle where everyone, including the women who were killed, and now the images of this last battle with the Cheyenne. Where did it get either side? The Cheyenne lost as many men as the troops and nothing was really settled. Is this what he had to expect, to look forward to in an Army career? He didn't like killing people. And more especially when the killing seemed so pointless.

The west was being opened by an endless horde of white settlers, trappers, hunters and worst of all were those who seemed to be stricken by a fever for the yellow gold. The natives from the Mississippi River to the Pacific Ocean couldn't understand where the hordes of these white skin people were coming from. But one thing was evident to all the tribes, with each passing season they were losing more and more of their land and culture. And Lucien Jandreau was worried for the natives. *Where will it stop?* Did he really want to be a part of the Indian demise? If he did, that would make him more like his father. A bully, and he could not live with that.

For no particular reason he purchased some new clothes at the trading post and a new 1860 Colt .45 pistol, a Sharps rifle, horse, saddle and saddle bags. He wasn't sure yet what he was going to do, but by purchasing these things he began to feel more human, more normal.

When he had time off he'd change his clothes and take his horse out for a ride. And to think, once he was away from people.

Two weeks after everyone had been released from the hospital, Major Merrill requested everyone change into clean uniforms and in formation in the compound yard.

Major Merrill requested Corporal Lucien Jandreau to come forward. Lucien had no idea what this was all about. Major Merrill awarded Lucien the Medal of Valor for his undying courage when he took on six Cheyenne braves at the same time and negotiating a truce of the battle, and using his medical skills to help save the lives of many of the combatants.

When everyone applauded, now Staff Sergeant Sanford stood with his hands to his sides.

He mumbled to himself, "I get demoted and he gets awarded the Medal of Valor." He hated Lucien Jandreau.

* * * *

Lucien was off the day after receiving the award and just like the other days when he decided to ride his horse in the open country, he packed a few things in his saddle bags. All of his money. He had Samuel in the kitchen fill one side of his saddle bags with food. He took his new rifle and holstered his new Colt .45. "I might shoot a deer or something, Samuel; if I do I'll bring the meat back." Then he mounted up and rode off and never looked back.

CHAPTER 8

A month after Lucien had deserted, the Portland newspaper had a cover story on the front page. Lucien's father Maurice had just finished his breakfast at his woods crew camp and with a second cup of coffee he sat back to read the newspaper.

When he saw the article on the front page about his son, he went pale, blood draining from his face and he began to shake. He read the article about Corporal Lucien Jandreau, how one day he was awarded the Medal of Valor for bravery in a Cheyenne Indian attack and how he deserted the next.

His father remembered vividly the last words Lucien had said to him, "If I hear from mom or my brother and sister that you have been abusing them like you have done to me, if I have to I'll desert and I'll come after you and kill you."

He finished reading the article and then he harnessed his horse and buggy and headed for home. The early morning air was cool, but by the time he arrived at his home he was bathed in sweat. He opened the kitchen door and sat down at the table, "Bertha, I know you and the two kids have been writing Lucien. What have you said to him:"

"What on earth are you talking about, Maurice?"

"Damn it, woman, what have you been telling Lucien?"

"Just chit chat, Maurice. I don't understand."

"What exactly have you said to him?"

"I tell him about your work in the woods, how Becky and Laurence are doing in school and what goes on in the village."

Maurice got up and started pacing back and forth in the huge kitchen. "What is wrong with you, Maurice? You're acting like a crazy man."

Maurice stopped and turned to face Bertha, "Have you been telling Lucien that I've been mean to you and the kids?"

"No, of course not. In fact I've told him how much you have changed since he left. What's this all about, Lucien?"

"Maurice showed her the newspaper and when she read the headlines she sat down at the table. "Oh my word. Why would he desert the Army?"

"Before he left he said that if you, Becky or Laurence ever tell him that I have been mean to you, if he had to he would desert and come and kill me. Now what have you been telling him!?"

"Nothing like that, Maurice, I promise."

"I don't know whether to believe you or not, Bertha. Then why after receiving the Medal of Valor, would he desert?"

CHAPTER 9

1860

When Lucien didn't return to Fort Kearny that day or present himself for duty the next morning, Sergeant Quinlin talked with Major Merrill.

"Do you know where he goes riding, Sergeant?"

"I only know he heads out on the Laramie Road. I have no idea from there."

"Okay, take two men and see if you can cut his tracks. It's possible he may have been ambushed by Indians."

With no wagon trains using the Laramie road recently, it didn't take Quinlin long to find Lucien's trail.

About two miles from Fort Kearny Lucien's tracks left the Laramie Road and made a wide circle to the north and then east.

"What in hell is he doing?" John and Bill rode with Quinlin.

* * * *

Lucien was no dummy. He made sure people at Kearny knew he often rode out the Laramie Road and since there were no wagon trains expected through the next week, he knew it would be easy to find his track. After two miles he gradually turned north while still leaving an obvious trail. Then he swung east and his trail was still obvious.

He was traveling just south of the Niobrara River. He

made camp and rested well that night with no confines around him or smelly snoring soldiers. This was real freedom.

When he left in the morning he made sure to leave his fire pit and the bough bed he had made. Satisfied, he mounted and continued towards the east. Then into a grassy prairie and he made a fast ride to the Niobrara River and crossed where he would leave good tracks going into the river and going out on the opposite shore.

Then he began hiding his trail. He walked beside his horse, brushing out any tracks left in the soft soil. He headed west following the river until he found shallow water and a good place where he and his horses walked out into the water on the ledge rock just above the water. Satisfied he had left no tracks he walked his horse upstream until just before dark. Then he left the river being careful not to leave tracks and he started a fire and ate some food and slept really well.

* * * *

Quinlin, John and Bill followed Lucien's trail to his first campsite, "Nothing out of the ordinary here, Sarg," John said.

"And the only fresh tracks are his," Bill added.

In the morning they picked up his trail again. The tracks indicated the horse was walking in a hurry. Quinlin was puzzled. *What is he doing?*

They weren't concerned until all of a sudden they lost his trail on the other side of the Niobrara River. As hard as they looked they could not see where he had gone. So they made camp there that night. "Is he up to something, Sarg? For days we have been on his trail that is so obvious that a blind man could follow, right up to the top of the river bank and then he disappears," John said.

"Sarg, do you think he has deserted?" Bill asked.

"I'm not sure, but for his sake I hope not. But I don't have any idea what he is doing."

"He was heading north when he came to the river, do you think, for whatever reason he is going back to the Cheyenne River where we fought the Cheyenne?"

"I would doubt it, but in the morning we'll check it out."

The next morning, after thinking about it all night, Quinlin said, "John, you and Bill go down river along the bank about a half mile and then make a half mile arc and back to the river upstream from here. Watch the river bank, in case he recrossed the river again. I'm going to walk along the riverbank up stream. He couldn't have just disappeared. We'll meet back here when we're done."

Quinlin waited until John and Bill were out of sight, then he took the reins and began leading his horse along the riverbank. He stopped often to turn over leaves and part the plants and bushes looking for a track. In some places it looked as if something had been dragged across the ground, only slightly disturbing the ground fauna.

He had not searched very far by mid-noon. It took time to over turn grass and leaves looking for a track. If he had been captured by yet another band or hunting party of Cheyenne there would have been a clear trail to follow.

He stood up to stretch and looking down something didn't look right in the accumulation of dead leaves and twigs washed up from the river. He was on his hands and knees, looking at each twig and leave. He found a broken stick and there was sand on top of some leaves. He picked up the leaves and there it was. One clear imprint of a shoed horse and not that of a Cheyenne pony. "You hid your trail well, Lucien. But why? What are you doing?" He said aloud.

Now he was more able to follow his trail by looking where it looked like something had been dragged across the ground. *Probably Lucien was dragging a bush behind him,* he thought. He was now able to follow this slightly visible trail to the rock ledge that protruded out into the water. Quinlin tied off his horse and walked out on the ledge and found where something, probably a horse shoe, had scratched the rock and in the sandy bottom of the river was a very clear trail where a horse was now walking upstream.

Quinlin sat down on the riverbank and laughed aloud and said, "I'm at least two days behind you Lucien. I don't see any chance of ever catching up with you. You have been out here long enough now so you think like an Indian. I know you deserted, Lucien, but some day I'd like to know why. Good luck, Lucien," and Sergeant Quinlin mounted his horse and rode back where he waited for John and Bill.

John and Bill showed up about mid-afternoon.

"Anything?" Quinlin asked.

"Not a track anywhere, Sarg. How about you?" John asked.

"Same here. Not a track."

"What do we do now, Sarg?" Bill asked.

"We return to Fort Kearny and let the major handle it however he sees fit."

As they were crossing the river, John said, "I don't understand how someone who was leaving such a clear and obvious trail for us to follow, all of a sudden up and disappears without a trace or wisp."

For the rest of Cedric Quinlin's life he would keep secret about what he had found in the river that day.

CHAPTER 10

Sergeant Quinlin, Corporal Adams and Private Anson were all standing at attention in Major Merrill's office. "What do you mean he disappeared, Sergeant? No one just up and disappears."

"Once he crossed the Niobrara River there were no more tracks. We circled and checked up and downstream." Sergeant Quinlin replied.

"What is your personal take on all this, Sergeant? You two were close friends."

"We were friends, Major, but I had no idea he was planning to do something like this. I had always figured Lucien liked Army life. Did he desert, Major? I'd have to say yes. But I haven't any idea why."

"How about you two?" and the major looked at John and Bill.

"We talked about this on the way back, Sir. We had no idea either, that Lucien was going to desert. He surprised us as much as anyone, Sir," John replied.

"What in hell do you think Washington is going to think about a corporal who was just awarded the Medal of Valor deserting? Damn it, I want some answers!"

Quinlin, John and Bill stood silent. Finally the major dismissed them.

"What will the Army do to Lucien, Sarg, if he is ever found?" Bill asked.

"He'll be court marshalled and sent to prison at Leavenworth."

"It ain't right, Sarg. Maybe Lucien did desert, but damn it, Sarg, the man is a hero. How's that going to sound when the public reads about it in the newspapers?" John said.

"If I knew where he was, Sarg, and if he needed help, I'd help him and never tell the Army. I'm sure he has a good reason for leaving," Bill added.

As they walked across the compound they met Sergeant Sanford. "What do you think of your hero now, Master Sergeant Quinlin?"

"I think that he is twice the man that you ever hope to be. And if I ever hear another derogatory mark from you about Lucien I'll find the nastiest jobs possible for you."

They continued on, Quinlin smiling to himself. From what he had seen of Lucien's abilities in the wild while trying to follow him, he didn't think the Army would ever find him.

* * * *

Lucien formulated his plan the first day out from Fort Kearny. He continued following the Niobrara River upstream for three days. When the footing was too dangerous for his horse in the river he traveled along the north side. When he figured he had traveled beyond Fort Laramie to the south, he turned south hoping to come out to Douglas on the Oregon Trail.

He finally found the trail just south of Douglas, which was good to have people see him coming in from the east. He wasn't afraid of people knowing who he was, as he had never talked with anyone whenever he was passing through. And he knew few soldiers at Fort Laramie. He was feeling safe.

He tied his horse off at the trading post and went inside to buy some supplies. "Can I help you?" The storekeep asked.

"Yes, I need a pot, a fry pan, beans, coffee, a coffee pot, fifteen pounds of bacon and ten pounds of oats for my horse. I'll need some rain gear and another blanket."

"Will there be anything else?"

157

"I think that'll do it," Lucien replied.

"How do you wish to pay for this?"

"I have a little army script and the rest in cash."

"That'll be just fine. Where you heading?"

"I'll follow the Oregon Trail for two more days and then turn north for the Montana Territory. I'm going to do some prospecting."

"You be careful, young fella. That's Blackfeet country up there. That'll be $21.50."

"That's a bit steep, isn't it," Lucien gave him the army script and the rest in coin.

"It costs plenty, young fella, to freight all this stuff out here. Good luck and watch them Blackfeet."

Lucien tied his supplies on behind the saddle and then walked his horse over to the saloon and tied it at the railing. Before getting something to eat he took out the small package from his saddle bags. He was sending his mother his Medal of Valor award. And no explanation about his desertion. The only place to drop it off to be mailed was a stage coach terminal.

He went inside and walked up to the bar. "Do you serve food here, mister?"

"Yes Sir, what's your pleasure?"

"I want a thick steak, boiled potatoes and green beans and plenty of coffee."

He drank coffee while he waited for his meal. Waiting made him even hungrier. There were five other men in the saloon, all drinking heavily. Two more men came in. They were dirty and needing a shave. They smelled also. They were both big men, but by the looks of them it was clear to Lucien that probably most of their work was done sitting on their backsides.

None of the men in the saloon looked particularly friendly. He would have to keep his eye on all of them. The barkeep finally brought Lucien his meal. It smelled and looked delicious.

The others were watching Lucien eat. It was certainly

as good as it smelled and looked. While he ate he couldn't help thinking that there would be trouble here before he left. When he had finished his steak he asked the barkeep, "Do you have any pie?"

"Yes Sir, the little woman baked an apple pie this morning."

"I'll have a slice and some cheese if you have any."

"I do." And the barkeep was soon back with a hot apple pie and a large slice of cheese. Lucien finished this and filled his cup with more coffee. He was wondering how many of these men were going to try something. He didn't have long to wait. The two standing at the bar turned and walked over to his corner table.

"Hey mister, my friend and I would like a meal like you just ate, except we don't have enough money."

"Then you should have bought food and not whiskey," Lucien answered.

The other said, "Hey mister, how about a little money so we can buy a meal."

"As I said, you should have bought food and not whiskey." And Lucien looked directly at them both. And much to Lucien's surprise they left the saloon.

That still left five men counting the two late comers, who were swallowing whiskey like it was going out of style.

Lucien got up and walked over to the bar and asked, "How much do I owe you barkeep?"

"$3.00 even."

Lucien gave him the money and said, "Thanks." He turned around to find all five men blocking his way. "Give us the rest of your money mister or we'll beat the living hell out of you!"

Lucien looked him up and down and then directly at the others and then he said rather calmly. "I have smelled cleaner outhouses than you pigs. You men stink so bad you're making my eyes water. And there's probably not one of you who might have enough sense to pound sand in a rat hole." The barkeep didn't know what to think. Five men threatening Lucien as he stood alone and he insulting them so, like he wanted a fight.

The one who had been doing the talking doubled his fist, which Lucien saw, and he started to throw a punch at Lucien's face. Lucien blocked the punch and hit the man in his face with the palm of his hand, breaking his nose and sending him backwards against two of his friends and the three of them fell to the floor. Blood was still spurting from his broken nose and covering him and his friends.

Lucien backhanded another sending him through the window and he picked up another and threw him through the window also. The last man started to throw a punch and Lucien snapped his arm and it broke and the man screamed. Two of the dolts got their wits back, and now rushed at Lucien, and much to their surprise Lucien turned around and charged at them and pushed them back against the back wall and knocked their heads together and they both slumped unconscious to the floor. The barkeep stood there speechless. He had never seen anything like this before.

Lucien walked outside and mounted up and rode west on the Oregon Trail for two miles and then turned north. He rode fast and long into the night to put as much distance from Douglas as he could. There was no doubt in his mind that reports of what happened at the saloon would soon reach Fort Laramie and then Kearny. If someone came to investigate they would learn of his purchase supplies. This was good, as it would throw them off from his real destination.

Two days later he was close to the Cheyenne River and he stopped for the night. As he was pouring a cup of coffee a stranger hollered to him, "Hey mister at the fire, can me and my friend come in?"

"What's your business?" Lucien asked.

"Only that we're cold and hungry. Hope to share your fire and warm up. That coffee smells awfully good."

"You can come in but your hands better be empty."

As the two walked into the fire light Lucien recognized them from the saloon earlier. They were not acting as though they had yet recognized him.

"Take your guns out and lay them on that rock," Lucien pointed.

They did and one of them said, "Don't blame you for being cautious mister, but all we want is to warm up by your fire. Your coffee smells good."

"Have a cup," and Lucien tossed him his only cup.

"What's your names?" Lucien asked.

"I'm Finley Bates and this here is Seth Bond."

"I'm Charles Hubert, II."

"Hello Charlie," Seth said.

"It's Charles, not Charlie."

"Where you heading, Charles?" Finley asked.

"I'm going to try prospecting. Going to look in the Black Hills in the Dakota Territory and then up to Montana. How about you two?"

"Canada, or the Red River, then take a canoe down the Red River to Winnipeg, Canada."

They talked for quite a while. "You warming up yet?" And Lucien put more wood on the fire.

"Yes, but I think it's going to be a cold night," Finley said. "Maybe we could bed down for the night beside your fire."

"As long as you two stay on that side of the fire."

"Fair enough."

Lucien was still suspicious of them. But to refuse them the warmth of his fire he felt would only agitate them until they did something stupid. But he still planned to only catnap and keep one eye open at all times.

Seth got up to get their bed rolls and they spread them out on the ground on their side of the fire.

Lucien put some green wood on the fire to last the night and then he pulled his blanket up under his chin and settled back to catnap, while holding his new revolver in his right hand.

Finley and Seth both stretched out their bed rolls. Lucien was wide awake watching the stars above and listening to the night sounds. A bat kept flying back and forth through the fire light chasing bugs. An owl overhead in a dead tree hooted and a lone coyote way off answered the owl. The night air was clear and Lucien suspected that by sunrise the temperature would be cold.

Finley and Seth dropped right off to sleep. At least they were snoring. Maybe. He wasn't yet trusting them.

Towards early morning Finley and Seth started moving and whispering. Lucien remained still with one eye partially open. He even began faking a light snore. "He sleeps," Seth said.

"We must attack before he awakens," Finley whispered. "Move slow and quiet." They both rolled out of their blanket and slowly inched their way around the fire to Lucien.

Not wanting to let either one of them get behind him, he acted now. He moved the blanket off him and pointed his gun at Finley's forehead. Lucien pulled the hammer all the way back cocking his .45. "Not one more move. Seth get back in front of me on the other side of the fire. Give me one reason why I shouldn't just shoot both of you right now."

Neither one of them answered. Lucien stood up. "You come in my fire wanting to warm up. I give you hot coffee and let you sleep beside my fire and now you try to kill and rob me. Get on your horses and leave. If I ever see either one of you again I'll shoot you on sight."

Finley started to pick up his gun and Lucien said, "Leave it and your rifles in your scabbards."

"You can't leave us defenseless out here mister," Seth was almost begging.

After they had left, Lucien smashed their rifles against a rock and unloaded the handguns and put them in his fire.

He put more wood on the fire and made a pot of coffee and fried up some bacon. When he finished eating he geared up and left. Knowing that the Colonel at Fort Laramie would have received a message by now that he had deserted, and it wouldn't be long before word would be sent to Fort Kearny that he had been in Douglas. He now headed east across the Nebraska Territory.

* * * *

Major Merrill had requested that Staff Sergeant Sanford report to his office. "Sit down, Sergeant. Lucien Jandreau was seen in Douglas. I'm going to detail you and one other man to travel to Douglas to see what you can find. He probably won't still be there but you might learn where he has gone. You are authorized to find Corporal Jandreau and bring him back. And I don't want any excuses why you can't bring him in. Is that clear, Sergeant?"

"Yes Sir. I'll take Private Mosby.

Sanford left the Major's office and found Mosby. "Private Mosby, you and I have been ordered to find Corporal Jandreau and bring him back. We leave in one hour. I'll get a pack horse and supplies."

At Douglas, Sanford and Moseby talked with the storekeep at the trading post, the livery stable and the saloon. "It was Lucien alright and he went west on the Oregon Road but turned north at the forks. It hasn't rained and maybe we might pick up his trail."

They rode hard and they found a trail, a trail of four horses.

"Maybe he's following two men or two men are following him. You did say he has now a pack horse," Moseby said.

"I'm not positive about the pack horse, but I think we should follow this trail," Sanford said.

The next morning they found an old fire and two burned out handguns. "What do you make of this Moseby?"

"I'd say two men were following Lucien and he got the jump on 'em."

163

"Look around on foot, Moseby, and see if you can see in which direction the three went. I'll look around here."

Sanford found the two smashed rifles and had a gut feeling that this was the work of Lucien Jandreau. But what surprised him most: if they had jumped Lucien, he was surprised not to find their bodies here.

"Sergeant Sanford! Over here, Sir!"

"What is it, Moseby?"

"Look here," and he pointed to tracks. "Two sets of tracks went left and a lone rider, without a pack horse went right."

"Good work Moseby. We take the lone track that went right."

They mounted up and started following the lone track east. "Sergeant, I don't understand why he is criss-crossing this whole territory?"

"I would say, Moseby, that he is trying to confuse whoever might be following."

"He's a smart one ain't he, Sergeant."

Sanford had no comment there.

* * * *

Lucien rode in no particular hurry. He wanted to travel across Nebraska and turn north before Freemont and Council Bluffs.

That night as he sat by his fire eating beans and bacon and hot coffee, he was feeling good about himself now, in spite of the fact that he was now a wanted fugitive. He unsaddled his horse and brushed him down lovingly. He didn't have a brush so he used his hand. His horse was responding to Lucien's care.

After he finished he spread out his bedroll and sat watching the fire. "It'll be another cool night. Wish I'd thought to get a coat."

He didn't fall asleep until after midnight. Then he fell into a deep sound sleep. And just before awakening at sunrise he started dreaming about a dark haired, beautiful woman. This woman was giving Lucien advice and instructions and all the while Lucien's mind was interpreting this encounter as physical love. When he awoke, he was smiling, feeling this physical love from this woman. But as the seconds passed the dream was fading rapidly, until it was no longer there. But he was happy.

He picked up his pace from the last couple of days. During the day he often would see an Indian or two on high ground watching him pass. That night just before dark, as he was warming up beans and bacon and a pot of coffee, he noticed three Indians walking towards him.

Lucien didn't panic. He didn't reach for his handgun and he didn't stand up. He continued warming up his food. There were three of them walking towards him. They stopped about twenty feet away and Lucien indicated for them to come in and sit. They talked briefly with themselves and then came forward cautiously. The leader, the one in front looked familiar, but he wasn't sure. They were close now, they stopped for only a brief moment. Heton, the leader of the previous war party, thought he recognized Lucien, but he didn't have his blue uniform.

Now in the fire light, Lucien recognized Heton, only he didn't know his name.

"Come in and sit. Would you like some coffee?" Lucien only had the one cup, so he filled it and handed it to Heton.

Heton took it and sipped it. Then he let his two friends try it. They shared the one cup.

Lucien cut off pieces of bacon and gave them to his visitors. "Put the meat on a stick and roast it." Heton explained what Lucien had said.

"You obviously can understand my words. Can you speak my tongue?"

"Yes." He patted his chest and said, "Heton. You army. Where Blue Coat? Why you here alone?"

"My name is Lucien. I quit the Army. Do you understand quit?"

"You no longer Blue Coat."

"That's right. I am alone, because I like being by myself."

"You not Blue Coat now?"

"No."

"Why you stop fighting. No kill me?"

"There was too much killing. No one else had to die that day. It was a stupid act for both of us to kill each other. So many died that day."

Heton finished the coffee and held the cup out for more. Heton took a sip and passed the cup to his two friends. "You help Cheyenne braves before Blue Coats injured. Why?"

"You needed help."

"Not understand. You fight Cheyenne enemy. You stop fighting so no more die. Then you help my wounded. No understand you Lucien. Why you quit Army?"

"I didn't like all this killing. The leader of the soldiers I was with wanted to kill all Indians. This is wrong."

"Where this leader?"

"He was reduced in rank and no longer leads soldiers."

"This is good."

"Why are you and your friends out here now, Heton?"

"Look to see if Blue Coats looking for Indian."

"They won't be, Heton. They want peace with the tribes."

The bacon on all the sticks was cooked and everyone was busy eating. "Good. What animal this come from?" Heton asked.

"From a farm animal called a pig."

When the three were done eating. They stood up to leave. Lucien stood also, "You, Lucien, have permission to travel on Cheyenne land, but not Blue Coats." Heton and his two friends turned to leave.

"Thank you, Heton."

When the three were out of sight Lucien sat back down on his bedroll and put more wood on the fire. He was watching the flames and musing how peculiar life could be some times.

He and Heton had once tried to kill each other and now there was no animosity between them.

Lucien made another pot of coffee and he put more wood on the fire. When the coffee was ready he poured a cup and sat back leaning against his saddle. He sipped his coffee and watched the flames in the fire. His mind was racing with that evening's encounter with Heton and his friends. "All it would take to start a full blown Indian war, would be if the Army made another blunder like Sanford's two. The Cheyenne, according to Heton, would not attack any more soldiers, but neither did he want the Army on Cheyenne land."

Lucien put these thoughts out of his mind and began watching the stars. The belt of stars that crossed the night sky was really bright that night. He stopped thinking about the Army and began wondering what was out there. The universe overhead.

It was about midnight when he emptied the coffee pot and lay down to sleep. He lay on his back and pulled the blanket up and under his chin. He was still fascinated with the bright stars overhead and he didn't fall to sleep until a couple of hours before sunrise. As he was awakening he could remember dreaming about a beautiful woman. He could see her face in his mind and she was saying something to him but he could not make out what she was saying. This dream was not fading.

Even though he did not sleep much, he was well rested and ready to start another day. While he was warming some food, he fed his horse and made sure it had some water. After everything was picked up he kicked sand to cover his fire and he left, heading east.

He didn't ride hard but he wasn't wasting anything either. Cold weather was coming soon and he had to be somewhere to hold-up for the winter. He just didn't know where. But he was being drawn to the east.

Just before awakening one morning he had another dream with the same dark haired woman. He wished he knew her name. Again in this dream toward the end, she was telling him something and during that day while riding his horse, it suddenly came to him what this woman was saying, "Look for me in this life." That's all. He wondered what it was that allowed him to remember now, hours after the dream ended while he was riding his horse and not even thinking about this woman. But now with her words stuck in his mind there was very little else he could think about.

He looked down at the ground and saw two different sets of tracks going ahead of him. He wondered how long he had been following these tracks. He stopped and dismounted and got down on his knees to examine the tracks.

The horses were both shoed, so they were not Indian ponies. And he doubted very much if they would be Army. Since the tracks were going in the same direction as he, he decided to follow, but cautiously. Not wanting to be ambushed.

The tracks led to a more used trail, going in the direction of Fort Kearny. Maybe a two or three days travel away. He followed the new trail northeasterly and the two sets of tracks he had been following had also turned in the same direction.

By mid-afternoon he saw a few head of beef grazing in a glade and from on top a knoll he could look down and see a small farm. There were animals about but no people. He rode down still being cautious.

As he rode into the farm yard he hollered, "Hey! Anybody home!"

No answer, he dismounted and tied his horse to a railing near the house. He knocked on the door and no answer. Things were not as they should be here. He knocked again and still no answer. He opened the door and hollered, "Hey, anyone home?" No answer.

He closed the door and walked over to the barn. "Hello, anyone here?!"

In the tie-up he found a man lying face down in cow manure. There was a puddle of blood under him. Lucien felt for a pulse. He was dead. He withdrew his handgun and began searching the barn. Cautiously. In the upstairs hayloft, there was a naked young girl lying in the hay. She too was dead and it was obvious she had been raped.

He searched all the out buildings before returning to the house. There in the larger bedroom was a naked woman lying on the bed and she was dead and had been raped.

There was no doubt in his mid that the two men from the other night, Finley and Seth, were responsible here. He had pretty much followed their tracks all the way here. Behind the house on a knoll he found two graves. He spent the rest of that day digging three more. The soil was sandy and digging was easy. After he had filled in the last grave there still was about an hour of sunlight left.

He walked around the farm and buildings looking for clues to who had done this. In the corral, he found two horses that looked a lot like the horses Finley and Seth had been riding. They probably took fresh mounts.

Someone had been searching for something in the house, by the looks. Probably looking for money. There were fresh foot prints in the dirt by the root cellar door. He opened the door and stepped in. There was ham and bacon hanging and a number of canning jars and cabbage and squash on the dirt floor.

He went back inside the house and made a closer look. He couldn't find any firearms so Finley and Seth had probably taken those.

The sun was setting so he decided to stay the night. The cook stove was still hot and he fixed a meal of ham and eggs and there was fresh bread in the kitchen. After eating he went out in the barn and laid out his bed roll in the hay. He had earlier given his horse some grain he had found, and hay.

At first he was going to sleep in the house in the parents' bed. But after thinking on it, he wouldn't feel right, so he chose the barn. He lay awake a long time that night thinking about the dead family and the two men responsible. They were nothing more than animals.

At first daylight he was still awake. He got up and tended his horse first, then he went inside the house and fixed himself a good breakfast. While he waited for the fire to get the stovetop hot, he found paper and pen and wrote a letter to leave behind:

I rode into the farmyard yesterday and no one was around. I eventually found all three had been killed. Smashed in the head by a heavy object. The woman and young girl had both been raped. I buried all three on the knoll behind the house where there was already two graves.

Three nights ago two men Finley Bates and Seth Bond came into my camp. They were cold and hungry. Later that night they tried to kill and rob me. I smashed their guns against a rock and drove them off. For two days I would cross their trail which led to this farm. When I leave here I'll try to follow their trail and if I catch up with them I'll settle the score for these poor people. They may be heading for Montana prospecting.

Sincerely, Charles Hubert II

He hoped by signing the letter Charles Hubert II he would be left out of it.

Before leaving he did take a shoulder of cured ham and the three loaves of fresh bread left on the sideboard. He packed the ham and bread and then walked his horse around the yard until he figured he had Bates and Bond's trail.

By the tracks the two didn't seem to be in any particular hurry. Lucien decided he had better remember that the two could possibly have firearms now. Since he could not find any at the farm. He didn't run his horse but he kept up a fast walk all day. The trail was still easy to see. That night he chose a high knoll for his camp, so he could look out across the flat for their camp fire. He kindled his fire behind a rock and warmed up some ham and fresh bread. He didn't see anything for a fire that night.

Instead of traveling north for Montana the trail was going east. Maybe they thought they had fooled him by saying they were going north.

At daylight the next morning there was a light drizzle that only lasted for a couple of hours. Then the air cleared; their trail was still visible.

The sky was overcast with gray clouds all day. Lucien was sure a rain storm was coming. The leaves on all the hardwood trees had turned backwards which was a sure indicator of rain.

Lucien pushed on as long as he could that evening before stopping. He wanted to close the distance between them before he lost their trail entirely. With no light to see by, he had to give it up. He made a small shelter with his slicker and spent a wet miserable night.

As soon as there was daylight the next morning Lucien was on the move. It had rained hard during the night and their trail was gone. He kept an easterly direction and he kept up the fast walk pace as the day before.

The rain or drizzle stopped by noon, but Lucien was wet and cold and he figured the two he was following would also be wet and cold and would probably build a big fire to dry their clothes and to warm up beside. He found a knoll and he made his camp on top with a fire. He had stopped early and now as the sun was setting his clothes were dry and he was warm. Then he put his fire out.

With a blanket wrapped around his shoulders he walked around the top of the knoll looking for their fire. When he saw it, he laughed. They had a bonfire going. Oblivious of the one who was following them. He figured they were about two miles to the east. Still going east. He checked his compass for a heading and then mounted his horse.

When he figured he was about a half mile from the fire, he dismounted and tied off his horse and continued on foot. As he came closer, he could hear the fire snapping as it burned. A little closer and he could hear them talking. He recognized Finley and Seth's voices. Seth was talking about taking the young girl and then having to kill her, "She just wouldn't stop screaming," Seth said.

Lucien was sickend to his stomach. These two were nothing more than brutal animals. He unholstered his .45 colt and walked silently into their camp. He just stood there silently in the firelight with his pistol pointing at them, waiting for them to see him.

When Finley Bates turned so he was facing Lucien, he dropped his plate of beans. Seth looked over at Finley and also saw Lucien standing with his gun pointing at them. "We ain't done you no harm, mister! You don't need to be pointing that there big gun at us," Finley said.

"I buried the family you two pigs left behind. I doubt if you even knew who they were."

"They kin of yours?" Seth asked.

"It doesn't matter who they were. Except they were probably hard working people and didn't deserve to die like that."

"What you going to do with us, mister?" Finley asked.

"I was just going to shoot both of you, but now I'm not so sure."

Finley saw a slight chance there and he drew his gun. But Lucien already had his pointing at Finley. Lucien's bullet took Finley in the chest. Now Seth, being scared, went for his gun and Lucien shot him also.

He didn't have a shovel to dig graves so he piled rocks on top of them and left a note describing that these two, Finley Bates and Seth Bond, had killed the farmer and his wife and daughter and he signed it Charles Hubert II.

He unsaddled the horses and turned them loose. It was midnight before he had finished rocking up their graves. He put more wood on the fire and walked back after his horse. He made a pot of coffee and warmed up some ham and bread. He was down to his last loaf of bread. He drank coffee most of the night and he didn't sleep at all. Partially because of the coffee, but mostly because he was thinking of the farmer and his family. How could anyone be that sadistic and cruel. He had killed two men tonight but he was not at all concerned about them.

Come daylight he mounted up and rode east.

CHAPTER 11

Sergeant Sanford and his sidekick Moseby picked up a lone track after the campsite, figuring this one would probably be Lucien's. The rain the next day had washed out all the tracks, but always the trail was heading east. So Sanford had no choice now but to continue in an easterly direction.

"Moseby ride up on top of that knoll and see if you can see anything. I'm going to walk around here and see if I can pick up any sign."

Sanford dismounted and tied his horse off and began to make circles around the area. He wasn't having much luck. The rain had washed away everything, leaving the sandy soil smooth and undisturbed.

Moseby found where a fire had been made behind a rock. He hollered to Sanford, "Hey! Sergeant Sanford! Hey!" Sanford was too far away to hear him. Moseby took out his pistol and fired one shot. This got Sanford's attention and Moseby signaled him to come up.

"Moseby now everyone within a five mile radius would have heard that shot. If Lucien is within a five mile radius he now knows someone is following him."

"Sorry, Sarg." Moseby pointed to the fire pit.

"Sheltered behind this rock. What does that tell you Moseby?"

"Well he camped on top of this knoll so he could look around like we have done and he didn't want his fire seen."

"That's good, Moseby. And maybe he was looking for another fire."

They made camp on the knoll that night and after dark they walked around the knoll looking for a fire on the flatland that stretched out below them.

In the morning they continued on in an easterly direction and came to the same trail leading to the farm and like Lucien they turned north and followed it to the farm. The farm looked in good condition but there was no one there and none of the buildings had been closed up.

Sanford knocked on the kitchen door and hollered, "Is anyone home! Hello there, anyone home?" When no one answered he and Moseby entered the kitchen. "Looks like someone had eaten here recently but didn't clean up," Sanford said.

"The fire in the stove is out and the stove is stone cold."

Moseby saw the letter on the table and said, as he picked up, "Sarg, here's a letter," and he handed it to Sanford.

"Someone killed the farmer, his wife and daughter. Raped the two women first. He buried them on a knoll behind the house. It is signed by a Charles Hubert II. Let's go have a look at the graves, Moseby."

On the way out to the knoll Moseby asked, "Who is this Charles Hubert II? I have never heard of him."

"I don't know for sure. It maybe Lucien using a false name to throw us off. Whoever it is is going after Bates and Bond"

"Hey Sarg, would someone who is on the run for desertion take the time to hunt the men who killed these people?"

"That's a good question, Moseby. An ordinary man, I'd have to say no. But I don't think Corporal Lucien Jandreau could be considered ordinary. All we can do is try to find his tracks leaving the farm and continue eastward."

Circling on foot Sanford did see where some horses, he couldn't tell how many, had left the farmyard and headed east. Moseby was looking for food they could take with them. "What did you find, Moseby?"

"A few canning jars of vegetables, a shoulder of smoked ham and a dozen fresh eggs. No bread, although from the looks in the kitchen I'd say the Mrs. had recently baked several loaves."

* * * *

Two days later they made camp near where Bates and Bond lay beneath the rocks. After eating that evening Sanford started walking around the area and stumbled upon the two graves. "Moseby, come here!" he hollered.

Sanford pointed at the two graves. "What do you think of that? And here is a short note Mr. Charles Hubert II left."

"This Jandreau fellow leaves dead bodies behind everywhere he goes," Moseby said.

"At least we'll have tracks we can see and follow tomorrow morning."

"Even if this Charles guy is Corporal Jandreau, Sarg, we are not gaining on him. We always seem to be two or three days behind him."

This started Sanford thinking. Moseby was correct. Lucien was staying two or three days ahead of them. "In the morning, Moseby, we change our tactics."

Sanford folded the note and put it in his pocket with the other letter. The next morning Sanford and Moseby headed east at a fast pace and not looking for Lucien's trail.

* * * *

Lucien stayed on the north side of the Niobrara River. He wasn't sure if anyone was following his trail or not, but he had to assume someone was. He found a nice spot to hold up for a couple of days and rest. His horse needed a day of grazing and he, too, needed rest.

He found a stream-fed tributary with a gravelly bottom and there were pockets of brook trout looking to spawn and they formed a solid black ribbon in the water. Once in a while one trout would turn and show its orange belly. They were not large brook trout—just right for a fry pan.

As night was approaching Lucien let his fire die out. His belly was full and he had a pot full of hot coffee. The air was warm, but he still wrapped a blanket around his shoulders. He started looking at the star filled sky again and wondering what was out there and what was life all about. Did his life have a specific purpose?

He sipped his coffee and then held his tin cup in his hands warming his fingers. As he sat there warming his fingers he began thinking about the woman he had been seeing in his dreams. She was always the same woman, but he had no idea who she was. Last time he saw her in his dream she was telling him something, but for the life of him he couldn't remember what she had been saying.

Just then this beautiful woman was standing now before him. She was dressed like an Indian princess and her smile was so beautiful. Divine love from her was engulfing Lucien, and now everything in his life was temporarily forgotten.

She was talking to him, but not with words. Her lips were not moving. They were carrying on a conversation in his mind. Only as thoughts.

He shifted his sitting position; his muscles were getting sore. He opened his eyes and he was still holding his tin cup; only it was now cold. And darkness had turned to daylight and he realized that he had been dreaming about this woman.

"Wow, it all seemed so real. Like I was awake," he said aloud as he stood up and stretched. He stood there in the morning light, but the last thing he could remember before seeing the woman standing in front of him was holding the hot tin cup in his hands, the darkness all around him. "What the hell happened?"

He didn't feel like eating. The experience seemed so real at the time and one moment it was dark and the next daylight. "How could this be?"

Confused he mounted his horse and turned north, following the Missouri River towards Lakota Lands.

* * * *

Sergeant Sanford and Private Moseby rode their horses as hard as they could for eastern Nebraska. They had no idea what they would find there. Hopefully something that would lead them to Lucien Jandreau.

They looked first at Omaha, across the river from Council Bluffs. They checked out the trading posts, the many saloons and liveries and no one had seen Lucien.

From Omaha they rode to Fremont and no one there had seen Lucien or a man calling himself Charles Hubert II. Before leaving Fremont, Sanford sent a telegram to Major Merrill at Fort Kearny explaining briefly what they had found so far and they soon would be going to the Lakota Territory.

They stopped at Covington at the junction of the Missouri and the Mississippi Rivers. This time they checked with the Sheriff's office, plus the saloons, trading posts and liveries for either Lucien Jandreau or Charles Hubert II and nothing.

"Where do we go now, Sarg?" Moseby asked.

"We go into the Lakota Land. He may be trying to avoid the populated areas on his way east. But we need to stop at the Pawnee village first."

* * * *

Lucien found a trading post on the west side of the Missouri River and he was needing some supplies and warmer clothing. He decided to change his name again to Marcel Gervais. And he would talk with a French accent hopefully to throw off any pursuers. Lucien tied his horse and walked inside. The interior was dingy and smelly, because of all the animal hides. "Bonjour Monsieur, I ah need supplies, me."

"Yes, Sir, my name is Alfie—and yours?"

"Marcel Gervais. I'll need a warm coat, hat, mittens and boots." Lucien waited until Alfie had those items on the counter and then said. "I need ten pounds of the bacon, beans, *pain* and coffee."

"Excuse me Mr. Gervais, what is *pain*?"

"Oh pardon me—ah—bread. Four loaves."

"Anything else Mr. Gervais?

"*Qui*, two cans of the peaches. I think that will be all Alfie. Maybe you would wrap the food into a package, no?"

"Sure thing, Mr. Gervais. Anything else?"

"Ah, *qui*, maybe a wool pant and shirt and bundle those too, please. Ah, the horse needs grain. Twenty pounds *s'il vous plait, monsieur.*"

While Alfie was wrapping them he asked, "Where you going from here Mr. Gervais? Winter will be here soon. You're a little late to be going west."

"I come from southwest, going home to Canada now. Was on a ship and got off in San Francisco. I not like the ocean, me. Too much water.

"How much money, Alfie?"

"$39.50."

Lucien counted out the money and gave it to Alfie and picked up his packages and said, "*Merci, Monsieur* Alfie."

Lucien tied the packages onto his saddle and mounted up and rode over to the little ferry on the Missouri River. He had decided to travel north for a while and then swing northwest. He still had no idea where he was going to winter. He stood by his horse on the ferry, he was hoping by pretending to be French he had delayed his pursuers some.

It was only mid-morning and already the air was unseasonably warm. He turned to the ferryman and asked, "Pardon me, *Monsieur,* what is the date?"

The ferryman began laughing and then said, "Frenchie, it's October 30th."

"*Merci, Monsieur.*"

Lucien walked his horse ashore and mounted and rode off. He decided to follow the river for a while before heading west so he wouldn't get trapped.

179

His hair was longer than he had ever allowed it before and he had a coal black beard. Maybe this would hide his features. He had to start thinking what he was going to do for the winter.

As he rode along at a fast pace to put some distance between him and Covington, he kept thinking about the woman in his dreams. *Who is she?* After two hours at a fast pace, Lucien stopped to feed and water his horse and to walk around himself to wake up his muscles. He gave his horse a hand full of grain and then he let it graze. He just drank a little water.

Lucien followed the river north for two days before swinging away from the river. He was careful not to leave any sign where he was going.

The sky was looking like another storm was coming, so he began to look for a place to build a shelter to wait out the storm. He found a small spring fed stream with plenty of trees to build a crude shelter. He started by cutting small trees and leaning them up against a ridgepole and the two sides forming an A-frame. He cut many more trees and stood them up to fill in the cracks. It might leak a little but it would certainly keep out most of the rain. He cut boughs for a bed and then started a fire and cooked a pot of beans with the last of his ham. He had worked hard and had worked up a sweat. In the morning even if it was still raining, he figured it was time he bathed.

The clouds opened up about midnight and it rained heavy all night with flashes of lightning and thunder. The roof of his A-frame shelter only leaked a little so he was able to get a good night's rest.

In the morning it was only drizzling and he decided to stay where he was for another day. He found brook trout in a spring and downstream he found an active beaver flowage and he made a drainage ditch across the top of the dam and sat back with his pistol to wait for a beaver to come and repair the dam.

He didn't have long to wait when a big beaver swam up to investigate and Lucien shot it in the head as it was in the trench. He wanted to smoke cure the meat and take it with him, although that meant staying there for another two days. He made a smoke rack and sliced off the meat and hung it on the rack to cure. He saved enough fresh meat for supper.

* * * *

Sanford and Moseby were two days traveling to the Pawnee village. They were taken immediately to see Chief Mato.

"Lieutenant Sanford, good see you again," Chief Mato said.

"Hello, Chief. It isn't Lieutenant anymore. I was demoted to Sergeant."

"How am I to help you, Sergeant?"

"We are looking for a deserter. A Corporal Lucien Jandreau. He may be using the name Charles Hubert II. He will be wearing plain clothes and not the blue coat."

"Not see the Jandreau or the one called Charles. Where they go?"

"We do not know for sure. We have been following his trail from Cheyenne land."

"No come through here like that. You wait here I go talk with runners."

Mato disappeared for a while, talking with the different runners. There were two there from the Dakota Land and no one had information about Lucien Jandreau or Charles Hubert II. "No one knows these two men. Not hear anything. What you do if you find them?"

"I have orders to take him back to Fort Kearny for trial."

Sanford and Moseby stayed at the Pawnee Village that night and in the morning they headed north following the Missouri River. Once in a while they would meet someone heading south and they would stop and ask if they had seen anyone fitting Lucien's description. No one had seen anyone fitting that description. Sanford stopped at each farm and inquired and again no one had seen him. They met an Army patrol heading south and they had not seen Lucien or anyone fitting his description. Nor had they heard anything about someone on the run.

At each settlement they checked the saloons, dining halls and trading posts. No one had seen or heard anything about Lucien or Charles Hubert II.

They finally made their way to Covington. It was late so they waited until morning before inquiring about him. They were up early and found a place that served breakfast. Sanford asked the owner and the cook if they had seen Lucien and he described him to them, "Sorry, no one like that has been here or traveled through Covington. You might try at the livery and the trading post. That's on the Sioux west road about a mile from town. There's a ferry there also, that crosses the Missouri River.

"Where to now, Sarg? No one has seen or even heard about Lucien or Charles Hubert II. It's like he just disappeared," Moseby said.

"Look, Moseby, we were on his trail a week ago and he was heading east, we beat-footed it and I think we got here before he did. He hasn't been seen or heard of north of Fremont. Maybe he turned north before coming this far east. I think we should check out the trading post west of Covington," Sanford said.

The trading post was a dingy looking place and the inside smelled as bad as the outside look. "Hello, I would like to speak to whomever owns or runs this establishment."

"That's me mister. What do you need?"

"Your name?"

"Alfie. And yours?"

"Sergeant Sanford and Private Moseby. We are looking for information."

"Shoot."

"We're looking for a deserter. Lucien Jandreau. He may be using the name of Charles Hubert II. Have you seen either of those men or anyone by those names?"

"There ain't been but a handful of men go through for

a month now. And no one by either of those names. I know because I ask everyone their name. What's this fella look like?" Alfie asked.

He's twenty-two—twenty-four, stands over six feet, weighs two forty-five, he's always well groomed and clean."

"Over six feet, aye. There was a tall drink of water come through here, but he won't your man. This one was French. He had a difficult time with English words. And he won't well groomed at all. He smelt worsen the inside of this place with all the animal hides. His hair was long and scraggly and he won't none two forty five either. He'd be lucky to top out at two hundred."

"What was his name?"

"Gervais, oh let's see his first name was—let me think. Oh yeah, it was Marcel. Marcel Gervais.

"Where was he going from here?"

"He said home to Canada."

"How was it he happened through Covington?"

"He said he was on a ship and didn't like all that water. His exact words were 'Too much water, me,' said he left ship in San Francisco."

"How long ago, Alfie?"

"Four days ago now."

"Anything else you can remember, Alfie?"

"Oh yeah, one more thing. He won't none twenty-two— twenty-four either. This guy was much older. You know I see a lot of trappers come through here each season and I never smelt one that smelt worse than Gervais."

"Which way did he leave Covington?"

"Not sure. I didn't go outside to watch him leave. Maybe the ferry, since he was heading for Canada. If'n he don't make it before it starts to snow, he'll never make it. Those open prairies are no place to get caught in when the cold wind blows. Besides that's all Dakota Sioux land up there," Alfie said.

"Sarg, don't you think maybe we should get some

supplies while we're here. We're almost out."

"Good point, Moseby. Alfie, we'll take twenty pounds of bacon, beans and we'll need warmer clothing also."

While Alfie was figuring how much to charge: "Moseby, pack the supplies on the pack horse while I square up with Alfie."

"How much, Alfie?"

"Everything, that comes to $45.75."

Sanford gave Alfie a voucher. "Alfie, how did Gervais pay for his supplies?"

"$30.00 in gold coin, the rest in silver. I have the gold coins right here."

Sanford was thinking how strange it was for a soldier to be carrying around that much gold and silver coin. There was a lot here to think over. "Thank you, Alfie," and Sanford went outside and closed the door.

"What now, Sarg?" Moseby asked.

"We talk with the ferryman."

"Do you think this Gervais was him?"

"At first I thought so, but now I'm not so sure. There was just too much that wasn't right. For one thing, the gold and silver coin Gervais used to purchase supplies. Most soldiers have very little money and then it is usually paper money, not hard currency. And the physical description of Gervais also."

As they rode over to the ferry, Sergeant Sanford said, "I'm beginning to believe everyone has sadly underestimated Lucien Jandreau."

"How do you mean, Sarg?" Moseby asked.

"Well...don't repeat this, but I honestly believe there isn't anyone in the union Army who can ride Lucien down and bring him in for court marshall.

"If it was up to me we would turn back now and forget about Lucien."

"Then why don't we head back for Fort Kearny, Sarg?" Moseby asked.

"I was given strict orders from the major not to come

back until we had him."

"Surly the major would understand that from here on we'd just be wasting our time and the Army's."

"Not exactly, Moseby. When Lucien deserted he embarrassed the major after he awarded Lucien the Medal of Valor. He'll have some tough questions to answer to the Defense Department. But the likelihood that we'll ever ride Lucien to ground is almost nil."

One look at the ferryman and Sanford didn't know if they would get any straight answers from him or not. His clothes were filthy and there was so much dirt on his hands you couldn't see the skin.

"You two wanta cross?"

"We'd like to ask you some questions first."

"What questions? I ain't nothing."

"We're looking for someone. Lucien Jandreau or Charles Hubert II. Have you taken these men across?"

"Nope."

"How about a Marcel Gervais?"

"Nope. Wait a minute, was he that Frenchman that's going home?"

"That's him. How many days ago did you take him across?"

"What's today?"

"Today is Wednesday."

"I'm not sure. But it was before Wednesday."

"One day, two, three or four days?" Sanford was beginning to lose patience.

"Maybe three days...I'm not sure."

"Did he say where he was going?"

"Oh yeah, he's on his way home, I think. He was awful hard to understand. He didn't speak much English and I ain't so good understanding his words. Oh, there were something strange about Frenchie—that is what I called him. He don't know the date. And I thought this funny."

185

"Okay, will you take us across?"
"Sure thing—a dime apiece."

* * * *

Lucien was up most of the night tending the curing fire and turning the meat occasionally, to cure thoroughly. He actually enjoyed this time. The night air was almost cold. The temperature had dropped. He wrapped a blanket about him and leaned back against his A-frame shelter feeling good.

The night sky was clear, with an occasional shooting star. He looked up—*how I wish I knew what is up there.*

He would catnap and then make a pot of coffee and more wood on the fire. He held his hot tin coffee cup in his hands, warming his cold fingers. He had no idea where he was going or what he was going to do. *It's like something is guiding and protecting me. Am I being guided to somewhere special. What will I find once I'm there?*

Then he began to think about the dark haired woman in his dreams. Could she be the one who was guiding and protecting him? He wished he knew. Hell, he wished he knew where he could find her. "Is that where I'm being guided to, taken to, where I'll find her?" he said aloud.

He catnapped some more. In the morning the meat wasn't quite cured yet, so he decided to stay another day. The rain had stopped, and there was a thin film of ice on the tree branches. But it melted and disappeared soon after the sun was up.

He saw that his horse had plenty of feed and water and he gave it an occasional handful of grain. He needed a rest also. He stayed close to camp all day tending the fire. By mid-afternoon the meat was fully cured and he wrapped it up and put it in a saddlebag.

The next morning he mounted up and left. As he was leaving the big river behind him the countryside began to change. To the north he could see tall mountains. Here, away from the river, the land was drier with fewer streams. He was glad he had taken the time to catch and smoke the meat.

He turned away from the Missouri River not knowing where he was going. He had surrendered to trust whatever entity was guiding him.

On the second day out away from the river he came upon two sets of horse tracks. The horses were shoed so that could only mean they were white men. But what were they doing out there? Out of curiosity he decided to follow. They were leaving the plains and prairies and traveling through the foothills. They sure weren't settlers, for they had passed by excellent farm or ranch land. And they were not trappers either. They shied away from the wetland where beaver would still be working on their winter feed beds. That left prospectors or miners.

From a hilltop he could see smoke rising in the afternoon air and he could smell coffee and bacon. He rode up close and stop and hollered, "Hey! You there by the campfire!"

He waited a minute before there was an answer, "Who are you and what do you want?"

"My name is Jean Corriveau. Saw your smoke and smelled your bacon. I'd like to come in and share your fire." He decided it would be wise to change his name again.

"Come on in, but your hands better be empty."

"Fair enough."

Lucien rode slowly and cautiously as he neared their campsite. There were two men in their 30's maybe. Their clothes were clean which told Lucien they were just making their way into this country. They each wore a side arm and were holding a rifle in front of them. They too were being cautious. "Step down, mister."

"It's Jean," and he got down off his horse.

"We have a cup of coffee for you, but we're running a little shy on food."

"Coffee would be okay. What's your name?"

The one who had been talking said, "I'm Ben Seams and my partner Howard Carter."

Howard handed Lucien a cup of coffee. "Thanks"

"Where you riding to, Jean?" Ben asked.

"Montana. I'm meeting some friends where the Big Muddy crosses the border into Canada. How about you two?" Lucien asked.

"We're prospecting. During the summer we met two guys who had good luck panning gold in the Black Hills. They panned enough so's they're set for life."

"Good deal. Do you know exactly where to go?'

"These guys told us just start panning at the first stream we come to."

"You going to winter out there?"

"We'll have to now. There won't be enough time before cold weather to do our panning and get out of here before snow."

"You seem to be traveling light, if you plan to winter out."

"We plan on building a log shelter and killing elk and deer for food."

"Have you two done any panning before?"

"Some," Howard replied.

"You know the Lakota Indians really don't like it when white men, miners, come onto their land without asking. Gold, yellow rock to them, means nothing and they can't understand why it drives white men crazy. I would be very cautious if I were you."

"Well Jean, these two guys we talked with said they never saw an Indian all the time they were out here."

"Where do you come from?" Lucien asked.

"Ben and I both come from Ohio. We came out here five years ago for a three year hitch in the Army. We were stationed at Des Moines, Iowa. It was three years of hell. Army life just was not for us," Howard said.

"This is the life we like," Ben added.

"Well I wish you two luck, and I must be going. The Big Muddy is still a long ways away. Remember, use caution; you are on Lakota land now."

Ben and Howard both nodded their heads and Lucien turned his horse and continued his journey. After leaving an obvious trail for the Montana Territory, he swung back towards the northeast. Not really knowing why. Only there was now an inner voice that was guiding him.

He put about five miles between him and Ben and Howard. He couldn't help but worry what the Sioux would do to those two if they find them panning in the Black Hills. He had warned them though. But he doubted if they would take his warning seriously.

The air was already getting colder and he stopped early for the night to make a lean-to shelter with spruce and fir boughs. He also made sure he had enough firewood for the night before he lost all of daylight.

He sat up late into the night sipping coffee, putting wood on the fire and watching the flames. He was feeling really good about himself now. He doubted if even the Army would risk sending someone onto the Lakota Land to find him. He was feeling safe and his mind was no longer listening to the crackle of the fire, the night sounds or watching the flames. Lucien was once again on the inner, with the same woman.

There was so much love coming from this woman that he was totally engulfed in it. He somehow knew he was dreaming, but he was also there in the dream as a third person watching himself and this woman. He had never had this kind of experience before, and he found it overwhelming and he awoke. Still holding a now cold cup of coffee and the fire had almost burned out. He put more wood on the fire and then laid down on his bed of boughs in the lean-to.

He awoke the next morning long after the sun had risen. While his breakfast was warming he tended to his horse and packed everything that he could. When he finished eating he finished packing and left.

This was beautiful country he was now riding through. It reminded him much of his home in Maine. He found a well-used game trail following a valley through the mountains and he decided to follow. The higher mountains were snow covered and the breeze had a cold bite to it.

When he stopped at noon to rest his horse, he built a fire and made a pot of coffee and was cooking some bacon on a stick.

Up ahead about fifty yards, he could see four Indians that had been riding towards him and had now stopped and were looking at him. He remained cool. There was no need to get excited. He remained sitting and waved to the four to come in. They looked at each other questioningly. After all there was only one of him and four of them.

They dismounted and leading there ponies they walked cautiously towards Lucien. They stood in front of the fire and saw the meat being cooked and understood what this stranger was doing.

Lucien motioned for them to sit. They did and Lucien poured some coffee in his cup and took a sip and passed it to the one who seemed to be the leader. He took the cup and a sip and handed the cup to his friends.

"What you do here?"

"You understand my tongue, good."

"Some," he said.

"My name is Jean Corriveau. What are your names?"

"Me—*Tate*, the wind. *Uta*—acorn, *Hoka*—the badger, *Kangi*—crow. Only me know your words. What do you here?"

"I'm only exploring, looking at things."

"You want the yellow rock?"

"No."

"Beaver?"

"No

"You Blue Coat, long knives?"

"No," not a real lie.

"Where you live cold and snow?"

"I don't know."

The bacon was cooked and Lucien shared it evenly with his new friends. They seemed to really enjoy it. "What animal this meat?"

"Pig."

"Know no pig."

"Boar?"

"Yes, know about boar. Never eat one. Good."

When the four had finished eating they stood and said, "Jean Corriveau you come with us."

Lucien stood up and he towered above the other four Sioux. "You big Jean Corriveau."

They all laughed.

"Where we go, Tate?"

"To village at Standing Rock."

* * * *

Much to Lucien's surprise he was not asked to surrender his firearms. He rode with them freely and he was excited about the direction his life was now taking. And he understood there was no more worry about being discovered by the Army and taken back. "Tate, what were you and your friends doing out here when you saw me?"

"Tall Feather said take friends, scout this valley and hills."

They rode at a much faster pace than Lucien had been traveling. He was wondering if they always traveled this fast, or if there was a special urgency to return him to their Chief, Tall Feather. On the eve on the third day they rode into Tall Feather's village. The first to notice their arrival were the children playing at the edge of the village. Then they went off hollering and the entire village was told of their arrival.

The first thing that caught Lucien's attention were a small girl and boy, both of the same age, about five or six, and they each had astonishingly red hair. Lucien looked around, these two were the only ones with red hair.

His four escorts dismounted and so too did Lucien, and Tate said, "Horse taken care of. No worry your things brought to you. Come follow me."

Lucien fell in behind Tate and the other three behind Lucien. The evening meal was just being served and Lucien was hungry. His food supplies ran out quickly, feeding his four escorts.

Tate said, "Sit, food will be brought for you."

He had not been introduced to anyone yet, except his four escorts. But everyone was hungry and ready to eat. A pretty young woman served Lucien first. There were several different kinds of meat. Some he knew and a few he just as soon not know. But whatever it was, it was all good. When he had finished that platter of food, another young woman gave him another and smiled at him.

"Thank you," he said. Never expecting that she would understand.

"You are welcomed," she said and when Lucien looked surprised, everyone started laughing. He finished eating that platter and another was given him. The village people had never seen anyone eat so much.

Lucien stood up and carried the empty platter over to the woman who had given it to him. "Thank you, thank you all. The food was delicious and I was hungry." The young woman smiled at him again. At that moment Lucien figured he had found a home that he had been subconsciously been looking for, for a long time. These were truly good people and he would try to learn everything he could about them and their way of living.

Lucien turned around and there stood the Chief. Tall Feather was the tallest person in the village but Lucien stood three or four inches taller. Tall Feather stood silently in front of Lucien, assessing him. "I am Chief, Tall Feather, you—you Big Jean Corriveau are welcomed in our village. Come, we much talk." Tall Feather turned and led the way to his lodge.

"It is customary that we smoke the pipe before we talk

about things of importance, but my body is old and my lungs are no longer young. I have many questions, Big Jean Corriveau. You travel light, not many supplies. This is beginning of cold, snow and the mighty wind. You travel alone, not afraid that you are on Lakota land

"You do not carry with you tools to look for the yellow rock, so you are not here to mine. You are not a trapper. You have no traps. You are not a settler, you have no tools to build you a house.

"You travel light like a man running from something. But you not travel fast. You stop often to rest your horse and make food. So, Big Jean Corriveau, what in your life makes you travel to Lakota land?"

Lucien was silent for a minute, thinking how best to answer Tall Feather. Tall Feather knew Big Jean Corriveau was thinking how to answer.

"I will not lie to you, Tall Feather. I am running from the Army. I deserted. Do you understand when I say I am a deserter?"

"It means you quit Army and left without anyone knowing. Why did you desert, Big Jean?"

Lucien told Tall Feather about the rescue of the women and massacre at Niobrara River and the battle at Cheyenne River and how the order was to kill everyone and how this had sickened him. That he didn't expect to be killing so many native peoples when he didn't think it was necessary.

"I know about the battle with the Cheyenne at the Cheyenne River, but I knew nothing about the massacre at Niobrara River. So who hunts you now?"

"I don't know, only that I know someone is following me. But I don't know if they will come to Lakota land."

"What would happen if they catch you?"

"They will have orders to take me dead or live back to Fort Kearny for a court marshall."

It was Tall Feather's turn now to remain silent as he thought about Big Jean's story. Then he surprised Lucien with his next statement. "There are two blue coats who follow you. One is a Sergeant."

When Lucien looked surprised, Tall Feather continued. "I have had runners following you and those who hunt for you." Lucien thought that it was probably Sergeant Cedric Quinlin who had been following him.

"So, Big Jean Corriveau, where is it that you travel?"

"At first I had intended to go to Canada. Now I don't know. I would like to stay here with your people for the cold and snow season, with your permission."

"There is much to consider, Big Jean. I cannot give you my answer now. Tomorrow I will council with all the elders and afterwards I will give you their answer. Tonight you stay in my lodge. Now you must leave me, I am tired and must rest."

Lucien left Tall Feather's lodge. Everyone had gone to their own lodge. He was surprised that so much time had passed. He sat by the fire, alone, listening to the night sounds. These people were completely trustworthy. He was still wearing his holster and .45 colt.

After a while Tall Feather's woman Wicahpi (morning star) walked up to Lucien and said, "Big Jean Corriveau, Tall Feather is asleep. You come back to lodge now," she turned and went back to her lodge and Lucien followed her.

* * * *

Everybody was up early the next morning and after eating everyone had their chores to do, to prepare for the coming cold season. "Big Jean Corriveau, you help get wood for fire. Come." Six men with two horses pulling a travois each headed for the forest. Lucien wished he had an axe and a bucksaw.

Much to Lucien's surprise once they found a nice stand of dead and dying trees three of the men suddenly produced an axe each they had been carrying. It didn't take long to cut enough wood to fill the two travois. While the wood was being hauled back to the village, Lucien took one of the axes and began felling trees. Tate and Kangi stood back and watched Lucien work. They each were amazed at the strength and power as Lucien wielded the axe. He had more than enough wood down by the time the travois were back. Lucien kept felling trees. He was enjoying the work out and stretching his muscles.

When the travois returned the next time they brought with them a third horse and travois. But still a third horse could not keep up with Lucien. By the end of the workday there was still wood down that didn't get hauled to the village. Lucien along with the others walked behind the horses dragging the travois.

Lucien stopped and picked up the butt end of one of these trees and tucked it under his right arm and dragged it along with him. The others saw what Lucien was doing and they all knew they did not have enough strength to do the same.

When they reached the village Lucien was surprised how much wood they had worked up. And also to his surprise one of the men did have a bucksaw and was busy chunking up the wood. "Tate," Lucien asked. "Where did you get the axes and the bucksaw?"

"Missionary come here some. Some white man trading for hides."

After eating Lucien was again invited into Tall Feather's lodge. "Sit." After Lucien had sat down Tall Feather continued. "Council Elders say you can stay here this season."

"Thank you, Tall Feather."

"Everyone in the village works. We all help each other. You too, Big Jean Corriveau, will have a work. My people need new blood, so that my people will survive. White man's way of life is so different than Sioux. You know things we do not. You're task while you are here is to leave your seed in two of our women. This way your blood will become Sioux and make Sioux stronger. New ideas, new ways of doing things and knowledge of things we do not have.

"My woman Wicahpi has chosen two young women who will take care of you in your own lodge until you leave. These two women have agreed to this. It will be a great honor for them to have your baby.

"You will also teach my people your words, your tongue and your ways. You see if we are to survive we need new blood for my people and we must understand the white man. Learn how to talk and understand his ways and words.

"Do you agree to this, Big Jean Corriveau?"

"I would be honored, Tall Feather."

"Good, Kyla and Hanka are preparing a lodge now for the three of you.

"I am old man, Big Jean Corriveau. My time to walk to the spirit world will soon be here. I am glad you will help my people. My son *TaTanka*—buffalo bull, will be chief when I leave.

"Do you have any questions?"

"Yes, you speak English so well. How?"

"We have had visitors before you, who have help our people and taught us their words. Carajou, Big Red Beard Not Afraid and there have been missionaries. Big Red Beard Not Afraid left his seed in two women like I have asked you to do and he taught many to speak this English."

"The girl and boy with red hair?"

"Yes, Big Red Beard Not Afraid's son and daughter. He was a great man and good friend. I'm tired and must rest. We talk tomorrow," Tall Feather said.

Kyla and Hanka were waiting for Lucien when he emerged from Tall Feather's lodge. They each took Lucien by the hand and Kyla said, "Come, Big Jean Corriveau, we take you our new lodge." Each girl was giggling. Others were watching as the three walked into their lodge and disappeared inside.

Lucien stood in the entry looking at the inside. The floor was covered with soft elk hides and a huge bear hide was spread on top of a thick bed of cedar boughs and pine needles. The inside smelled like a walk through a spring glade. "You two alone make all this?"

Hanka spoke first, "You like?"

"We change if not happy," Kyla added.

"No change. I like this. I'm surprised, that's all."

"You leave your seed in each of us, we take care of you, Big Jean Corriveau," Kyla said.

"We want make you happy. You our man now. We take good care of our man. You see," and both girls laughed and Lucien hugged them.

Suddenly there was a noisy distraction at the west end of the village. Everyone was rushing over to see what was happening. Even Lucien, Kyla and Hanka. It soon became clear. Four Sioux braves had two men tied across their horses and were being escorted to the center of the village.

TaTanka was helping his father Tall Feather from his lodge to the two bound strangers. One of the four braves, Running Bear, said, "These two men were found on our land looking for the yellow rocks that drive the white man crazy with greed."

Seams and Carter were untied and given water and something to eat. Lucien thought it best if he stayed away from them at the present. He did notice that the Council Elders, TaTanka and Tall Feather had all gathered in Tall Feather's lodge. Probably to decide what to do with the two.

Lucien saw Tate and walked over to talk with him. "Tate, what will happen with these two men?"

"That up to Council Elders and Chief Tall Feather. The two not kill any Sioux. This is good. They will live," Tate said.

"Thank you."

The Council Elders and TaTanka counseled for a long time with Tall Feather. After two hours Lucien was summoned to join them. This really surprised him.

"Come, Big Jean Corriveau. We would ask you what white man government would do with these two?"

"It might be a good idea to have them explain why they

were on Lakota land. Then maybe the elders could see a clear picture in their minds what to do."

"What would you do, Big Jean Corriveau?" TaTanka asked.

"I would not harm them, and I would send them back where they came with a message to tell others not to violate Lakota lands and rights."

"The one called Seams said they know you," TaTanka said.

"I shared their fire one day before I was found by Tate and his friends. Seams and Carter had been given some bad, wrong, information from a friend of theirs who said he had been on Lakota land looking for the yellow rock and said the Sioux didn't bother him. This may have been a lie. This friend may never have been on Lakota land. Seams and Carter listened to the wrong person. I don't think they meant the Sioux any danger. Only if they found the yellow rock they would tell their friends and more people would come here looking for the yellow rock. They should have used better judgment."

"We will talk about what you say. Now leave us, so we talk."

Lucien left. Outside, he scratched his chin. He had been so use to his beard he had not consciously thought much about it. But now he would be sharing a lodge and his life with two young women, he thought maybe it was time to bathe and shave.

"Kyla can you heat up some water for me in a bowl?"

"Yes, why you want hot water?" she asked.

"I want to shave off my beard."

She didn't understand, but she warmed up water and then she and Hanka watched while he lathed his beard and shaved. He had attracted the attention of the children also and they all gathered around him to watch. When he had finished he took Kyla's and Hanka's hand and rubbed his cheek. They were surprised how smooth his face was now.

Then he gave his straight razor to Kyla and had her trim

the hair on the back of his neck. She only cut him once. Hanka wanted to help also so Lucien asked her to trim his hair. Both girls had to work on this. But when they had finished Lucien was looking like a different person. He hugged and kissed them both and said, "Now I need to bathe in the stream." While he was bathing the girls washed his clothes and laid out his only clean ones.

As he was dressing Hanka said to Kyla, "We make new clothes from deer hide—"

The Council Elders were finished talking about what they were going to do with them when they saw Lucien. At first they all thought a stranger had come amongst them.

TaTanka said to Lucien, "Big Jean Corriveau, you come with me." Lucien followed him to a quiet spot where they would not be interrupted. TaTanka told Lucien how they had decided to handle the matter with Seams and Carter and asked Lucien to explain the conditions to Seams and Carter so they each would understand.

TaTanka and Lucien talked for a long time before TaTanka explained to Lucien what the Council Elders wanted. Then they walked over to the lodge where Seams and Carter were staying. There were no guards. They went inside and sat down.

"Big Jean Corriveau speak for Sioux, and in your words. Tell you we decided. So you make no wrong, and you understand."

TaTanka and Lucien sat down with Seams and Carter.

"Ben and Howard, this is Chief Tall Feather's son TaTanka. He will be the Sioux Chief when Tall Feather walks into the spirit world. TaTanka can understand and speak English, but he has asked me to communicate the Council Elder's decisions concerning you two. I am Jean Corriveau. You shared your fire with me.

"Before I tell you the Elder's terms I want you to tell TaTanka why you were on Lakota land in the Black Hills. He needs to hear in your own words."

199

"A year ago we met a man who said he had found a lot of gold, in any stream bed in the Black Hills. We knew this was Sioux land, but this man said the Sioux didn't care. When he was there. He said he had not seen any Sioux all the time he was in the Black Hills. We believed what he said and we decided to come out to look for gold," Ben said.

"What was this man's name that you met?" Lucien asked.

"Jim Hartley," Howard said.

Lucien looked at TaTanka and he nodded his head. "You two need to understand, this is Lakota country and white man's law is no good out here. The Sioux have the final word here and we set the rules that they expect everyone to live by. Lakota are the law out here.

"The Council Elders, TaTanka and Tall Feather have decided not to kill you." He let those words hang there for a while to let the concept set into the minds of Ben Seams and Howard Carter. TaTanka remained stoic.

"It took a lot of discussion to decide what to do with you two. They have every right to protect their land. Tomorrow morning you two will be set free to return where you came from. But there is a condition to being set free. You are to take word back to the nearest Army depot and anyone who thinks they can come onto Lakota land without first asking for permission. You are to tell the commander at the Army depot that the Army is to keep all prospectors off Lakota land. You make sure you tell the commander that the Sioux wish to live in peace. But if the white man seeking gold keeps coming to Lakota land there will be trouble and it won't be the Sioux who starts the trouble. This gold makes the white man crazy and they'll do anything to get this gold. You two will be set free so you can take this advice back with you, but you make it clear to the Army that if any more miners come onto Lakota land they will not be treated so kindly.

"Do you two understand this so far?"

"Yes."

"When you are set free tomorrow morning you'll have only one rifle, your horses and that's all. Everything else is confiscated.

"I want to stress one thing. The Council Elders were very close to agreeing to having you two killed as an example. When you leave there'll be runners who will be watching you and they will know if you take this word back to the Army. If you don't, you may be killed. You'll never know when the runners are watching you. So take my advice go straight to the nearest Army depot.

"Until tomorrow you'll be free to walk around the village and food will be provided for you until you leave.

"Do you have anything you want to add, TaTanka?"

"You come back, you die." TaTanka and Lucien then left.

* * * *

Ben and Howard spent the rest of that day wandering around the village, and they found it odd how none of the people seemed to show any hostilities toward them. They were also feeling very appreciative that the Council Elders had decided not to kill them.

After Tall Feather's noon nap Lucien was summoned to his lodge. "Sit Big Jean Corriveau. We talk. It was good you help TaTanka talk with those two. My son says you did good."

"I believe they will take your words to the Army. And for a while the Army will keep miners off Lakota land."

"While I slept, I had a vision. The one who hunts you is close and soon he will be here. I can send some braves to tell them to leave."

"No, Tall Feather, let them come. This needs to stop now. I will not be chased anymore."

"This is good. You take care of hunters that chase you and not run any longer."

Randall Probert

"I afraid for my people, Big Jean Corriveau. We have lived on Lakota land for many seasons. I have visions while I sleep some times that the blue coats and white settlers will push my people from our land. I won't be here to hold my people together when this happens. I will be in spirit world. I worry for my people."

"Tall Feather, this is why it is important that the Sioux learn to read and write and understand the ways of the white man. This will be your only defense against losing your land, your home. Some of your children need to go out to the settlements and go to the white man's schools. This is the most important thing you can do for your people.

"If you try to fight the blue coats and the settlers, you may win a few battles, but in the end you will lose the war. There are just too many whites for you to defeat. This is why your people need to learn to read and write."

'Big Red Beard Not Afraid said this. When missionaries come to Sioux village, I or TaTanka will send some of the children back with them so they can learn these things.

"You good for my people, Big Jean Corriveau. Now leave, I must rest."

Lucien walked around the village thinking about his future. He really enjoyed living here with the Sioux and he also knew some time in the future these people would be fighting against the Army. If he stayed and became a member of the tribe, could he fight alongside the Sioux against the white man's Army? He wasn't so sure he could. And if he couldn't, then did he really belong here?

That night to work off some of his frustrations and anger for not knowing where his future was taking him, he made love to Kyla and Hanka, over and over until the two girls finally said, "No more tonight, Big Jean Corriveau. We all tired and need sleep now."

Lucien laid on his back holding his arms around both girls. They were soon asleep. He wished he was asleep also, instead of the confusing thoughts and images in his mind.

When Lucien finally did fall asleep he was met by the beautiful woman that he only saw in his dreams. This time she was talking to him. Saying he could not stay with the Sioux, that come spring he would have to leave. And she would be there to guide him as she had always been there to guide him.

* * * *

Moseby put another piece of wood on the fire and then poured himself a cup of hot coffee. "We haven't seen any tracks made by Lucien or any information for a few weeks now, Sarg. What are we doing? We keep traveling north and we haven't seen any clues of his passing through here. Cold weather will be here soon and I don't think we want to be without a shelter in this country."

Sanford threw out his cold coffee and filled his cup with hot coffee and took a sip before answering. "We have never been sure that we were ever following Lucien. The trail we were following has now disappeared. We have no way of knowing for sure if the trail we were following was ever his. We've traveled a long way north and I just don't know any more. I do know Major Merrill said not to come back until we had Lucien.

"So if we turn around now, Moseby, where do we go?"

"What would happen if we went back to Fort Kearny without Lucien?"

"The major would probably court marshall us."

"What else can we do, Sarg?"

"I don't know, maybe go north to Canada like Lucien may be doing."

"Maybe we should have gone with Lucien, instead of hunting him," Moseby said in jest. Sanford didn't answer him, but he too was thinking the same thing.

Nothing more was said that night about Lucien. The ground was covered with a heavy frost the next morning and Sergeant Sanford knew they would have to make a decision soon.

Two hours after leaving the campsite that morning they were suddenly confronted by four serious looking Indians. *Probably Sioux,* Sanford thought. He and Moseby sat their saddles and made no attempt to arm themselves.

"What you do here, Blue Coat?"

"We are looking for someone."

"Who?"

"Lucien Jandreau," that did not get a response. "Charles Hubert II?" Still nothing. "Marcel Gervais?" Still nothing.

"Have you seen any white men in Lakota country?"

"Chief Tall Feather told two miners looking for yellow rock to leave Lakota land or they die. Big Jean Corriveau living with Sioux now. You come, Tall Feather said bring you back."

Two Sioux rode in front and two more rode behind them. They still had not asked for their firearms. "We might come out of this okay yet, Moseby. They don't seem to be too hostile."

Sanford and Moseby were rather quiescent as they were escorted by the four Sioux braves. But they each were wondering where they were going and what would happen to them.

At mid-afternoon they rode into the Sioux village. Sanford was surprised to see how the village was built within a grove of tall spruce trees. The village was well protected from the cold winter winds.

There was a lot of excitement as the two Blue Coats were escorted through the village to Tall Feather's lodge. Lucien came out to see what all the excitement was about.

Sanford and Moseby were told to dismount and wait beside their horses. As Sergeant Sanford was stepping down he saw Lucien Jandreau. And he was walking towards them.

"Sergeant Sanford, Private Moseby. I am surprised to learn that it is you that Major Merrill sent after me. I would have thought he would have sent Sergeant Quinlin."

"What are you doing here, Lucien?" that question caught Lucien off guard, and he didn't answer.

Tall Feather had stepped out from his lodge and said,

"Gentlemen, you two will join me in my lodge," and he went back inside. TaTanka pointed to the two and then to the lodge. His meaning was quite evident.

"Sit down, gentlemen."

Still no one had told them to remove their side arms, and this puzzled Sanford.

"Now Sergeant, why you hunt Big Jean Corriveau?" So Lucien had changed his name again.

"You names." Not a question. Tall Feather maintained a stern expression.

"Sergeant John Sanford and Private Moseby."

"You hunt for Big Jean Corriveau. Why?"

"He deserted from the Army. He left without permission."

"You know why Big Jean Corriveau left Army?"

"No."

Tall Feather then asked that Lucien come.

"Sit, Big Jean Corriveau. You tell Sergeant why you left Army."

"I didn't join the Army to kill innocent Indian natives. What we did to the Cheyenne when we rescued the women and then the battle at Cheyenne River, both were not necessary. I found it difficult to accept as something righteous and I was full of quilt. I knew the only way to escape this was to leave. And there is another reason also. I wasn't going to be drawn into a war between the north and south over slavery. But there was nobody who would listen to me. So that is why I decided to leave on my own.

"I was right? Maybe not politically, but I was right for my own well being."

Sanford and Moseby remained silent, even after Lucien had finished.

"Leave us alone, Big Jean Corriveau, so we talk." Lucien got up and left.

After Lucien had left Tall Feather said, "What you think now, Sergeant?"

"I can understand why he left and I don't know if he was right in doing so or not. That is not my judgment. We were ordered to find him and bring him back. But at the same time I think I can now understand why he deserted."

"You must know, Sergeant, we will never let you leave with Big Jean Corriveau.

"Now you must leave my lodge. I old man and must rest now. I will talk with Council Elders and we will make a decision about you."

Sanford and Moseby left Tall Feather and Lucien was waiting for them. "Go for a walk, Sergeant and Private?"

"Considering everything, Lucien, I think you had better start calling me by my first name, John."

"Just call me Moseby, Lucien."

John and Moseby followed Lucien to a nearby stream and they sat down. "Lucien, no one has asked for our side arms. And I find this confusing. To them we must be the enemy," John said.

"They trust that you know that to use your handguns would be futile. They respect you enough to realize this."

"What will they do with us?"

"I have no idea. But I don't think you'll be harmed."

"We have only been here a short while and already I'm seeing the Indian differently than I did as a lieutenant. I wish I had known the difference then. Then maybe we wouldn't be where we are today."

"How did you come to find me here?"

"The truth is we didn't. The Sioux party found us and brought us here. We lost your trail weeks ago. At least what we think was your trail. If you be Charles Hubert II and Marcel Gervais, then we were on your trail for a while. Then we lost it.

"Lucien, what are you doing here?"

"A Sioux party found me also and brought me here. Tall Feather said he knew I was coming. "

"You led us on quite a chase, Lucien," Moseby said.

"Why did you go to Douglas, Lucien, and after you tore that saloon into pieces everyone there remembered you."

"I was trying to throw you off my real destination. I thought you might think I was heading west. That's why I went east."

"You didn't answer my question. Lucien, why are you here?"

"I needed a place to winter and I like these people. They are like family to me."

"How long are you planning on staying?"

"Tall Feather said I must leave come spring.

"You must realize one thing, John."

"You won't go back with us," John said.

"You figured it out already. What about you and Moseby? What will you do?"

"The major said not to come back without you. Moseby and I have talked about this. We don't think we'll be going back. Major Merrill isn't the same person since you deserted. You embarrassed him after he awarded you the Medal of Valor. Now he has to answer to the Department of Defense. He would be unbearable as a commanding officer."

"Well, if you two aren't going to return to Fort Kearny, then you can't continue to parade around with Army uniforms. Do either of you have civilian's clothes?"

"No."

"Me neither," Moseby said.

"I'll see what I can do. Maybe some of the women here will make you some deer skin clothes and a coat. It'll cost you though. Probably your pack horse and your supplies. And maybe a rifle or two. I'll talk with TaTanka for you.

"Where will you go?" Lucien asked.

"The only place we can go and be safe is north into Canada," Moseby said.

"How about you, Lucien?"

"I'm not sure exactly, but there's something that seems to be pulling to the Montana Territory or even Canada north of there. I would really like to stay with the Sioux, but I don't think that is possible.

"Come, we don't want to be late for supper."

Much to Sanford and Moseby's surprise, they were served first. "They are honoring both of you," Lucien said.

"Well, if that don't beat all. These people truly surprise me. And I mean that in a good way," Sanford said.

Lucien, John, Moseby and TaTanka sat up talking near the fire long after everyone else had gone to bed. Lucien could tell that the two were honestly interested with these people or they would not have asked so many questions of TaTanka. And TaTanka was also enjoying talking with them.

That night Lucien laid between Kyla and Hanka with his arms around each girl. Just happy to be there with them. He knew he would have to leave in the spring and he also knew it would be difficult to leave Kyla and Hanka behind, as well as the entire village.

* * * *

The next morning the Council Elders met with Tall Feather and TaTanka and talked for a long time about the Blue Coats. But Tall Feather became tired and they had to stop and let him rest. They would continue talking after he had awoken and taken some nourishment.

In the meantime, John and Moseby were enjoying themselves looking at everything in the village and talking with the people. John Sanford was learning that as backward as the natives might seem, they were in no shape or form a bunch of ignorant savages. He was sorry about leading the two raids against the Cheyenne.

The next day John Sanford and Moseby were told, "Sanford and Moseby you will speak before the Council Elders."

They were escorted to Tall Feather's lodge and were asked to remain standing. The Elders were concerned that

Sergeant Sanford might in fact be there scouting for the Army and they had a lot of explaining to do. And they both were becoming worried about their fate.

Finally they were told to leave the lodge, "...and tell Big Jean Corriveau to come."

Tall Feather was tired so TaTanka did most of the talking. "Sanford and Moseby say they were after you for deserting Army. They were found not following your trail but coming towards Sioux village. The Elders are worried they are scouting for Army for an attack like the massacre at Cheyenne River. We have much to fear from these two blue coats as Sioux. Council Elders ask for you thought. What do you say, Big Jean Corriveau?"

"While Sergeant Sanford was following me, he had a lot of time to think about what he was doing and his part in the massacre and the later battle at Cheyenne River, and he and Moseby, like me, were disillusioned about how the native Indians are treated.

"Sanford and Moseby, if allowed to leave, will not be going back to Fort Kearny, nor back to the Army. They, like me, have seen too much killing. When they lost my trail several weeks ago they had decided to travel north to Canada. If you release them that is where they will go."

"You leave us now. Let us talk among ourselves," Tall Feather said.

John and Moseby were nowhere to be seen, but this didn't worry Lucien. He found Hanka working with deer skins and Kyla was inside the lodge. "Kyla will you walk with me?"

"I do all you say, Big Jean Corriveau. Where we go?" she asked.

"Let's walk by the stream." When this seemed to confuse her he said, "Walk by the water." She understood this okay.

They followed the stream, upstream until they were well beyond the busy noise of the village. Lucien found a nice dry place under a huge spruce tree where the dry needles covered the ground like a thick carpet. He sat down with his back against the tree and motioned for Kyla to sit on the ground between his legs and she leaned back against him and he wrapped his strong arms around her.

Kyla was enjoying this interlude of intimacy. She had never experienced this kind of intimacy before where the man only wanted to hold her close and talk.

"What word when woman have baby inside her, Big Jean Corriveau?"

"Pregnant?"

"Yes. That word I want. Hanka and me not pregnant yet. We must try more—ah, more harder. Tonight I excite you all night and you make me pregnant okay?"

"Okay," and they both laughed.

"How do say—sometimes I have this feeling that I want you inside me now. This good funny feeling that makes me want you, how do you say this?"

"The word is horny. When you want sex with me, this is horny."

"You get this horny with me and Hanka too?"

"You bet I do. Sometimes all I have to do is look at you," Kyla giggled and turned to face Lucien and she kissed him long and hard with passion.

"Okay, Big Jean Corriveau. I much horny and I want this sex with you now." And she took her clothes off and then undressed Lucien. Then she pushed Lucien down on the soft needles and made him lay back and she sat on him and muffled a soft scream of delight as he entered her.

They made love and had sex over and over all afternoon. As it was getting close to the evening meal, Kyla said, "We stop now. Must help prepare food. I'm not horny now. This I did for fun, Big Jean Corriveau. You understand this?"

"Yes. I had fun too, Kyla."

"Tonight you make me pregnant, okay?"

"Okay."

* * * *

The next morning John, Moseby and Lucien were summoned to Tall Feather's lodge. "Sit. Council Elders have decided. If not for you, Big Jean Corriveau, the Elders would not have believe the story these two told. You," and he pointed, "would have been killed. We listened to you and Big Jean Corriveau and found merit with your words. You are free to leave anytime you wish. TaTanka, he say if you go to Canada he will give you four braves to escort you across Lakota land, so you will not be harmed.

"I have spoken, so you must leave me now."

* * * *

As everyone was preparing to turn in for the night, a brilliant display of northern lights began to dance across the north sky like a ballerina dancing on a cloud. Lucien went to his lodge. "Kyla, Hanka, come here," and he motioned with his hand.

"What you want?" Hanka asked.

"I want to show you something," and he walked with them to a small clearing in the forest where they could see better.

"Look at those lights. Aren't they beautiful?"

Hanka said, "*Manitou's hin.*" She was excited.

"What did you say, Hanka?" Lucien asked.

"*Manitou's hin.*"

When Lucien still looked confused Kyla said, "*Manitou*——Great Creator."

"Okay, my people say God."

"*Hin*—I don't know your word for this." Then Hanka grasped her hair and said, "*Hin, hin.*"

"Hair," Lucien said.

"Yes, hair."

"Manitou's hair, God's hair," Lucien said.

"He dances with spirits who have walked to spirit world."

The three of them stood there watching God's hair dance in the heavens. The lights were exceptionally bright tonight, with a variety of mint green, pink and yellow shades.

As they stood there watching, a micro-burst of wind suddenly swept down and blew over the village. There was a large snap when a huge spruce tree broke near the ground and it began to wobble in the wind like a top that wobbles just before it stops. There was no safe place to run, so the three stood there holding onto each other. Then the spruce tree began to fall. The top branches catching the other tree branches breaking its descent. The tree dropped onto Tate's lodge. He, his woman and daughter were inside. There were screams from inside the destroyed lodge.

Lucien instinctively ran over and without stopping to think what he or anyone else should do, he reached down and wrapped his arms around the trunk and lifted the tree off the destroyed lodge. Then he began to back up dragging the tree with him until it was away from the lodge and no longer in the way.

John Sanford, Moseby, TaTanka and many others stood and watched as Lucien, alone, lifted the tree and dragged it away. Everyone was stunned with Lucien's display of his enormous strength.

Lucien dropped the tree and rushed over to see if anyone was seriously hurt. Everyone remained silent as Lucien pushed his way through the throng of onlookers. They were all amazed at Lucien's tremendous strength. No one spoke as he cleared a path to Tate. He was still moaning in pain.

Lucien finally reached the lodge and saw the daughter was okay. Just scared. Tate's woman had been hit by a fallen branch and she only had a bruise on the side of her head.

"Step back, people; let me through." Tate was holding his left leg. "John, sit behind Tate and wrap your arms around him and pin his arms to his body."

John did and Lucien sat down facing Tate. "Hold him

upright, John, and hold on."

Lucien put one foot against Tate's crotch and pulled Tate's left leg out straight until he felt the bones set.

"Moseby, we're going to need two flat slats to put on either side of his leg. About three inches wide, half-inch thick and twenty-eight inches long."

"Okay Lucien, but I may have to rough 'em out of a piece of slab wood."

"Kyla and Hanka, I need some cloth or hide strips or leather strapping to tie everything together." They disappeared without saying anything.

TaTanka was impressed how Big Jean Corriveau, John and Moseby had taken charge to help Tate. He knew his people would not know how to do this. And that bothered him. He could truly see what Big Jean Corriveau had said about learning the ways of the white man.

Tate had stopped moaning and he relaxed. He looked at Lucien, somehow knowing he was in good hands. He slightly nodded his head at Lucien. Another way of saying he understood what Lucien was doing and that he trusted him.

Someone was tending to Tate's woman's bruised head.

It didn't take Kyla and Hanka long to find what Lucien needed to bind the splint together. Moseby was a little longer but he had two perfectly shaped splint boards. "I had to carve these from a piece of cedar with an axe. I hope they'll be okay."

"They're perfect, Moseby. Now crouch down here and help me place a board on each side. When I move my hand, slide one board into place. Okay I have that one, now the next one. Okay. Moseby, you'll have to tie the splint together. Use those hide strips. Tie one just above the break and another just below the knee. Okay, keep tightening the knot until you see Tate wince from the pain."

Moseby kept tightening the knot and he saw Tate wince. He stopped and finished the knot. "That's good, Moseby, now tie another one just below the break."

Tate had relaxed again.

"Tie another above the knee, Moseby."

"How are you, Tate?"

Tate nodded his head. Meaning he was okay.

"Okay, Moseby, now tie one just above the ankle and one around his foot criss-crossing the ties with the ends of each board.

When he had finished Lucien said, "Okay, John, you can let go of the patient now. He won't feel any pain now. That was a good job, Moseby."

Moseby looked at Tate and said, "In the morning, Tate, I'll make you some crutches and show you how to use them." He had no idea what a crutch was but he nodded his head and smiled.

"I didn't know you were that talented Moseby," John said.

"I worked with my father making cabinets before the Army, crutches won't be a problem."

Lucien addressed Tate's woman and TaTanka, "Tate must lay on his back for seven days," and he held up seven fingers. "He must stay off his feet, okay?"

Tate's woman said, "Okay."

TaTanka asked, "Will he walk again, Big Jean Corriveau?"

"If he'll stay off his feet and let the bones heal, he'll be running soon." This brought a smile to TaTanka's face.

Kyla and Hanka were standing together happily smiling. They were proud of their man, even if he was only theirs for the winter.

TaTanka, Uta, Hoka, Kongi, Waglula and Ptan tried to lift the tree and move it out of the way. The six of them couldn't even lift it, let along move it. They looked at each other and turned to look at Lucien. He was walking away with Kyla and Hanka back to their lodge. They stood there watching him walk away and all six of them wondering the same thing. *How could he alone lift the tree and move it when the six of them couldn't? Who was this man they called Big Jean Corriveau? He certainly wasn't any ordinary man.*

TaTanka returned to his lodge thinking about Big Jean Corriveau and what he had seen that night.

As Lucien, Kyla and Hanka laid together with the glow of their small fire, Hanka said, "You good work tonight, Big Jean Corriveau. I proud of you and proud I have your *wakan yeja.*"

"Oh, you mean baby," Lucien said.

"Yes, I have your baby. My English get better, no?"

"Yes, your English is better."

The three curled up together and were soon asleep.

* * * *

After eating the next morning, Moseby took an axe and walked out into the forest looking for some small trees he could carve into crutches.

When he showed Tate the crude crutches, he wanted to try them out immediately. But his woman reminded him he had to stay off his feet. He thanked Moseby and put the crutches by his side.

Lucien was talking with John Sanford. "If you and Moseby are going to Canada, TaTanka says you need to leave now so your escorts can make it back to the village before there is too much snow.

"We'll leave at noon. I'll go tell Moseby."

John and Moseby had to leave their pack horse not as payment for new clothes, but as a trade. Everyone was happy. What helped the trade go smoothly though was the way the two had helped with Tate. Everyone knew they were leaving, but as was their custom there was no great fanfare.

Lucien said to John Sanford, "You know John, when we first met I didn't think much of you then. Seeing how you have changed and your demeanor here at the village, you have changed a lot. And I am proud to call you friend. You two have a safe journey."

215

They shook hands and John said, "You're a better man, Big Jean Corriveau, than I'll ever be. You take care of yourself also."

That was all there was for goodbyes. Lucien stood and watched until they had disappeared.

Lucien went back to teaching. He had several children in the morning and in the afternoon he helped the adults to speak and understand English more fluently.

Two days after John and Moseby's departure, TaTanka said, "Big Jean Corriveau, today we hunt buffalo. Is cold day and night so meat not spoil. I send out scouts to watch herd to the east that is starting to move south for winter. Not far."

Lucien sharpened his knife and strapped on his .45 handgun and with his rifle he mounted his horse and joined the others. He rode up front with TaTanka. There was no talking and they walked their mounts so not to spook the herd. The buffalo were only an hour away.

TaTanka set up an ambush where the herd's trail would take them through a narrow pass. Everyone concealed themselves behind bushes and tall clumps of grass.

Lucien marveled at the patience the Sioux had as they waited for the herd to come close enough for their arrows and spears. They all were functioning as one. Everyone knew what their job was and it would be TaTanka who would signal when the kill would begin.

So far everything Lucien had seen of the Sioux impressed him. They certainly were not like he had imagined or what was written about them in newspapers.

The buffalo were in sight now and they were feeding as they moved. Slowly. Lucien's knees were beginning to hurt, but if he moved he would only embarrass himself. The lead buffalo now were only about fifty feet away. An easy kill with his rifle, but not with arrows and spears.

The lead buffalo was out of sight now and more animals were funneling in and bunching up in front. TaTanka only nodded his head ever so slightly. This was the signal. Arrows whistled through the air until they found their mark. Lucien sighted in on a huge bull and fired. The beast dropped where it had been standing.

As Lucien was reloading his rifle he saw another huge bull, with arrows stuck in it, was rushing head down towards TaTanka. Lucien dropped his rifle and drew his pistol and fired at the charging bull. The bull then sighted in on Lucien. The bullet had hit him in the right shoulder, but the bull never broke stride. Lucien fired again and the bull lowered his head, still charging at Lucien. He fired again, and again and the bull stumbled, but he was still coming. Lucien knew he only had one more shot. There was no time to sight in his last shot. He concentrated on a spot just behind the bull's head where the spine joined with the head. He fired his last shot and the bull fell and skidded towards Lucien and came to a stop five feet from his feet.

Lucien breathed a sigh of relief. TaTanka was grateful for Lucien saving his life, but even more for the courage Big Jean Corriveau showed as he stood his ground as the huge bull was charging at him.

Ten animals in all had been killed. Some had run off a short distance before dying from their wounds. Apparently only about half of the men had actually been the hunters, the rest, mostly the younger men, were there to help. While the animals were being skun and quartered, others were making travois to haul the meat and hides back to the village.

Lucien helped with the skinning and butchering. There was enough meat here to feed the entire village during the cold months.

All of the meat and hides could not be hauled back to the village with one trip, so Lucien volunteered to stay behind to keep the wolves, bears and mountain lions from stealing the meat. TaTanka said he would stay also. He wanted some time to talk with Big Jean Corriveau. TaTanka was as impressed with Lucien, as Lucien was with the entire tribe. Big Jean Corriveau

ÂÂÂÂ

certainly was unlike any of the stories he had heard about of the blue coats or the white man.

The two built a fire to ward off the animals looking for food and they roasted heart and liver and feasted and talked until the others returned with the travois to haul the rest of the meat back.

The sun was just beginning to peak through the early morning fog as the last of the meat was brought into the village. No one slept that night. Everyone was too excited about the kills and everyone helped to take care of the meat.

It took three days before all the meat and hides were taken care of. Lucien was given the hides from the two bulls he killed. One he gave to TaTanka. The other one became a rug in his and his two women's lodge.

Nothing went to waste, if it could be used. The intestines were cleaned and washed and hung up to dry. It would later become bow stings, sewing thread and rope.

The eyeballs and brains were cooked together for a soup. The tongues were skinned and roasted. The skulls were cleaned, washed and left in the sun to dry and turn white.

There was snow on the ground now and the temperatures at night were so cold, the sap in the spruce trees would freeze and the freezing wood would snap. Lucien was really enjoying his life here. And every day Tall Feather would ask Lucien to sit with him in the warmth of his lodge so the two could talk.

"Sit. We smoke the pipe first. Loosens the tongue and mind." Tall Feather lit the pipe and handed it to Lucien. They handed it back and forth until there was no more smoke and Tall Feather set the pipe aside.

"Today Big Jean Corriveau, I tell you a story. What I tell you now, I never tell anyone. Not even Wicahpi. Many seasons ago, before I was chief, I was only young brave. I started seeing this beautiful woman in my visions. In time she told me how she was called. We would talk a lot, of many things. She told to me that no harm would ever come to me. She would always watch over me.

"I knew her words were true. I began doing things other young braves did not have enough courage to do. This made me good standing with Sioux people. I only wanted to be good leader for my people. I wanted my woman to bring new blood to Sioux people. So I by myself went to Cheyenne village. I hid for days until I saw the woman I wanted. Wicahpi. One day I see her alone near river and I took her. She was daughter to Cheyenne Chief. Cheyenne chased after us for days. She gave me two sons and a daughter. Her blood has been good for my people." Tall Feather paused and sipped some hot berry tea.

"This woman I see in my visions, she same woman you see, Big Jean Corriveau." He was silent then and Lucien couldn't image how Tall Feather knew he had been seeing a beautiful woman in his dreams that also said she would always take care of him. Tall Feather saw the bewildered expression on Lucien's face.

"I see you, your spirit body, in my visions sometimes. This how I know.

"You see in your visions this same woman I see, then you have good spirit or you would not see her."

Tall Feather sipped his tea. "Do you know who this woman is, Tall Feather?"

"Yes. I know."

Lucien waited for him to continue and tell him who she was. But after a while it became evident he was not going to.

"Who is she, Tall Feather?"

"I can not tell you. This you must discover for yourself."

"Where will I find her?"

"Have you not found her already? If she talks with you in your visions and tells you she will always watch over you—she has found you. Maybe you need to understand this."

"Where should I go to find her? What should I do, Tall Feather?"

"The choices must be yours. You make wrong choices you may never find her or know what it is you must do. The choices are yours and yours alone. You must learn to trust your spirit. Learning to trust your own guidance and knowledge may only be a test for you to see if your spirit is true."

"You have given me much to think about, Tall Feather."

"You have become one of our people, Big Jean Corriveau. Kyla and Hanka both would make you good mates and you them. I will tell you this, Big Jean Corriveau, if you decide you wish to stay, you already have my approval and the Council Elders. The choice will have to be yours. Or your spirit may want you to travel somewhere beyond here. The choice will be yours.

"Now my friend, this old man needs to rest. We talk again tomorrow."

Lucien walked around the village in a daze. Just as he figured he had found his place in life and his understanding of things, Tall Feather lays all of this on him. Even though the ground was covered with snow he walked down to the ice choked stream and sat down on a rock.

As hard as he tried to think about Kyla and Hanka his mind would surely drift away from them and he would start thinking about this woman he sees in his dreams. And much more than this, Tall Feather more or less said that wherever he went or did, he would be guided by this woman. He would have choices to make. Whether they were the right choices or not, he would have to make them. "But if I make the wrong choices?" he said aloud.

After a while, and he was getting chilled by the north wind, he wandered back to the village. His afternoons were busy helping the adults with their use of and understanding of the English language.

One day he found Kyla and Hanka scraping the fat and sinew from the buffalo hide. When he offered to help they drove him off saying, "This woman work."

But he stayed and watched. It was a slow process scraping the entire hide. When they had finished they staked it to the ground to finish drying. In this cold weather it would soon freeze dry, which would help turn the flesh side of the hide white.

When he saw Kyla and Hanka pee on the hide he was shocked. *What are they doing?* But he remained silent. Then the two girls began rubbing the pee into the hide.

Kyla saw the questioning look on Lucien's face and explained, "What you call yellow water?"

"Pee."

She repeated the word "Pee. Pee helps make hide white like snow and makes soft."

After the hide had thoroughly freeze-dried, the girls took it inside their lodge and began the tedious task of preening the hair. Untangling the clumps and snarls and then combing it with a special comb made from bone. When they had finished the robe was clean and soft. "Not use on floor," Hanka said. "We use it keep warm on top of us when we sleep."

That night the wind howled outside and the temperature had dropped significantly. But inside their lodge Lucien and the two girls sat naked on the new buffalo blanket watching their small fire. The soft hair felt good to their bare backsides and Kyla said, "Watching fire, warmth, feel this soft blanket on my *san*," Kyla placed Lucien's hand between her legs and said again "*San.*"

Lucien nodded his head he understood.

"All this, Big Jean Corriveau, make me very horny."

"I horny too, Big Jean," Hanka added. Before their love making stopped they each were bathed in sweat.

"Okay Kyla, Hanka, now we sleep."

* * * *

Little by little the fallen spruce tree was worked up into firewood and because of the sap, it was used mostly for outside cooking, weather permitting.

Tate's broken leg healed and he had adapted easily to the crutches.

One day Lucien strapped on his handgun and told Kyla and Hanka that he was going for a walk, exploring. "I'll return before dark."

The snow was dry and fluffy and not deep. He decided to follow the stream upstream. Even through the stream was mostly iced over there were pieces of peeled sticks and branches which meant somewhere upstream were beaver.

The further upstream he traveled the tall spruce trees were left behind. Most of the vegetation was bushes and small cotton wood, which beaver cherished for food. He eventually came to a beaver dam and there was a large beaver on top of the dam repairing a leak. When the beaver saw Lucien it went back into the water under the ice. He found a spot to wait for the beaver to return, as soon as Lucien was quiet.

He didn't have long to wait when the beaver crawled out of the water onto the dam. It was looking downstream where it had seen Lucien earlier. He took a careful bead with his handgun and fired. The beaver dropped and didn't move. He pulled the beaver off the dam and was rolling it in the snow when another beaver crawled up on the dam. Lucien shot that one also and then rolled it in the snow to soak up the water. He figured there would be more beaver here but he wouldn't be able to carry anymore back to the village without a backpack.

He carried a beaver under each arm and headed for home.

Kyla and Hanka wouldn't let him skin them inside where it was warm so he built a fire in the outside fire pit and when he started to skin Kyla and Hanka came to watch. He showed them how to flesh the hide while he skun. "When I'm done you will not have to scrape the fat and meat off."

He finished one beaver and warmed his hands before starting the other one.

Instead of keeping the beaver for himself he gave them to Tall Feather's woman, Wicahpi. She said she would make a communal stew and she thanked Lucien repeatedly.

Lucien watched as the woman cut the beaver meat up

for a stew. There wasn't much of the beaver that didn't go into the pot. The brains, eye balls, the tail was skinned and cut into small pieces, the heart, liver, kidneys and the leg bones were cracked open for the marrow and then all the separate bones, to cook the meat off the bones. The stew was quite excellent and there was enough so everyone had a bowl. The hides of course he gave to Kyla and Hanka, knowing they would use them to make clothing. "This good thing you give Wicahpi beaver so all people enjoy eating them."

"You know, Big Jean," Hanka said, "You more like us, more Indian than you white," and she laughed and Kyla and Lucien also laughed.

Later that evening when Lucien and the girls were alone in their lodge Kyla said, "Take clothes off, Big Jean."

When he just stood there dumfounded she said again, "Take clothes. Me not horny. Take off clothes."

This time he did, standing there naked Hanka produced a deer skin shirt and pants that she and Kyla had been making.

"They fit good. When did you two find time to make these?"

"When not working or learning your words."

Hanka then held out a deer hide fur lined coat with hair on the outside so rain would run off and not soak through. Lucien pulled it on. It was heavy, but it would surely be warm.

He had noticed though that during the cold and snowy months, the men did not do much traveling.

The four escorts that rode out with John and Moseby had returned and a runner had returned from another tribe and that would be the last runner until spring. A lot of time was spent napping arrow and spear heads, arrow shafts, bows and making flint knives which were actually sharper than Lucien's steel blade.

Lucien noticed that everything anyone did was for the benefit of the whole tribe. If someone needed help, help was there. Food, clothing, hides and firewood was shared amongst everyone. No one tried to progress and better the next person. The Council Elders were much like legislators and Tall Feather as Chief was like the president, except those positions were permanent and not elected posts. And they each worked towards the structure and well-being of the tribe, with no sense of personal gain.

He marveled at their simplicity and form of government. Their honesty and trustworthiness. If only his own people could be like the Sioux. There was no stealing, no lewd behavior, no fighting, no drunks or bickering. Yes, he had found a wonderful land and people.

What Tall Feather had said to him earlier about making the right choices, he tried to push the idea out of his mind whenever he found himself thinking about the choice he would have to make come spring. He just didn't know how he should choose. There were significant factors on both sides of whatever choice he would have to make.

He still talked often with Tall Feather and it seemed he could see how Tall Feather's strength and health was beginning to leave him with each new visit. Tall Feather knew his time was near when he would take his walk into the spirit world and he actually found comfort in that. But he was more worried about the fate of his people and the onslaught of more white settlers and the blue coats coming west.

"Big Jean Corriveau, I know in the white man's world there are many things that my people do not have and can not even imagine. I worry if they try to discover some of these things and forget the ways of their people, their elders and the tribe breaks apart."

"I think I can understand how you feel, Tall Feather," Lucien said.

"Why can you know how I feel? You come from the land of the white man with things and ideas my people know nothing about."

"I understand, Tall Feather, 'cause sometimes I feel like

I'm opening my eyes for the first time and I see huge grassy prairies and everything looks the same and I have no idea where I am or which direction I should travel."

Tall Feather smiled then and said, "Then you do understand, Big Jean Corriveau."

"Yes I understand, Tall Feather. Let me ask you a question, Tall Feather."

Tall Feather only nodded his head.

"Do you want to take your walk into the spirit world with these troubles and worries or do you want to walk there as a happy free spirit?"

"You make good talk, Big Jean Corriveau. Like I said before, you more Indian then you are white man. You understand our ways, good. Like Indian."

"When you take your walk, Tall Feather, I understand your son TaTanka will take your place as Chief."

"Yes, he does now some of my work."

"TaTanka is a good and righteous man. Maybe you should trust in him to do the right thing concerning your people and not worry that your people will be no more."

Tall Feather was silent for a long time, then he said, "I see now why this woman in your vision has brought you here. To comfort an old man in his last days. Go now, I need rest."

Lucien left and went back to his own lodge. Kyla and Hanka were there also.

* * * *

Lucien figured it must be about mid-winter. A cold wind from the north blew in frigid artic temperatures. It was so cold no one ventured outside their own lodge. There was no communal cooking and everyone was using extra firewood. Lucien decided he would brave the cold and go after more wood. A few others saw what he was doing and joined him. They found a tall dead pine tree and when they had it on the ground, the center of the trunk was hollow rotten. The wood was dry and still good and just as Lucien was about to chunk up the trunk Hoka stopped him, "No, make good canoe."

Hoka paced off on top of the trunk and said, "Cut here."

The trunk was still hollow rotten but the wood was dry and good. It took all day to work up the tree into useable pieces of firewood. The men did the same the next day and the next.

After the extreme windy and cold weather had passed the men still worked on getting more firewood. No one wanted to run out and be cold.

The days began to get warmer and longer and the children began playing outside again. Lucien had to put away the furlined coat for a much lighter one.

Tall Feather had stopped asking to talk and TaTanka and Wicahpi were both spending more time with him. He seldom came outside now. Wicahpi brought his meals to him. Lucien knew Tall Feather would soon walk away. TaTanka knew also as he seldom showed his happy disposition now. He was concerned about his father and if he could live up to his father's expectations. TaTanka knew there were troubling times ahead of them, with the encroaching white man and blue coats.

As Tall Feather grew weaker and weaker there was a somber cloud that hung over the tribe. But no one wanted to talk about it. But they all knew he would soon be taking his walk. This made them happy, but he was so loved by everyone, they all would miss him.

The ice had broken up in the stream and there was bare muddy ground in the village as the snow began to melt. Lucien was surprised. He thought there would be more snow here so near the tall Black Mountains than back home. With the warm nights and warmer days the snow was soon gone.

One day TaTanka came to see Lucien. "Big Jean Corriveau. My father wishes to see you."

Lucien entered his lodge. Tall Feather was lying down with a rolled up hide for a pillow. He told Wicahpi to leave,

"I wish to talk with Big Jean alone." After Wicahpi left, Tall Feather said, "Sit."

Lucien sat and Tall Feather said, "My time is near. I will not live through the night. Wicahpi and TaTanka know this too." Just then Tall Feather winced from pain.

He was several minutes before he could continue.

"Feels like buffalo sitting on my chest. Each time the pain comes is worse. I wanted to thank you for coming to Sioux village. You helped my people. Have you decided which choice you'll make?"

"I have, Tall Feather." That's all Lucien would say.

"This is good. Remember let this woman in your visions guide you. She has always been here for me. Although I find it troubling that a woman spirit has been my guide and not a man. Maybe I listened more to this woman than I would have man. You learn to listen too.

"You have great spirit, Big Jean Corriveau. Now leave me. Send in Wicahpi."

When Lucien stepped out Wicahpi stepped in front of him and she began to cry. Lucien hugged her to comfort her and he said, "Tall Feather wants you, Wicahpi."

TaTanka came over and sat near Lucien. "Tall Feather like you, Big Jean Corriveau. You like son. You my brother. Our skin different color, but in here," and he tapped his chest, "we are alike."

"I will miss him, TaTanka. And I will miss you and all of your people."

"You have made your choice. Father said you would. Where will you go my brother?"

"I'm not sure. To the Big Muddy in Montana? Canada? I'm not sure yet."

"When you go?"

"In a few days. I will miss Kyla and Hanka. They have been good to me."

"You will always be welcome here, if you ever want to

come home. This is your home now."

Then on another note, TaTanka said, "When ground is dry, I move village. Firewood hard to get now. We go *wiyohpeya*—west, towards Black Hills. Already scouted land and I found good place. Many elk and buffalo."

Just then Wicahpi started wailing from inside the lodge. TaTanka jumped up and said, "Tall Feather has left us. He is walking now to the spirit world." Just then a wind blew in from the north for just a few moments and then it was gone.

"Good-bye, old friend," Lucien said.

TaTanka went to comfort his mother.

CHAPTER 12

Before the body became cold and rigid, TaTanka helped his mother dress Tall Feather in his new walking clothes. There was a celebration that night around a huge fire where the people danced and told stories of Tall Feather. Lucien felt greatly honored to be able to partake in this celebration of life, not death. There was sadness of course and a few tears. Not because Tall Feather had died, but because they would miss him.

Early the next morning TaTanka asked Lucien, "Big Jean Corriveau will you help me put my father on his horse?"
When they had him tied on securely Lucien asked, "Do you want me to come along and help you?" TaTanka turned and left without answering.

Wicahpi said, "It is a son's duty to take body to chosen place. There TaTanka will leave his father; with his bow and arrows. When it is my time to walk to the spirit world, my body will be placed there also."

It was well after midnight before the celebration finally ended and everyone strolled back to their own homes.

Lucien, Kyla and Hanka took their clothes off and laid down on the buffalo blanket, and in the glow of their fire he caressed the girls growing bellies. "You'll be leaving us soon," not a question. Kyla was simply stating something she and Hanka already knew.

"Yes, in a few days."

"You could stay here, Big Jean," Hanka said, "You people of Sioux now. You family."

"I know. But we all knew what my job was, for Tall

Feather to let me live here during the cold season. I was to make you each pregnant so my blood will mix with Sioux blood, and to teach English. I do have the choice to stay, but there is something which is making me understand that I must leave. Maybe someday I can return, but I don't know."

Kyla and Hanka snuggled close to Lucien all night. They were in love with him.

Life at the village returned to normal and TaTanka assumed his new position as Chief.

A runner from the Mandan Tribe to the northeast arrived and Lucien was summoned to TaTanka's lodge. "Big Jean Corriveau, Little Squirrel is Mandan he brought paper from trading post near his tribe for you."

Little Squirrel gave Lucien a two month old newspaper. "You can read the words, Big Jean Corriveau, then you tell me what words say. Little Squirrel brings news that John Sanford and Moseby made it safely into Canada.

"He also says because of war between north and south, Blue Coats not so active out here. This good to hear. Maybe those after yellow rock will be fighting in this war and stop looking for yellow rock on Lakota land."

He brought more news about the tribes to the east, and many blue coats had been recalled to the east to fight in their war.

Lucien found a quiet place where he read the two month old newspaper from cover to cover. He had forgotten how much he had in the past enjoyed reading.

That evening in the glow of their fire Lucien showed Kyla and Hanka the newspaper. And page by page, he showed them the pictures of the white man's world. There were photos of the, now called Civil War, photos of huge sailing ships unloading cargo from Europe. And he had to explain where Europe was.

Lucien turned the front page and one article on page two caught his attention. He read the article to himself, Major Merrill had officially listed him, John Sanford and Moseby as deserters and a reward of $300.00 each for their capture. Dead or alive. He was so glad he had seen the article. Now he knew to be cautious. Had the woman in the dreams guided the Mandan runner to bring him the newspaper? Or was it only a coincidence?

Kyla began to cry. "Kyla what's wrong?" Lucien asked. "Why do you cry?"

She held up the newspaper and said, "This frightens me. Pictures of things I know nothing of. How are we Sioux to survive in a world that frightens us so much? It is so different."

"You'll be okay, Kyla. TaTanka tells me he is going to move the tribe close to the Black Hills soon. You'll be safe there."

This seemed to calm her down.

He eventually left his lodge and went to talk with TaTanka and tell him the news that he read in the paper.

That night Lucien, Kyla and Hanka laid down on top of the buffalo blanket wrapped in each others arms. There was very little talking, but they each were enjoying the moment in their own way.

* * * *

Two weeks after Tall Feather walked to the spirit world, the snow was gone and the ground was drying and the grass was beginning to turn green. Lucien decided it was time for him to leave. "TaTanka, I would like to talk with you."

"Come, we go near stream." Nothing was said until they were sitting on the stream bank in the shade of a spruce tree. "TaTanka, it is time for me to leave."

"When?"

"Tomorrow morning. I would very much like to stay, but there are reasons why I can't." TaTanka waited for Big Jean Corriveau to continue.

"I am being guided by a spirit that I see often in my dreams. I do not know where this guide wants me to go, but I

231

must trust her." TaTanka nodded his head that he understood.

"And I have read in that newspaper that I am a wanted man with a price on my head. Dead or alive."

"You stay here, we protect you."

"That's why I cannot stay, TaTanka. Someday people will learn about the white man who lives with the Sioux and they will come looking for me. And I do not want this trouble for my Sioux family. If I leave, then no one will come looking for me and you will not have this trouble."

"I understand what you say, Big Jean Corriveau. This makes you great man, great Sioux man." TaTanka's eyes were red. He and Lucien had been good friends and now they must say goodbye.

"You come back some time, no? We tell stores and you be welcomed."

Lucien's eyes were red and watery also; he hated the idea of leaving, but he knew he could not stay.

That night as Lucien, Kyla and Hanka were lying together on the buffalo blanket Kyla said, "Big Jean, Hanka and me not horny, but we wish you to have sex with us all night. When you leave we no have this horny sex for long time. Okay?"

Tonight Lucien took the girl's clothes off and then stood up and took his off. He caressed and kissed them both until they could not with stand it any longer and first Kyla pulled Lucien on top of her and then Hanka.

When they were not making love they would lay back and talk, laugh and giggle. Anything, so long as they did not think about the morning.

* * * *

After eating breakfast the next morning, Lucien saddled his horse and packed his few belongings. He removed some powder and shot from his saddlebags and pulled his rifle from the scabbard and presented it to TaTanka. "TaTanka, I would like to give you this rifle as a token of my friendship and as trade for all you and your people have done for me. I hope this rifle will help you shoot more buffalo for winter survival."

TaTanka took the gift and all he could do was nod his head. He was too emotional to say anything. Lucien hugged Kyla and Hanka and then mounted his horse, waved good-bye and rode off towards the north. Not a word was spoken by TaTanka or his people until Lucien was out of sight. Lucien had a lump in his throat and his eyes, too, were watery.

He walked his horse in a northly direction but was not much aware of his surroundings. His mind was still back at the village and his spirit was with Kyla and Hanka. But by high noon he had brought himself around to conscious thinking and his surroundings. He tried to outdistance his longing by running his horse until it was tired. "Okay boy, we're okay now," and he patted its neck.

He was feeling better now. He had no idea where he was going. He knew he was headed northerly when he left the village but now he wasn't so sure. And he decided not to check his compass either. He would let his woman guide show him where to go. He would put his full trust with her.

By mid afternoon he was getting hungry and he didn't have any food. He would have to stop and find something. His horse had plenty of fresh new grass to eat. He found a quiet stream and tied his horse to a tree and he went hunting. All he had now was his pistol.

He was gone about an hour and had shot a rabbit and a sage grouse. He was hungry enough to eat both. He made a fire and peeled the skin off the rabbit and put it on a stick to roast over the fire and then he did the same with the sage grouse. While they were roasting he made a shelter of fir boughs for the night.

After he finished the shelter, the rabbit and grouse were still roasting, so he walked along the stream to see if he could see any fish. There were no fish, but he found a bucketful of crayfish. He decided these would make for a good breakfast in the morning.

He was wishing he had some coffee to go along with the rabbit and grouse. His last cup coffee was before he was taken to the Sioux village. Maybe he could find a trading post somewhere. He surely hoped so. He really needed a few supplies.

Instead of coffee he made some hot tea with teaberry leaves. He made it strong. Just before dark the rabbit and grouse were finally cooked. In the warmth and firelight glow he enjoyed his meal and hot tea. When he had finished eating he went after more firewood.

He sat up long into the night staring into the flames. He hadn't thought about Kyla and Hanka or the Sioux people for hours now. His mind was confused and troubled. Wondering where he was to go and would he choose the right direction. That is why he would not check his compass. He would let his guide show him where to go. *But where was it? And once there what am I supposed to do? Tall Feather said I would know when I found it.*

He still had his cooking utensils, and in the morning he boiled a pot of hot water and put the crayfish in to cook. He hadn't eaten any since he was a boy and he had forgotten how good they were to eat.

When he had finished the crayfish, he packed up and moved on. He could remember studying reference books at Fort Kearny and the many maps of that part of the mid-west. He knew the great Missouri River swung west, then south to Fort Benton, an American Fur Company fort and not a military fort.

But what he wanted was Fort Union at the junction of the Yellowstone River and the Missouri. Fort Union was a fort built by John Jacob Astor and the American Fur Company in 1828. The Northwest Fur Company now owns the fort. The fort was originally built at the request of the Assiniboine Indian Nation.

The Assiniboine people saw the value in the fur trade and they needed an outlet in which to trade and sell their fur.

Lucien's book reading and studies were beginning to pay off. And he wondered if the woman spirit guide had directed him in his interest of reading and studies.

In the information Lucien was able to learn about the fort, i.e. trading post, was that Fort Union soon became the most profitable fur trading post on the Missouri River.

Again Lucien's thoughts returned now to his earlier desire for reading and learning. He was convinced it all came down to this. He finding his way to Fort Union on the Missouri River. He would have to travel a little west of the Big Muddy River to reach Fort Union., but he needed supplies.

With that decision now made and seeing images of his trail ahead of him flash across his inner vision and hearing Tall Feather tell him his future would depend on the choices that lay ahead of him.

Lucien was no longer concerned or worried about making the wrong choice. Everything in his life had been preparing him for this journey and what would lay at the end. And he was no longer worried or wondering what he would find. All of his life he now understood that subconsciously he had been following this beautiful woman's guidance. He was escorted now as he spurred his horse into a run, Kyla and Hanka now forgotten. He had for once a purpose and a destination to his life and he was in a hurry to get there.

He would stop often to rest his horse and stretch his own tired muscles, and to feed and water his horse. One morning when he awoke it was raining and he stayed where he was until the next day. He built a water tight shelter and shot sage grouse and rabbit. They were both so numerous. He always made camp near a stream. He tried catching trout, but he wasn't very successful. He did often find an abundance of crayfish, which he'd rather have than fish. The meat was sweeter.

He had been pushing his horse for days and he needed a long rest and fatten up on green grass. Lucien spent most of his time laying in the cover for his shelter, looking for firewood and when he was hungry, looking for food.

He decided to stay longer and find a small deer or bear and cure some of the meat, so he would have a supply. He wasn't sure if he would always be able to shoot rabbit and sage grouse.

Not far from his camp he spotted a nice doe. But she had twin lambs with her and Lucien decided against killing her. A yearling doe would be just right. If there was one deer here there probably would be more. He kept hunting and soon found a spike horn reaching up and stripping new leaves from a yellow birch sapling. He took careful aim with his .45 and pulled the trigger. The deer fell where it had been feeding.

After cleaning out the stomach and intestines he carried it back to his camp. He skun it and removed the heart and liver and set the heart to roasting. Then he fashioned a crude smoking rack and began stripping the meat and hanging it on the rack to cure. When he was finished the rack was full. He would keep the clean hide to carry the meat in once it was fully cured.

He sat near the fire day and night, tending to the fire and meat. The rain had blown out and clear skies and sun returned. The meat wasn't completely smoke cured until late in the third day. Being so late he decided to stay another night. The heart was all gone and there remained only a little of the liver.

The second night out after leaving the smoke-curing camp, the night sky was clear and stars were as bright as Lucien could ever remember. There were a few shooting stars, but not many. Before midnight the big milky colored belt was exquisite. He laid on his back looking up.

Some time, maybe two hours after midnight Lucien got up and put more wood on the fire. To the north the northern lights were dancing a ballerina's dance. "Manitou's hair," he said. "Manitou dancing in the heavens tonight."

That got him thinking about Kyla and Hanka. He laid down on his bed roll and went to sleep thinking of his girls.

He only had a few hours of sleep, but he was up early and after some of the cured meat, he saddled up and was moving north towards the Missouri River. The closest that he could figure, it had been at least five weeks since leaving the Sioux village, "I must be getting close to the river."

He had journeyed through some beautiful country. He wished he had had the time to explore. But for now there was a more pressing destination.

The following day when he crested a high pinnacle, he could see the river off in the distance. He figured the river was two or three miles away. There was a river steamboat heading downstream. *It'll probably bring back a boat load of settlers and those looking to get rich quick from gold. The Lakota don't stand a chance against this invasion. In thirty years the native Indian's empire probably will have fallen. I feel so sorry for all of them.*

He made camp that night on top of the pinnacle in a thicket of softwood. His fire was made of snapping dry firewood so there'd be no smoke.

The air was cool this night and Lucien gathered plenty of wood. He tried to sit up like he had the night before. But he was sleepy and he kept dozing off. He laid back and pulled his blanket around him.

It didn't seem as though anytime had passed at all and he suddenly found it difficult to sleep. He kept turning over and over and finally he sat up to watch the fire again. The flames were blazing high, so he didn't have to add any more wood.

The woman in his dream filled his thinking. She was all he could think of. Looking up from the fire he saw this same beautiful woman standing behind the fire. "I have waited so long to see you," he said calmly.

She smiled and said, "From this day on, Big Jean Corriveau, you will be known as Jean Corriveau. Lucien Jandreau is now only a memory. When you enter Fort Union, go with caution. I will not be able to be with you to protect you. You have made good choices, so far. I will not be with you after tonight, Jean Corriveau. There is a good reason. There are more choices you have to make, and after this night for a while you'll be alone to make those choices on your own. You have come a great distance, Jean Corriveau, in your understanding and in your journey. But your journey is not yet over." She smiled radiantly at him again and she seemed to glow with a soft luminous light.

"What is your name?" Jean Corriveau asked.

She didn't answer. She turned around and she took one maybe two steps and she was gone.

Jean Corriveau opened his eyes and he found himself laying on his bed roll. The fire had burned out and daylight was filtering through the tree tops. At first he thought he had only had another dream (vision) of this woman. But he could remember distinctly of getting up and sitting by the fire and seeing how high the flames rose above the wood. "I could remember everything she had said. But when she left, the fire was still burning brightly and then I opened my eyes and the fire had burned out. He couldn't remember laying back on his bed and where did all the time go. She had come to him before he had fallen asleep.

She was real, I know that. And I know she was here.

He had to remember from now on, he was Jean Corriveau, and Lucien Jandreau was in the past and forgotten. He remembered asking her her name and she never replied. That's when she left.

There was too much to think about to even think about eating.

As he rode off the pinnacle he had no idea where on the river he was. But instinctively he knew he would have to follow it upstream to find Fort Union. Rather than riding straight for the river, he went diagonally off to the west. Once he could see the river he set back away from it, so he would not be visible from the water, in case of a passing river boat or a canoe.

He rode the high ground when he could; always watching the river, the grass plains on his left and the forest that followed the river. Maybe he was only being paranoid, but he remembered what his guide had said about using caution.

Before stopping for the night he looked for high ground

where he could see around him. He waited until after dark to kindle a fire to warm up the smoked venison. Then he put the fire out for the night.

He traveled like this for three days. Going slow and using caution.

As he laid on his bed roll that night looking up at the stars. The words, "Look for me in this life," kept echoing in his mind. He remembered hearing this one night before he went to prison and only now he was remembering, he could hear her saying this to him many times when they would meet after he had fallen to sleep.

The next morning instead of following the Missouri River to Fort Union he decided to go across country and hit the Yellowstone River and follow that to the fort.

As he rode off the high ground he saw a small group of men hunting between him and the river. It took him a day to reach the Yellowstone River, and being in no particular hurry he stopped for the night on a high point where he could watch the river.

He felt safer with a fire tonight. He wasn't sure why, but he was. But he kindled it with dry wood that wouldn't smoke. Just before dark he saw four canoes in a group float downstream. They each were loaded heavy with winter fur.

He made some more hot tea from teaberry leaves and sat up long after dark sipping tea, listening to an owl across the river and watching the fire.

The next morning he ate a little cold smoked venison and then mounted up and rode off the high ground for the river. At the bottom of the knoll, he found a well used trail and decided to follow it. As he rode, he was thinking it would appear better to anyone who might see him ride into the fort if he was using this trail as versus coming in through the bushes.

The fort was still more than a day's ride, so he made camp early off the trail. He could have pushed on and maybe have gotten there late, but he heard his guide saying to be cautious.

Shortly after getting back on the trail in the morning he met four trappers who were on their way back into beaver country. They had been at the fort and sold their hides, outfitted again with supplies and were now going back to their camp.

They were friendly and didn't ask Jean Corriveau his business. They were blurry-eyed and smelling of whiskey. Probably a lot of celebrating after being in the wilderness by themselves for a year.

By noon he caught up with two more trappers on horseback heading for the fort. "Hello there," Jean Corriveau hollered.

They stopped and waited for him to catch up. "What happened to your catch, young fella? Run on bad times like we did?" Harry Walker asked.

"*Monsieur,* my name is Jean Corriveau. I, too, had bad trapping and a Sioux Chief felt pity for me and let me stay for the winter," Jean Corriveau replied.

"Well, Corriveau, you still have your hair and horse so that says a lot for you." Bill Stearns said.

"Where you heading now, young fella?"

"Back to Canada, when I leave Fort Union."

"Where's all your gear, Corriveau?" Bill asked.

"Still on my pack horse and my pack horse is on the bottom of the Cheyenne River."

"Oh."

By mid-afternoon Jean Corriveau asked, "How much further is it to Fort Union?"

"We should be there in another couple of hours," Harry replied.

"I think I'll stay the night here. I didn't get much sleep last night and I'm tired and so is my horse.

"Suit yourself mister. But Harry and me are looking forward to a nice meal," Bill said.

"Maybe I'll see you at the fort," Jean Corriveau said.

He waited until they were out of sight before looking for

a place to make camp, off the trail. There was still three hours or so of daylight left. Not sure if it would rain or not he had the time to make a water tight shelter and a fir bough bed. Then he saw to his horse. He let it eat and drink as much water as he wanted.

Jean Corriveau made some teaberry tea and he put in some hemlock buds for flavoring. Then he warmed up some smoke-cured venison. He was hungry and the meat tasted good.

It started to drizzle some just as Jean Corriveau laid down for the night. The air was so warm he didn't care if his fire went out or not. He was planning on having breakfast at the fort anyway. He awoke just as the sun started to peak over the hill tops, promising a nice day ahead.

He removed some coin money from his saddlebags and put it in his pocket. Then he tightly secured the saddlebags on behind the saddle and secured the deer hide rolled up with what venison there was left on top of the saddlebags. He made sure to tie everything in place tightly.

The first stream he came to he stopped and washed up some and ran his fingers through his hair to make himself look a little presentable. Once at the fort he'd look into taking a bath, getting his hair and beard trimmed.

When Jean Corriveau rode into Fort Union, it wasn't what he was expecting. There were only civilian people and the fort itself was more impressive than any of the Army forts he had visited.

He left his horse at the livery. "You *Monsieur* Harper?"

"Yes Sir, what can I do you for?"

"New shoes for the horse, feed some grain and I'd like to leave him here until I have finished my business."

"Yes Sir, I can do that."

"I can pay now or when I come back."

"You can pay when you come back."

"Where can I get a bath and my hair trimmed?"

"Directly across the compound."

"Thank you," and Jean Corriveau walked over.

"Hello, I would like a bath and then my hair and beard trimmed."

"Certainly, this way, the water is already hot. 50 cents for the bath and $1.00 for the trim. I'd like my money upfront please."

Jean Corriveau paid him and then removed his clothes and sat down in the tub of hot water. It took a little to get used to. He soaked in the tub until the water was lukewarm.

Then he got dressed, shaved and had his hair cut off his ears. He felt like a new man. It was time for breakfast. "Where is the best café for a hearty breakfast, *Monsieur*?"

"At the south end of the compound next to the trading post. Anabelle's. She's the best cook at the fort."

"Thank you."

"You staying long, young fella?"

"Doubtful."

At Anabelle's he chose a table in the corner of the room where he could see the front door, kitchen door and the room. "Sit down, mister, I'll be right there," a stocky woman said.

After a few minutes she returned with a cup of coffee, "You might as well leave the pot, *Madame*."

"Oh, yeah, fellas, we have here a Frenchie," she said jokingly. "What can I get for you? What's your name, young fella?"

"Jean—Jean Corriveau.

"Six eggs over easy, home fries and a ham steak and a loaf of warm bread, please."

"I must say you're a polite one. We don't get many like you in here. Or someone who can eat all that you have ordered. Are you sure you want it all?"

"Yes, *Madame*, I could eat a horse raw and have room for an apple pie."

Anabelle laughed again and said, "Sweetie, if you can eat every bit of that order I'll charge you only half price." She went off into the kitchen.

There were seven men there all looking at Jean Corriveau and sizing him up. He was a big one all right, but every man there doubted if he'd be able to eat every bite.

Anabelle had to use three plates to bring him his breakfast. When he tasted the eggs he said, "Maybe I should have ordered a couple more."

Anabelle's eyes opened wide. She didn't think he could finish what he had let along another two eggs.

She sat down at the next table, and watched as Jean Corriveau enjoyed his breakfast. "This ham is *bon magnifique.* 'Tis the best I have eaten in a long time."

"I'm glad you like it," she poured another cup of coffee. There was another cup left and one more slice of bread and he used that to sop up the juices.

He leaned back in his chair and finished the last of the coffee.

"I would never have believed it possible if I had not seen it for myself. You must have a hollow leg."

Jean Corriveau laughed and said, "That's what my mother said also. Said she couldn't wait until I left home. Said she couldn't afford to feed me anymore." Everyone laughed then.

"Where are you from, Mr. Corriveau?"

"Eastern Canada."

"What are you doing out here?"

"I went to trap the beaver, but my pack horse went through some ice while crossing a river. Lost all of my supplies and pack horse. Spent the winter with a band of Sioux."

Jean Corriveau stood up and stretched and asked, "How much for the breakfast, *Madame*?"

"A breakfast like that would usually cost you $2.00, but I said half, remember, if you finished every bite?"

"Here is $2.00. It was worth every penny. Good day *Madame*."

He hoped he had not overplayed the French part.

243

The many nights he spent watching the fire, he often wished he had had a drink of whiskey to help relax the day. So his next stop was at the Big Muddy Saloon. It was still comparatively early in the day, but the saloon was almost too full. He walked up to the bar and waited for the barkeep to notice him.

"Yes, what can I get for you, mister?"

"*Bonjour, Monsieur*, I would like a bottle of your whiskey please. And not that stuff you serve these fellows."

The barkeep removed that bottle and put another on the bar. "That'll be 75 cents."

Jean Corriveau paid him.

Two fellas down the bar from Jean Corriveau, a heavy-set fella who already had had too much to drink, noticed Jean Corriveau with his buckskin clothing. "Hey you!" he bellowed, "Indians don't get served in here!"

Jean Corriveau turned to look at this loud mouth. When the fellow saw Jean Corriveau's hard eyes, he said, "I guess you ain't no Indian, but you must have spent some time with them, the way you look."

Then a friend of the loud mouth chirmed in and said, "Hey, Luther, maybe we should show this Indian lover the door."

Jean Corriveau turned so he was square on to the two. The men who had been between them left. "I spent the winter with the Sioux and I have never seen a group of people as nice as they all were. You two foul mouth bastards could surely take some advice from them. But then I think you two are too stupid to learn anything, especially from someone who is so much better than you two."

The entire saloon went quiet. No one had expected Jean Corriveau to respond quite like this.

"Hey Benny, did you hear what he said about us?" Luther asked.

"I sure enough did. I think we need to show this upstart who's bigger," Benny said.

"I wouldn't advise it. You two have had too much to drink to be able to fight even a little girl, let alone me. Why don't you boys do yourself a big favor and leave before you get hurt."

They both stepped close to Jean Corriveau.

"Why don't you both go sleep it off somewhere?"

"You insulted us, mister," Luther said. And they took another step closer.

"Wow, you know something? You two really stink. How can you stand your own body odor?"

That was more than they could take. Luther doubled up his fist and started to swing at Jean Corriveau while saying, "You bastard!"

Jean Corriveau punched him in the nose with the flat of his hand, sending Luther backward screaming and blood running down his face. At the same time Benny tried to punch Jean Corriveau on the side of his head. It was a glancing blow and Jean Corriveau grabbed his arm and twisted it and broke it. Benny was now screaming. But he tried to land another punch with his left. Jean Corriveau caught his fist in his iron grip hand and began to squeeze until the bones in his hand broke. Benny fell to the floor screaming. He was done for.

Luther put his head down and charged. Jean Corriveau saw him coming and side stepped and Luther hit the bar with his head and fell to the floor unconscious. Jean Corriveau stepped over them and picked up the bottle of whiskey and walked out.

Another patron said, "These two have had it coming to them for a long time. I for one am glad I was here to see it."

"Yeah, but have you ever seen anyone fight like that before? Benny hit him beside his head and it didn't faze him. And he never threw a punch with a closed fist."

"He was so polite and quiet, you'd never think he would ever get the best of these two."

"He was so calm and collected about what he was doing. I have never seen anything like it."

The barkeep said, "Who in the hell was that?"

Another patron said, "I have never seen anything like it either."

Another said, "I guess no one should talk bad about Indians around him."

He walked over to the livery stable. He guessed he'd leave as soon as he could. He'd had enough of Fort Union's hospitalities.

"Have you changed the shoes on my horse yet?"

"Just finished. You leaving so soon mister?"

"There was a little trouble at the Big Muddy Saloon."

"Let me guess. Luther and Benny?"

"Yes."

"Figures. They are always trying to push their weight around. You don't look as if you've been in a fight."

"They do. Do you have a pack horse here you could sell me?"

"Sure do. $35.00. Pack harness—$5.00. $4.00 for the shoes. $1.00 for feed. Anything else?"

"Yes, twenty pounds of grain."

"That'll be $2.00, total—$47.00"

Jean Corriveau gave him $50.00 and waited for the change. "Thank you."

He led both horses over to the trading post and tied them off to the hitching rail.

"Hello there, can I help you with something?" Edwin Smith said.

"Yes, I need a few supplies. What do you have for new rifles?"

"I just got this here in yesterday, mister. It's brand new, lever action Henry .44 rifle. Holds fifteen shots. Uses the brass cartridge now and not the percussion cap. I only have two."

"I'll take one," he looked it over and liked how it handled. "I'll need:

10 lbs. of beans
10 lbs. of bacon

10 lbs. of ham
2 blankets
2 boxes of .44 cartridges
10 lbs. of coffee
How about fresh bread?"
"You'll have to get that at Anabelle's."
1 shirt
1 pair of pants
1 pair of leather boots
A piece of canvas

"How much is that?"
"That comes to $57.50."
"Do you have any pistols that use the brass cartridge?"
"Yes. .45 colt."
"One of those also and a box of shells."
"That all comes to $77.50."

Jean Corriveau gave Edwin the money and then started to secure everything on the pack horse.

"Where you heading mister?"

"Getting a little noisy aren't you?" He didn't want anyone to know instead of heading east to back home, he was turning northwest, once he was across the border.

He walked his horses back over to Anabelle's. "You back again young fella. You can't be hungry already?"

"No, *Madame*. I'd wish to purchase some bread, if you have some?"

"How many loaves would you like?"

"Four."

"That'll be 50 cents." She wrapped them in brown wrapping paper and handed them to Jean Corriveau. "Good luck to you, young fella, wherever you are going. Hope to see you back here some time."

"Good day, *Madame*."

He made sure everything was loaded and secure on the

horse and he headed for the ferry to cross the Missouri. He wanted to stay on the west side of the Big Muddy.

By now everyone at the fort had heard about his confrontation with Luther and Benny. A lot of folks were glad someone had beaten them so badly.

There was no mention or conversation about a wanted Army deserter.

* * * *

He rode fast and hard once he had crossed the Missouri. He'd ride hard for a while and then walk the horses. And once while he was walking them he had to stop and listen to something in his head. There was something else that this woman had been saying to him, what was it? And suddenly it was there. Sangreal. "SANGREAL MOUNTAINS," she said. He was so excited now. Now he knew where his destination lay. "Sangreal," he said again. He would have to inquire from someone once he had crossed into Canada.

Being this close to his final destination he rode faster than before. Some times even after the sun had set. As long as he could see where he was going. He didn't need a compass or map. He let his instincts guide him.

He liked the feel of the new Henry repeating rifle and the .45 colt hung differently on his side.

When he was near the border, he tied off his horses on a high knoll and explored on foot. He wanted to know what was ahead of him before he went any further. From the highest point on the knoll he could look down on the Big Muddy and upstream maybe three or four miles he could see a structure. He wasn't sure what it was, but he decided it had to be the border.

He stayed on the knoll that night, so he would be fresh and alert when he rode up to probably some sort of border security facility. After eating he enjoyed several cups of coffee before wrapping up in a blanket.

As he neared the river the next morning he found an often used trail that was heading in his direction. He followed it to the structure he had seen from the top of the knoll. As he rode closer, it was obvious a guardhouse of sorts. "Hello there in the guardhouse!" he hollered.

Two uniformed men came out. The uniforms made him uncomfortable. But they were Canadian uniforms and not the United States. They turned and waved him to come up.

"This must be Canada's border, no?"

"It is, *monsieur*. Where are you traveling?"

"Home, but first to the Sangreal Mountains to the west."

"Where is home?"

"I was born and raised near Woburn, Quebec. But my family moved to Maine. My father was looking for work. I am eventually going back to Woburn." He was thinking he was becoming a skilled liar.

"Then what are you doing this far west and in the United States?"

"My father and mother decided to move back to Woburn, but I wanted some adventure first. I wanted to try my hand in the gold fields and trapping."

"How did you do?"

"I was crossing a frozen river when my pack horse broke through the ice. The current carried the horse and all my supplies downstream under the ice."

"How did you survive the winter without any supplies?"

"A Sioux hunting party found me and took me back to their village. I stayed with them all winter."

"Maybe you should go home, *monsieur*. If you're going to Sangreal Mountains you'll need to go to Fort Macleod first."

"I've seen it on the map. I think I can find it okay."

"We'll need your name for our records."

"Surely, Jean Corriveau."

"Take this road north one mile and you'll come to a 'T'; the left goes to Fort Macleod."

"Thank you." Jean Corriveau said.

"Thank you, *Monsieur* Corriveau. Have a nice day."

At the 'T' Jean Corriveau paused for a few minutes, drinking in the joyous feeling of now being in Canada. But he had been Jean Corriveau for so long and he liked the name, he decided that's who he would be for the rest of his life. He inhaled deeply and let it out. "Life is good," he said.

He met freight wagons loaded with furs and hides. He passed others traveling to Fort Macleod loaded with everything from food to hardware.

It was easy to follow the gravel road after dark. Much easier than cross-country travel. He was making forty miles a day.

Two days out from Fort Macleod he saw a beautiful wilderness setting to the west. He wasn't sure why, but there was something that was telling him to take the time and check it out. Fort Macleod could wait.

It was getting late and he made camp in a small clearing of tall cedar and spruce trees. He inhaled deeply, smelling the natural perfume. There wasn't much here to feed his two horses so he fed them some grain and then water.

He had been traveling hard these last few days without taking the time to rest and eat a good meal. He leaned back and then he stretched out on the ground and he was soon asleep. He awoke during the night and he was cold. He spread out his bed roll and took another blanket from his gear and went back to sleep. Eating would have to wait.

When he awoke in the morning just before daylight he was cold and hungry. He kindled a fire and warmed his body before eating. First he needed a cup of hot coffee. While that was making, he warmed up the last of his beans and roasted some bacon.

Jean Corriveau ate his fill of beans, bacon and coffee. The sun was up and the air was clear and warming. He waited until his fire had burned out and then he packed up and mounted his horse and continued following the trail. The further he followed the trail the wider and more used it became. "Maybe this will lead to another settlement."

As he rode along the trail, at a walk, he began thinking of Kyla and Hanka. Would he ever see them again or his babies they carried in their bellies? *Probably not until I'm no longer wanted by the Army.*

Since crossing into Canada where the U.S. Army could not come after him, he had begun to sit in his saddle more comfortably, not always on the edge, jumping at every noise. He was sleeping better also.

As he rode along the trail, his thoughts changed from Kyla and Hanka to the woman in his dreams. If indeed those experiences had been dreams at all. They all seemed so real to life for him. *Visions?*

Just then he heard something up ahead. He stopped his horse to listen. Just as he thought maybe it had only been a scolding squirrel or something, he heard it again. This time he could clearly distinguish a man's voice and he seemed to be taunting someone else. He dismounted and tied both horses to a small tree and walked noiseless up a small knoll. There on the other side were two large white men. Both almost as tall as Jean Corriveau, but much fatter. They were taunting an Indian over a small elk that was dead and lying between the two parties. There was an arrow in the elk. And the Indian had a knife gash on his left arm and holding a knife in his other hand. The two white men were also holding a knife each.

Jean Corriveau walked quietly down the knoll to within a few feet of the two white men. The Indian saw him coming but not the other two. The Indian didn't seem concerned about Jean Corriveau's presence.

"Hey!" Jean Corriveau hollered.

The two men jumped in surprise. "What goes on here?"

The biggest of the two answered, "This dirty Indian won't give us this elk. We're starving and haven't eaten for two days."

"Is the elk yours or his?"

"He kilt it," the other one answered, "but he ain't nothing but a dirty Injun."

This infuriated Jean Corriveau and he walked up to the guy and back handed him so hard he fell over backwards unconscious. His friend started to withdraw his handgun and Jean Corriveau walked up to him and with the flat of his hand hit him as hard as he could in the nose. He too went over backwards. Blood spurting from his crushed nose and screaming bloody threats.

Jean Corriveau looked at the Indian and asked, "Do you understand my words?"

The Indian nodded his head that he did.

"How are you called?"

"Running Dog."

Before Jean Corriveau could tell him his name, Running Dog said, "I know who you are, you Big Jean Corriveau."

Jean Corriveau walked over to the guy with the crushed nose. "What made you think you had any right to this man's elk. I see an arrow in it and no bullet wound. You were trying to steal it. You were willing to kill for it. Why?"

In between gagging on his own blood, he said, "My friend and I were panning for gold and a bear ate all our supplies. We were hungry."

"So you think this gave you the right to steal Running Dog's elk? What are your names?"

When the guy hesitated Jean Corriveau picked him up by the shirt front and said, "I asked you a question."

"I'm Gerard Harvey and my friend is Earl Hayes."

"By the smell of you two I'd say the bear didn't drink your whiskey. You reek with the smell of it." Jean Corriveau reached down and took Gerard's handgun and walked over and took Earl's and then smashed them on a rock.

"Why did you smash our guns? You have left us defenseless."

"That's not my problem. I don't want to be shot in the back. Now get Earl on his feet and get out of here before I let Running Dog take you back to his village. And I don't think you want that."

As Gerard and Earl were staggering off, Gerard said, "Some day, Jean Corriveau, we'll meet again. I can promise you that."

Jean Corriveau cleaned Running Dog's wound. He poured some whiskey into the wound, Running Dog winced from the sting of the alcohol. It wasn't deep, and he tied some cloth around it to keep it clean.

"What tribe are you, Running Dog?"

"Blackfeet."

"I thought that was it. Do you have a pony?"

"Yes, but far from here."

"Okay. I'll put the elk on my horse and then we'll go find yours." Not wanting to get blood all over his horse and saddle Jean Corriveau left the innards intact. He bent down and lifted the elk and put it on his horse and then tied it off.

"You lead the way, Running Dog." Jean Corriveau followed behind Running Dog for about a mile before they came to his pony. "How far to your village Running Dog?"

"One day travel."

"Let's make as much distance as we can. You lead and I'll walk my horse behind you."

Running Dog did as Jean Corriveau said, but he was puzzled why this white man was so gracious and now he was walking without tiring.

They stopped early that evening and it was Running Dog's privilege to clean the elk. He removed the heart and liver and said, "Eat good tonight," and he held up the heart and liver.

Jean Corriveau made a travois to drag behind his horse and carry the meat and hide back to the village.

Before going to sleep that night Jean Corriveau looked at Running Dog's wound again. He washed it and was about to pour some whiskey on the wound when Running Dog pulled back and said, "No, no more whiskey."

Jean Corriveau laughed and said, "Okay". He took a drink and offered the bottle to Running Dog. He shook his head no.

* * * *

They rode into the Blackfeet village at high noon the next day. Running Dog's woman Cika came running when she saw Running Dog's bandaged arm. The people saw the elk that their visitor was hauling behind his horse. Everyone was gathering around them, all talking and wanting to know who this tall stranger was. Jean Corriveau dismounted. He was much taller than everyone there. But he did see one woman who was standing at the edge of the crowd who was also much taller than anyone else. Her hair was dark brown, almost with a red tint and shorter. When she noticed Jean Corriveau looking at her she disappeared. He looked everywhere for her, but he couldn't see where she had gone to.

Everyone was concerned about Running Dog's wound and at first, people thought the stranger who had come in with Running Dog had caused it. Some of the people were already taking care of the elk, skinning it and cutting up the meat. Running Dog turned to look at Jean Corriveau and said, "My father wishes to talk with you."

Chief Flying Eagle stood by his lodge and waited for Jean Corriveau. "Come, we sit inside, talk."

The Chief lit his pipe and passed it to Jean Corriveau. They smoked the pipe without saying a word, then, "I am called Flying Eagle Chief of my people Blackfeet."

"I am called Jean Corriveau."

"I was told you would be coming to see my people. My son Running Dog says you fought your own people to protect him."

"I fought two bullies. They were not my people, but they were white like me."

"Maybe all white men no so bad as stories told about them. You are welcome to stay with Blackfeet people as long as you want. I think you good medicine."

The two of them talked for hours. Because of the closeness to Fort Macleod the Blackfeet people had a better understanding of the white men and there was naturally less hostilities on both sides. But Flying Eagle was still concerned about the white settlers. But one thing the Blackfeet tribe had which the Sioux, Pawnee, Mandan and Cheyenne tribes didn't have, was an Indian agent who worked with them and for their native rights.

"I will share my lodge with you, Jean Corriveau, until one is made for you. My family will be honored. Tonight the women make feast, big celebration in your honor. Elk is being made ready as we talk. My daughter Nika will serve you your meals when we gather and she will tend to your needs. My daughter has a special gift. Since she was strong enough to walk she has this gift. She sees vision. I no tell others." Flying Eagle cleared his throat and added, "You will see."

"Chief Flying Eagle it is good that I am here with your people. I have traveled many days from the Sioux village. This is beautiful country."

Flying Eagle wanted to know all about his life with the Sioux. Also the Cheyenne, Mandans he had heard a lot about, and Pawnee. There were only a few questions about the white man's world. Maybe since the Blackfeet were so far removed.

Jean Corriveau's stomach started growling with hunger pains and Flying Eagle said, while laughing, "Soon my friend, soon the women will have the feast prepared."

They talked for a while longer and Flying Eagle said, "Before feast, might he wish to clean up?"

"Yes I would." Jean Corriveau left the lodge and took a towel and razor from his saddlebags and went down to the stream. He removed his shirt and washed up and trimmed his beard so it didn't look so shaggy, his hair was still short.

Just as Jean Corriveau was pulling his shirt on, the feast was being announced. He walked back up to the gathering and stood near Running Dog. "How is your arm, Running Dog?"

"Good! Cika cleaned and tied a new cloth. No clean with whiskey." They both laughed.

"This feast to honor our friend, Jean Corriveau. You are served first," and his daughter Nika walked up to Jean Corriveau with a big platter of delicious looking food.

"This food for you, Jean Corriveau," she said as she handed him the platter. She looked directly at him and they made eye contact. And then she backed away to let the others be served and all to enjoy the feast.

The food was delicious. Some of it Jean Corriveau had no idea what it was. After everyone had eaten everything was put away. The sun had set and a large fire was burning and everyone gathered around the fire. Jean Corriveau looked for Nika. He didn't see her.

Running Dog took center station at the fire and no one spoke. All that was audible was the burning wood as it snapped and crackled. Running Dog began telling the gathering about his hunting trip and how he had been accosted by two white men. He even used those two men's names. "Gerald and Earl had cut my arm with a knife when they wanted the elk I had killed. They were two big men and I would have been killed if not for Jean Corriveau. I never see any man who can fight like Jean Corriveau. He smashed their guns against a rock and told them to leave. Jean Corriveau by his self lifted elk onto his horse. I never see any man as strong. He cleaned and tie cloth to my arm to keep wound clean." He began laughing then and said, "He poured whiskey drink on knife wound. This hurt more than cut." Everyone laughed now and he continued, "Jean Corriveau never think about own self. He worry about Running Dog and take elk back to Blackfeet people.

"Jean Corriveau good white man. My friend."

It was Jean Corriveau's turn to entertain everyone. "I am called Jean Corriveau. I want to thank you all for this feast, I certainly wasn't expecting it. I have traveled here from the Sioux village much distance from here to the south. I learned much from Chief Tall Feather and watch every day events of the Sioux people. I found them all to be good honest people and I like them all." He didn't want to tell them that he had deserted from the Army. So instead he told them about his life back in Skowhegan, Maine, working in the woods.

They all were very interested and asked many questions. Finally Flying Eagle had to step in and pull Jean Corriveau from the center of attention. Now everyone could tell stories. And Jean Corriveau was sure some of the stories had been retold many times.

Someone started beating a drum. A soft rhythmic beat. This was the signal for everyone to get up and dance. They made a human circle around the fire. Nika pushed her way clear, and she took Jean Corriveau's right hand. They looked at each other and smiled, without saying a word.

Everyone kept beat with the drum and kept circling the fire. When the drum beat would quicken the people quickened their step. This went on for a long time until some from exhaustion had to stop. And when the drum beat stopped this signaled the end of the celebration and everyone went to their own lodge. The fire was left to burn out.

Jean Corriveau waited a few minutes before entering Flying Eagle's lodge to give him and Mika time to cover themselves in bed. Nika had left after the celebration had ended. Jean Corriveau looked for her but he didn't see her. He went to Flying Eagle's lodge and entered. A soft bed had been made for him. Nika was not there. Flying Eagle saw the disappointment on his face and said, "Don't worry about Nika, Jean Corriveau. Sometimes she stays up most of the night."

He laid down on what he assumed was his bed with his

hands under his head. The woman in his dreams had brought him this far and he began to wonder what was he in store for now. He was too excited to sleep, so he lay awake thinking about this mysterious and beautiful woman.

Flying Eagle and Mika were snoring, but this didn't bother him at all. Nika had not come to bed yet. Two hours before sunrise Jean Corriveau decided to get up and sit by the fire. He left the lodge quietly.

He put some wood on the fire and sat down on one of the benches. He thought he was there alone when suddenly Nika sat down beside him. He turned to look at her. She was wearing a headband around her hair. She smiled and Jean Corriveau was engulfed with her omniscience. He thought he had died and gone to heaven. He smiled back and stood up and took her hands in his. She didn't resist. She stood close—facing him. "It's you. You are the woman I have been seeing in my dreams all these years. There is no doubt in my mind."

"If I am this woman you speak of, then you have for all of your life made the right choices. Or you would not be here now," Nika said.

"Then my whole purpose for coming here was to finally find you?"

"That is part of your purpose, but you still have choices to make. And these you will have to make on your own."

She looked into his eyes with warmth, love and understanding, and she squeezed his hands. She felt good to hold, he was thinking.

"Jean Corriveau, I have always watched over you in my spirit body. I kept you from harm. Everything in your life had a purpose. Even you going to jail and the Army and why you left. You lived with Tall Feather for a reason too. You see, Jean Corriveau, everything we do in life has a purpose. We only have to understand and make the right choices."

"Do your mother and father know any of this?"

"No, only my father knows I have a special ability."

He put his arms around her then and hugged her and held her close. She didn't resist. "I'm so full of emotions now I can't think straight."

She laughed and said, "Maybe you need time by yourself to straighten things out in your mind?"

"Now that I have found you I don't want to go off by myself."

"Okay, I too do not want to be alone any longer. But we each have work to do for the village. Everyone has a job. Even you, Lucien Jandreau. I like Jean Corriveau better. Lucien is gone and forgotten."

He ran his fingers through her hair and inhaled her natural perfume. "You are more beautiful than in my dreams." She smiled beautifully.

"There is much I have to teach you, but not now. Not until the choices you still have to make are made. And then only a little at a time."

"I can live with that."

They were still standing together and talking when the sun rose and people everywhere were emerging from their lodges. When Flying Eagle and Mika came out and saw Jean Corriveau and their daughter together they both smiled at them when the two turned to look at them. Flying Eagle knew his daughter had special abilities, but he did not know to what extent. Mika was just so happy that her daughter had finally found someone. There wasn't one young man in the village who had even tried to get close to Nika. But now a strange man had come from far away, —*Maybe just to see Nika,* Mika thought to herself. Either way, she was extremely happy for her.

Nika would serve Jean Corriveau with a smile at each meal and she would always sit next to him. When not working they could be seen together. Usually a relationship within the village took many months to blossom, but this was Nika and a stranger that had come into their lives and somehow, for whatever reason, no one was holding them to the same tradition.

Jean Corriveau's duties were to help Running Dog provide meat for the village. Like the Sioux village, people here also had a particular duty. No one went off on their own to better themself. This was a collective where everyone worked for the betterment of everyone.

A lodge was being built for Jean Corriveau and Nika and Jean Corriveau was not allowed to help. As was the custom, the woman of the lodge made it and took care of it. "You go for a walk or something. This is woman work and I want to surprise you."

Jean Corriveau had not yet asked Nika to be his woman. But the entire village, Flying Eagle and Mika included, just assumed this to be.

That evening after eating and the cleanup and the new lodge was finished, Jean Corriveau and Nika went for a walk down by the stream. They walked hand in hand while talking and enjoying each other's company.

"You know, Nika, in the white man's world it is customary that the man asks the woman he loves to marry him, to be his wife." They stopped and he turned to face Nika. He took both of her hands in his and said, "I know we haven't been together for long, but I feel we always have been together. I love you, Nika, and I'm asking you to be my wife." She kissed him passionately then and said, "Yes, I'll be your wife. But we cannot be alone together until then. I mean no lovemaking."

"I understand. Just as long as we can be together like this."

They ran back to tell Nika's mother and father and they were excited about the joining of their daughter with Jean Corriveau.

* * * *

Nika and a cousin made Jean Corriveau a new set of buckskin clothes, and she had long ago made a white buckskin dress and blouse.

Two days later the village stood together while Jean Corriveau and Nika walked up to Flying Eagle and Mika who were standing at the front of the gathering. Flying Eagle raised his hand and the talking stopped.

"Jean Corriveau and our daughter have asked to join. Mika and I believe this to be good. Jean Corriveau came into our village a stranger. But I don't think he is a stranger to Nika. Is there anyone who disagrees with this joining?" Everyone was quiet and Flying Eagle waited the appropriate time before continuing.

"Since no one objects and Mika and I both think this is good, Jean Corriveau and Nika you are now joined."

Nika took Jean Corriveau's hand and ran for their new lodge. They were chased by the entire village. But once they had disappeared inside, the villagers dispersed and went about their business. Jean Corriveau and Nika would remain in their new lodge getting to know each more intimately.

* * * *

The next morning just before daylight as they lay in each other's embrace, Jean Corriveau said, "Do you know what a honeymoon is?"

"No."

"When two people marry or join, they go off somewhere together, just the two of them. Sometimes a trip. It's in celebration of their marriage."

"Do you have any ideas?" she asked.

"Yes, I would like to go see the Sangreal Mountains and then to Fort Macleod.

"I know the Sangreal Mountains. Though I have never been there. I understand they are beautiful. And Macleod. What is there?" she asked.

"I don't know. I only have this feeling that we need to go."

"I'll go anywhere you go my husband."

They got up and dressed and went outside. By then everyone in the village was already up and Nika went to help the women with the morning meal. Jean Corriveau went to see Flying Eagle.

"I understand Sangreal Mountains. I been there. Is pretty. What is in Macleod for you?" Flying Eagle asked.

"I'm not sure Flying Eagle. I only know I must go."

"You come back?"

"Yes, we will come back."

"You go then. I know Nika watches over you. You are family to Blackfeet now.

"Yes, Flying Eagle, Blackfeet are my family."

When they had finished eating, Jean Corriveau packed the pack horse with supplies and the food he had brought with him and the piece of canvas in case of rain. The Blackfeet had no saddles. He saddled his horse and asked Nika, "Do you need a saddle? I don't see any."

"I'll be fine without one. I have never used one."

As they were riding out of sight of the village he asked, "How many days travel to Sangreal?"

"Two days." They rode side-by-each.

On the eve of the second day they arrived at a clear spring fed inlet to a lake, and standing tall behind the lake were the Sangreal Mountains. "This looks like a nice place to make camp, my husband."

They made a lean-to and put the canvas on the top and then filled the back and the two sides in with evergreen boughs. While Nika was busy fixing something to eat, Jean Corriveau made a bed of evergreen tops and he laid their bedroll on top of that.

That night as they were sitting up talking and watching the stars, the northern lights started dancing in the northern sky.

Jean Corriveau said, "Manitou is dancing in the heavens tonight. That light is his hair."

"You know this legend? How?" she was surprised that he had known about it.

"I learned it from the Sioux." There was no need of saying any more. But he knew he would have to in time.

They both slept well that night in each other's embrace. A loon out front in the spring-fed stream started calling just as the sun was beginning to peak through. "Nika, look at Sangreal." They both watched in amazement as the snow topped peak of the tallest mountain turned blood red as the sun shone through the earth's atmosphere.

The top stayed red for a long time and both Jean Corriveau and Nika were silent as they watched. When the red had changed back to white again, Jean Corriveau asked, "Do you know what Sangreal means, Nika?" He didn't suppose that she would, but then again she knew so much and had abilities that most people do not have.

"It means Royal Blood."

"Yes, and I can understand why when Eben McNinch and Fred Michaud camped somewhere right here and when they got up the next morning, they saw the blood red top the same as we did and named it Sangreal Mountain. This was about fifty years ago. Eben and his wife Ada were legends, even among the many native tribes."

They camped there for two more days enjoying the excitement of their joining. Their food was getting low so they made the decision to start toward Macleod. Jean Corriveau was a little apprehensive about Macleod. He was supposed to go there, but for what purpose? As much as he tried to find the answers there just weren't any.

One day they had to stop early to find food. While Nika gathered wild herbs Jean Corriveau went hunting. Nika had filled the pot with herbs and Jean Corriveau brought back a rabbit and three partridges. Nika made up a nice stew and added a little sage for taste. "This is delicious, Nika."

Nika noticed how quiet and subdued Jean Corriveau had

become and at times a worried expression on his face. "What are you thinking my husband? You look worried."

"Not worried exactly, just wondering what we will find at Fort Macleod."

Nika knew what they would find at the fort, but she could not tell Jean Corriveau. She knew he would be faced with a huge choice to make and she could not help him to make the right choice.

Late in the afternoon from on top a knoll they could see the fort at a distance. "I think we should stay here tonight and wait for morning to ride in."

They made camp back away from the knoll near a spring-fed stream in amongst cedar and spruce trees. Here their fire would not be seen.

Jean Corriveau did not sleep well that night. He couldn't stop wondering what they would find at the fort. He, so far in his life, had made all the correct choices. And these choices had brought him west and then north where he finally met the woman who had watched over him for so many years. But he also knew that there was another choice to be made inside this fort. He understood Nika could not help him make the right choice. Would he fail or would he make the right choice, whatever it might be.

Morning came and after eating more stew and a pot of coffee he was ready. "Shall we go, my wife, and see what lays ahead?"

She didn't answer, she only smiled and that to him was his answer and support.

It didn't take them long and they rode through the main gate. There were log palisades encompassing the fort and inside was the Northwest Royal Mounted Police Barracks and a trading post, livery, hotel and eatery, saloon, almost anything that one would need.

They rode up to the livery and tied off their horses. The sign said Alfred Jones livery. "Are you Mr. Jones?" Jean Corriveau asked.

"Yes Sir what can I do for you?"

"Can you grain the horses and we would like to stable them here until we leave. Oh yeah, we'll be needing a saddle for this one. Nothing fancy, but a good one."

"Yes Sir."

"I'm still hungry. Shall we go over to the eatery?"

As they were walking across the compound Jean Corriveau and Nika both noticed two large men standing together at the far end of the fort who seemed to have a particular interest in them. But they stayed where they were.

Inside the eatery they chose a table in the back corner where they could see everything and the door. Nika also sat with her back to the wall.

A short pot-bellied guy brought over a pot of coffee and two cups. "What can I get for you?" he asked.

"I'll have six eggs over easy, a side of ham and a loaf of bread. My wife will have two eggs over easy and ham."

"My husband, everyone is looking at me."

"They probably have never seen anyone quite as beautiful as you." They also were looking at the size of Jean Corriveau. The size of his order and that his wife was almost as tall as he was.

It didn't take long for their food to come. They ate hungrily. "This I miss most of all, living in the wilderness. Fresh eggs. I suppose we could take back some chickens with us and then we would always have a supply of fresh eggs."

When they had finished eating, Jean Corriveau paid for their meal and they walked outside. The two men who had been watching them across the compound from the far end, Gerard Harvey and Earl Hayes, were waiting for them around the side corner of the eatery. Jean Corriveau and Nika started to cross the compound again and had only gone about twenty feet when the two stepped out and Gerard bellowed loud enough for everyone to hear, "Jean Corriveau! You dirty Injun lover, remember what I said I would do you if I ever saw you again?"

265

Jean Corriveau and Nika turned to face them and said, "Sweetheart you'd better stay clear. These two mean trouble."

She stepped to the side out of the way.

Everyone at the fort was now watching and there was one red haired man with an Indian woman standing at the livery watching.

Jean Corriveau's first remark took everyone by surprise. "You two stinking idiots smell worse that you did the last time I tried to beat some sense in you."

"We ain't drunk this time, Corriveau, and we're going to do worse to you than you did to us," Earl said.

"Drunk or sober, I think you two are too stupid to do much of anything. Hey, if you have to breathe turn your heads so I don't have to smell your foul-smelling breath." The red haired man was laughing.

"What is the matter, stupid? You two afraid of just one man? Either one of you will weigh more than I do. But then you're both probably filled with foul smelling pig crap."

This was more than either Gerard or Earl could stand. They both charged towards Jean Corriveau.

Jean Corriveau stepped to one side and stuck out his foot and tripped Gerard. He went down hard, his face in some fresh horse manure. He back handed Earl and sent him sprawling to the ground. Gerard put his head down and charged at Jean Corriveau. Jean Corriveau side stepped again and brought his doubled fists down on Gerard's collar bone. It snapped and he screamed with pain.

Earl picked himself up and swung at the side of Jean Corriveau's head. Jean Corriveau caught his fist in his powerful hand and began to squeeze. Then he hit him with the flat of his hand in the nose breaking it and blood spurted from his nose. He too was screaming, but he was too mad to give up. He tried to get his arms around Jean Corriveau to squeeze him. But Jean Corriveau picked him up by his shirt front and belt and threw him. He hit the ground hard and he had had enough of Big Jean Corriveau.

Gerard was still too mad to give up. Even with a broken collar bone he came at Jean Corriveau again. This time Jean Corriveau grabbed his right arm and broke it over his knee like a piece of wood. Gerard screamed some more and he now was through. He had had enough.

Jean Corriveau held out his hand for Nika to come to him. He took her hand and walked over to Gerard. "Mr. Harvey, you owe my wife an apology. And you'd better make it sound sincere, or we can do this all over again."

Gerard stopped screaming and managed to get to his knees, "Ma'am, I'm truly sorry for offending you. It will not happen again."

"Thank you, Mr. Harvey," Nika said,

Nika took her husband's hand in hers and they started walking across the compound when someone with a deep voice started laughing and saying, "Ha! Ha! My God! Big Jean Corriveau! You remind me of my grandfather." And he was still laughing.

Jean Corriveau and Nika stopped and looked at the red haired man and his woman. Nika said, "Big Red Beard Not Afraid!"

Jean Corriveau said, "Eben McNinch. You are real. I have read many dime novels about you and thought it was just a good story."

"That was my grandfather. You took care of those two just like my granddad would have. I was quite impressed. Excuse me, I'd like to introduce my wife, Wenonah. She is Cree and my mother was Cree."

Nika stepped forward and hugged Wenonah and said, "So pleased to meet you. I am called Nika and I am Blackfeet."

"There is no need of us standing out here talking. We should go to our quarters. We have much to talk about."

"You live here?" Nika asked Wenonah.

"We stay here some each summer," Wenonah said.

"Jean Corriveau, where are you and Nika going from here?" Eben asked.

"Back to her village."

"I can tell by your accent that you are not Canadian, where are you coming from?" Eben asked.

"I spent last winter in a Sioux village—"

Eben interrupted and said, "Ah yes, that would be Tall Feather's village. I spent a winter there when I was on the run. So what brought you to the village?"

Jean Corriveau took a deep breath and looked at Nika before answering. Maybe this was the choice he had to make. Better to come right out with it he thought. "I deserted from the Army."

"Why did you desert?" An honest question.

"I was a corporal stationed at Fort Kearny and our duty was to escort wagon trains." He told them about the Cheyenne massacre and then about the ambush at Cheyenne River. "I just couldn't go on killing the native people—for what reason? I felt sorry for them."

"I have seen posters about three deserters. But I don't remember one of them being Jean Corriveau."

"No, I changed my name. I was called Lucien Jandreau then. I thought it best to use another name."

"The U.S. Army will not cross the border looking for you. What will you do when you return to Nika's village?"

"Learn their ways and become a Blackfeet."

"What if you could do more good for the Blackfeet and all Canadian tribes?"

"I don't understand."

"I am the director of Canadian Indian affairs in the Northwest Territories. I answer to Governor Shelby Rigsby."

"He was with your granddad and grandmother," Jean Corriveau said.

"Yes, he is Governor of the Northwest Territories and his wife is Tika; she is also Blackfeet."

"I know this name," Nika said. "There are stories told about her and the man she took for her husband."

"You can do the tribes all over Canada a lot of good, Jean Corriveau."

"Where would we live?"

"Right here in these quarters. Although there would be travel to other tribes. You would answer to me."

Tears welled up in Jean Corriveau's eyes. He now understood this was the choice he would have to make. All this time, all of his life he had been training to fulfill this position. At last the quest had come to his final decision. He looked at his wife Nika and said, "This is the final choice isn't it? And you knew all along what I would be facing." Nika was smiling. "And there is so much more you have to teach me isn't there?" Again she only smiled radiantly.

"Of course we'll take it. I want you to understand I am a wanted man with a price on my head."

"I too am a wanted man with a price on my head," Eben said.

"I think before I start, Nika and I should return to her village and talk with Chief Flying Eagle and explain what we will be doing. Helping Canadian Native tribes."

"Certainly. Can you do it in a week? There is much I need to go over with you. Wenonah and I are here for another month before we have to return to Winnipeg."

"We'll make sure we're back here in one week. We'll leave this afternoon, in fact, when we are finished talking."

"Now that you'll be handling affairs in this part of the territories, Wenonah and I can visit our people more often.

"When you start back for your village, there is a more direct route. If you go out the west gate the road will swing to the north when you come to a Y in the road, take the left. It will take you very close to the village. I'm sure Nika will recognize the countryside there."

While Eben and Jean Corriveau talked business, Wenonah showed Nika the rest of the quarters. This was the first house she had ever been in and she was excited about living here.

"You must lie down and try this bed, Nika," Wenonah said.

Nika laid down and rolled over and over and she couldn't believe its softness. "I like this bed. Much better than lumpy ground," they both laughed.

* * * *

The Corriveaus and the McNinches said their good-byes and the Corriveaus traveled four hours on the road Eben had told them about and made camp off the road, and for once he was not afraid of his fire being seen.

That night sitting in the firelight, Jean Corriveau said, "There is so much I want to know and learn about you sweetheart, and I want to take the rest of my life to discover all about you. You are the most amazing woman I have ever met. Will you continue to watch over me?"

"Of course. Tonight while our bodies sleep and rest for the journey ahead of us, I will take you on a fantastic journey." He had no doubt that indeed she would.

He wrapped his arms around his wife and held her close. "You are the best thing that has ever happened to me."

EPILOGUE

The Corriveaus made the trip back to the village in a day-and-a-half. Flying Eagle and Running Dog were ecstatic that someone they knew and who was part of the Blackfeet tribe now would be helping them and other native tribes to adapt to the strange ways of the white man.

They were able to stay for two days, and in all honesty they both were eager to leave so they could get back to Fort Macleod and start their new lives.

Eben McNinch was true to his word. They stayed a full month before leaving, and both Jean Corriveau and Nika fully understood what their new duties would entail.

Whenever Jean Corriveau would have to travel to a faraway tribe, like Wenonah, Nika was always by his side. They were so well liked that soon they both became a legend among the Canadian Native Tribes. And there never was another confrontation with any white—or otherwise—troublemakers.

One evening while sitting in their quarters at Fort Macleod, Jean Corriveau said, "I think it is time that I send a letter home to my family. And tell them about you."

Dear Family,
I have traveled a long way, both in body and spirit since I said good-bye so many years ago. I want to explain about my desertion. I couldn't go on killing innocent people. It made me sick. I must explain about the Medal of Valor that was awarded to me, not for killing Indians, but for bringing an end to

the senseless killing in one battle with the Cheyenne. I negotiated a truce with the Cheyenne leader. I told him no one else had to die that day. We both had lost most of our men. I was wounded and so was he. I let him pick up his wounded and leave. I saved many lives that day by stopping the fighting and this is why I was awarded the Medal.

I lived one winter with a Sioux tribe and was taught many things. And now I know my life has a purpose and that I was always protected by the woman who is now my wife, Nika, of the Blackfeet tribe in western Canada. She is a marvelous woman.

And Dad, I can now forgive you for the way you treated me. I now understand that this had to be as well as my time in prison. These experiences were helping to create the person I am now, so that I could make the right choices.

Everything in my life was for this purpose. I have had to change my name. I am now called Jean Corriveau. I don't know if we'll ever be able to visit you, as I am a wanted man in the States. But here I am free.

Our headquarters is at Fort Macleod in the North-west Territories of Canada. I work for the Bureau of Canadian Indian Affairs and I answer to Eben McNinch.

I hope this letter will answer some of the questions you have about me and that it finds you all well. Mom and Dad I am happy.

Jean Corriveau

Jean Corriveau posted the letter the next morning. There were daily freight wagons and couriers leaving for Winnipeg. He guessed his family should receive it in six weeks or a little more.

Jean Corriveau and Nika settled into their new position very easy and everyone there at the fort were friends with them and had a great deal of respect for them both.

Nika continued to watch over her husband and sometimes helped to guide him. With each passing year, Jean Corriveau learned a little more about his wife's special abilities and loved her more with each passing day.

THE END

Author, Randall Probert

Randall Probert lived and was raised in Strong,Maine; a small town in the western mountains of Maine. Six months after graduating from high school, he left the small town behind for Baltimore, Maryland and a Marine Engineering School, situated downtown near what was then called "The Block". Because of bad weather, the flight from Portland to New York was canceled and this made him late for the connecting flight to Baltimore. A young kid and alone from the backwoods of Maine finally found his way to Washington DC and boarded a bus from there to Baltimore. After leaving the Merchant Marines, he went to an aviation school in Lexington, Massachusetts.

During his interview for Maine Game Warden he was asked, "You have gone from the high seas to the air. . .are you sure you want to be a Game Warden?" Mr. Probert retired from Warden Service in 1997 and started writing historical novels about the history in the areas where he patrolled as a game warden, with his own experiences as a game warden as those of the wardens in his books. Mr. Probert has since expanded his purview and has written 2 science fiction books, *PARADIGM* and *PARADIGM2,* and has written a mystical adventure, *AN ESOTERIC JOURNEY.* Mr. Probert is also currently working on another historical novel, which should be available in the spring, 2015.

Acknowledgments

I would like to thank Laura Ashton for her help getting this book published. And a special thanks to Amy Robertson for her help typing and corrections, and for letting me use her photo on the cover and captions in the book.

Other Books by Randall Probert

A Forgotten Legacy

An Eloquent Caper

Courier de Bois

Katrina's Valley

Mysteries at Matagamon Lake

A Warden's Worry

A Quandry at Knowles Corner

Paradigm

Trial at Norway Dam

A Grafton Tale

Paradigm II

Train to Barnjum

A Trapper's Legacy

An Esoteric Journey

The Three Day Club

Eben McNinch